# Model
# Behavior

A Charitable Endeavors Novel

## M.E. CARTER
## ANDREA JOHNSTON

Dedicated to Luke the Squirrel.

We miss you buddy.

Don't forget to look before you cross the street.

# Model Behavior

# Prologue

*Carrie*

I'm not sure if coming to the National Association of Narrators Awards – NANA for short - was the best idea I've ever had in my life, or the absolute worst. It could go either way.

It's always been on my forever changing bucket list to see what the ceremony was all about. The best of the best is here, after all, decked out in their finest duds. But as an avid reader and listener, I never want to ruin the fantasy in my head by seeing what a narrator looks like in real life. It's also why I've spent much of tonight's ceremony with my eyes closed. Seems like it would defeat the purpose of attending, but truly I've had a blast. One of my favorite authors, Pippa Worthington, treated me to this fantastic trip, which I could never have afforded on my own. I've been wined and dined and hobnobbed with more of my favorites, like Donna Moreno, while they wait to see if their story won any kind of narration award.

That might be a slight exaggeration. The wine was fourteen dollars a glass so I only had one and vowed not to spring for more. The dining options are severely overpriced for mediocre food so I Door Dashed lunch today instead. Of course, I kept my gaze down as I rushed through the hotel to meet the delivery guy. Like I wasn't taking any chances tonight, I sure as heck wasn't taking them this afternoon.

If you knew how much I love audiobooks, though, you would know why I couldn't risk seeing anyone's face. Don't get me wrong, I love reading. It's why I became a book blogger and why I'm so good at it. But audiobooks take things to a whole new level for me. A good voice can make the story come alive in a much more intense way. Plus, I'm very visual with the characters. Seeing the face of the narrator just ruins the fantasy for me because they almost never look like my imagination has made them out to be.

Or at least I assume they never do.

My only snafu was accidentally interrupting my favorite erotica romance author, Donna Moreno, while she talked, er, whistled, to the narrator with the sexiest voice, Hawk Weaver.

*Block out his face, Carrie. You didn't see anything. You did not hear her call him Todd. Push that waaaaay deep into the recesses of your brain…*

I still don't understand what all the whistling was for. Hawk mumbled something about her learning the language of his people and then they started re-enacting one of the make out scenes from Donna's books. It's all a bit muddled.

Before I could ask, I was dragged away by a hot guy who was kind enough to guide me through the crowd while my hand was over my eyes. He didn't even run me into anything, which is more than I can say for what I would do to myself.

Unfortunately, the hot guy is romance cover model, Matthew Roberts. Sexy face, lickable abs, perfect swoon-worthy smile, and according to anyone who has ever met him in person, always kind to everyone. Oh, and he's known to sleep with a different reader at every event he attends.

I hate guys like him.

Hate might be a strong word. Loathe would be more accurate, but fact of the matter is, I don't know him well enough to loathe him either. I just loathe his type. A type I know too darn well. The type we *all* know too darn well because we've seen it—the guy who spends his time counting his macros, doing crunches, and climbing ropes between flirty winks in the mirror at other gym bunnies. The type that has no interest in an actual relationship, just wants to flirt with women to get in their pants, then drop them like a hot potato while spouting "I was clear from the beginning that I have no interest in a relationship."

Most of the women I know fell for the game called "Scratch the Itch" a time or two in college. It sucked and now that I'm older I want no part of it. I'm perfectly happy sitting on the sidelines playing my own game called, "Not until you put a ring on it, and even then, maybe not."

Really, I'm not as bitchy as I sound. It just makes me uncomfortable that Matthew is so flirty with me whenever our paths cross, which doesn't happen frequently enough for him to even call it "friendly flirting." Hell, the first time we met he hit on me before even asking my name. I find that kind of thing counterproductive to my relationship goals, and yes, I have them. I want to be someone's one and only, not their one right now. And I'm nobody to Matthew Roberts. I'm a book blogger who loves to go to author events and was lucky enough to become friends with Donna Moreno. I have nothing to offer Matthew, especially if he's looking to get in my pants. Based on his reputation and my ideals, getting to know each other would be a waste of both of our time. I don't need him to flirt with me; I need some liquor.

"Okay, the coast is clear. You can open your eyes now."

Blinking rapidly as my eyes readjust to the light, I look around the room. Matthew has brought me to the hotel bar I've been avoiding. Mentally, I calculate how much is left in my bank account before choosing my very expensive beverage of choice. I was considering a whiskey, but one finger is probably more than my monthly light bill.

"What can I get you?" Matthew asks, because that's just the kind of polite crap he does. Offers to buy women he doesn't know drinks. The question is, what does he expect in return?

I furrow my brow momentarily, but quickly school my features. I don't like Matthew but that doesn't mean I need to be rude all the time. I can be nice. Fine... I can answer civilly.

"Ice water, please."

It's Matthew's turn to look confused. "After having our ear drums blown apart in the weirdest declaration of love ever? I thought you just mumbled something about wanting liquor?"

He heard that? Which means he was listening? Huh.

"Are you mocking the grand gesture Donna just made?" At least I assume it was a grand gesture. Based on how fast Hawk Weaver's tongue ended up in her mouth, anyway.

"Little bit, yeah." He grins like he's funny, which he isn't. At all. Maybe a little.

"It's called romance," I snark and yes, I make air-quotes, "which you would know if you read any of the books you're on the cover of."

Matthew only smirks at me. I don't like it. I'm trying to put up a good bitchy front so he doesn't get any ideas and instead I seem to be entertaining him.

"Are you always so hostile?"

"Yes." The word comes out a little too quickly, and we both know I'm lying. "Fine. No."

"So why are you so angry with me?"

I could go into all the reasons—I've known boys like him before. I've been hurt by boys like him before. I don't subscribe to this whole "sex can be just sex" thing. If he doesn't care enough to earn my trust, he's not worth my time. Et cetera, et cetera, et cetera.

I know how that conversation will end though. I'll waste my breath explaining my reasons. He'll zone out while I talk. We'll both walk away frustrated. It's better for both of us if I just get him to leave now. Which means I need to explain in a way I've discovered most men can understand.

"I'm not having sex with you."

Matthew laughs. Hard. Like the idea of getting naked with me is the most absurd thing he's ever heard. I wish I was relieved to know we're on the same page, but I'm not. I turn away from him so he can't see the hurt on my face and signal the bartender. Suddenly, I need a stiff drink, cost be damned.

"Hey." The laughter has stopped and his tone has changed to something more assuring. "I'm not laughing at the idea. I think you're incredibly sexy."

"Hmm." That's the only response he's getting from me. I refuse to let him get a rise out of me. I'd rather he thinks I'm irritated by the bartender flirting with yet another cover model at the end of the bar instead of getting me a drink. I begin waving, hoping to catch her attention this time.

"No really. I just think you're funny."

Now he has my attention. I look over my shoulder at him, crinkling my nose. "You think it's funny that I have boundaries?"

"No. I think you're funny because you just assume you need them. You're like a little chihuahua, barking at me to show how tough you are. It's cute."

He did not just refer to me as a yappy, nervous dog. I love chihuahuas, particularly our shelter dog, Noah, who makes no qualms about letting anyone and everyone know he's a permanent resident, but that doesn't mean I like to be compared to him. First of all, I have way better teeth. Second, I don't usually pee on chairs.

"You're not making a good case for yourself, Roberts." Waving frantically now, I still can't seem to catch the bartender's attention. It's starting to piss me off, especially since I may need alcohol to get through this conversation.

Matthew moves in behind me and I stifle a gasp caused by the heat of his body next to mine.

*No, Carrie. You will not have a visceral reaction to this man. Not this time…*

He flicks his wrist once and the same bitch I've been waving at flashes a huge smile and saunters our way. That's one more irritation I have about a pretty face and eight pack of abs—to be catered to while the rest of us fight to be seen. It's irrationally annoying. Any tingling in my lady bits has dried up.

"What can I get for you?" The bartender's voice comes out dripping of sexuality. If I rolled my eyes any harder, they'd get stuck in the back of my head. By the way she narrows hers at me, she didn't miss my reaction. Welp, I'm getting spit in my drink now for sure.

Matthew doesn't seem to notice the pissing contest in front of him, probably so used to women fighting over him. Instead he smiles kindly. "I need two whiskeys please. Neat."

Wait, did he just buy me a drink? Whipping my head around to clarify what's going on, he takes one look at me and startles like I reminded him of something.

"Sorry. Make it two fingers each please."

"Coming right up." I assume she bites her lip and looks him up and down because it takes a few seconds for the scent of Love's Baby Soft spray, circa 1990 to fade away. I don't know for sure, though, because I'm still trying to figure him out. "Just let me buy you the drink. I promise I won't try to get in your pants."

I'm both relieved and disappointed. Doesn't he *want* in my pants? He's not getting there, but a lady still likes to be wanted.

And I've lost my mind. Shaking my head, I try to filter through all my muddled feelings. So much has happened in the last five minutes; on top of the adrenaline high I've been riding all night, I feel like nothing makes sense anymore. Default bitch mode is clearly not working for me, so I just move right back into regular Carrie mode. Whatever that is. Right now, it's resolved.

"Thank you."

Matthew's eyes light up. "Ah! She can be polite after all."

I purse my lips and bite back a smile. "Don't push your luck, buddy."

My phone vibrates, and I pull it out to read the text from my bestie, Jamie, while our drinks are delivered.

"Thanks. Keep the change." Matthew says kindly and hands her some cash. I don't even want to know how much it cost for two hard liquor drinks. Next time I go to an event like this, I need to hit a liquor store on my way in.

"Everything okay?"

I find myself smiling at the picture Jamie sent me and rubbing my thumb over the cute little face on the screen. "Yeah. Just got a picture of my baby boy."

The words pop out of my mouth before I can stop them, and I immediately realize I've made a mistake. Clicking my phone off, I pray Matthew was distracted by Lady Love the bartender again and missed it. But no. I find Matthew swallowing a good-sized sip of his drink, his eyes lit up. "Mmm." He wipes a drop from his bottom lip, and I'm back to that lady bit issue again. "You have a son?"

"Uhhh… sort of?" I have no idea how to explain my weird situation to him. On the one hand, I'm not embarrassed. Quite the contrary. I love this little guy. On the other hand, I don't live in a normal life situation. I've gotten some weird looks before, and based on Matthew's face, he's already confused.

"How do you sort of have a son?" He snaps his fingers like the answer just occurred to him. "Oh! Are you a foster mom? I have such respect for people who do that."

Oh great. Now he thinks I'm a saint. This is about to go downhill. At least I don't have to worry about him inviting me to his room anymore. The crazy lady is about to be marked off his list permanently.

"I have a six-year-old daughter myself," he continues to ramble while I try and decide how to answer his actual question. "She's the absolute love of my life. See?" Matthew flashes me a picture of arguably the most adorable little girl I've ever seen. Dark hair like her daddy in a halo of ringlets. Light, chocolate eyes with long lashes women my age pay top dollar to emulate. This kid is a knockout. Of course, look who her dad is. It's not a surprise she takes after him.

"I don't understand how people can bring a child into the world and let it fend for itself. I would die for her, ya know?" I nod because I do know. Theoretically. "It takes a special person to bring someone else's child into their home to raise and love. I really admire that."

"Umm... yeah. Thanks." I try to leave it at that. Now that he's come to his own conclusions, I have no reason to correct him. I won't see him again after tonight until the next event, and hopefully only in passing, so I can just let him believe what he wants, right?

But no. I can't be so lucky. Matthew wants to keep

pushing the issue. Damn interested charmer. "How old is he? And what's his name?"

I close my eyes and realize I'm not getting out of this one without an explanation. "He's, uh, about four weeks old…"

Matthew's eyes light up again. "Oh, he's little!"

I snort a laugh. "You have no idea."

"Sorry. Continue."

Feeling a burst of confidence, I decide to just go for it. Like I said before, I may never see him again anyway, so who cares what he thinks of me?

"Listen, Matthew. I think you've misunderstood some things."

Now he looks confused. "Like what? You're not a foster mom?"

I bobble my head. "I am. Sort of. But not the way you think."

"I don't understand. At all."

Sighing, I pull my phone out again and pull up Jamie's text. "I'll show you his picture but promise me you won't laugh."

"Why would I laugh at a child?"

Enough. Time to set the record straight. I flash the phone his direction and see it the moment the pieces come together. He looks at the picture, his face takes on sort of a contorted look, like he's not sure what to feel. Then he looks at me, back at the phone, back at me, a couple more times until he finally points at it and speaks.

"That's a squirrel."

At least he's not laughing.

Clicking off my phone, I drop it back in my clutch. "Yes, he is."

"So you don't have a baby. You have a squirrel."

"A *baby* squirrel. I do wildlife rescue. Someone found him when he was a newborn and brought him to me. His name is Luke, and I'll raise him until he's old enough to go back out into the wild."

"So you have a squirrel."

I give him my best "eat shit" look. "You can stop saying that like it's the weirdest thing you've ever heard."

"But it just might be."

"No, the weirdest thing you've ever heard is Donna Moreno whistle that she loves Hawk Weaver."

He opens his mouth to argue but thinks better of it. "You got me there. This might be a close second though."

"Well then, it's a good thing I don't care what you think."

I turn back to face the bar and take a quick sip of my whiskey. It burns from the back of my throat all the way to my stomach, which is a welcome feeling to the embarrassment I'm trying not to focus on. But really, it's not my fault Matthew jumped to these massive conclusions.

"You're right."

Is he still talking? I thought for sure he'd have ditched me by now. For the life of me I can't figure out why he keeps coming back for more.

"It's admirable that you take these defenseless creatures and raise them to go back out on their own." He slides onto the recently vacated stool next to me. "It took me by surprise is all."

"Usually does," I say, still refusing to make eye contact with him, and tossing back the rest of my drink. Of course it throws me right into a coughing fit.

I have to give Matthew credit—he doesn't seem fazed by my lack of couth, instead patting me on the back while I practically convulse on the bar. "Geez, Carrie. Drink slower next time. Are you okay?"

I nod and take a few more seconds to pull myself together. When I can finally speak through the burn, I grab my clutch and stand up. "Thanks for the drink, Matthew, but I have an early morning flight so I need to run."

He looks confused, but at least he doesn't try to stop me. "Um . . . okay. It was nice talking to you again and good luck with that little guy."

With a curt nod, I turn on my heel and hightail it to my room.

My intent is to pack and hit the hay. But as soon as my face is washed, there's a knock on the door.

Furrowing my brow, I see someone from room service through the peep hole. Weird. I didn't order anything.

I open the door and she immediately hands me a small, but hefty package. "Delivery for Carrie... Mibooks?" She looks up at me, confused by my blogger name, then shrugs and leaves without giving me time to tip her.

Huh. Who could have sent me a gift? I pull the small note card out of the envelope and read.

*Please accept this as my apology for embarrassing you earlier. I love that you love your baby. And I hope Luke likes his gift.*
*-Matthew*

Inside the package is the last thing I expected to see—

It's a bag of walnuts.

Damn that Matthew and his charm. Now I have to like him.

# Chapter 1

*Matthew*

Somewhere in the country it's the perfect fall day. Leaves are turning various shades of yellow, orange, and red. The breeze is light but crisp, making everyone shiver and reach for a coat. That somewhere is not here.

Nope, here in Texas, it's a cool eighty-three degrees with the sun high in the sky and my skin already damp with sweat. Off on the far end of the house I can hear the sounds and frustrated groans of my little girl scouring to find her sandals before school.

Miss Independent refuses to accept my help, and like every other morning I let her stomp around searching every corner of the house for whatever it is she can't find. Yesterday it was her favorite pink hair clip. Today it's her shoes. If I were a betting man, I'd say tomorrow will be her favorite leotard for ballet. Which is why I know exactly where it is—in my room until tomorrow when I'll place it on top of her bed while she's at school. I've learned a few things as a single dad and the number one on that list is being one step ahead of her. Of course, that knowledge only came after an epic meltdown over missing ballet slippers. The same slippers that are secure in her little gym bag currently behind the seat in my truck.

That's a move I like to refer to as "kicking this dad thing's ass."

Slicing half a banana into small chunks and dropping them in the blender with my protein powder and ice, I chuckle as she shouts "Victory is mine" from her room. I assume her declaration means she's found her lost shoe. The whir of the blender fills the quiet of the house, but it's not enough to keep me from hearing Calypso enter the room and climb up on the stool at the counter. With deep sighs, she shakes her head from side to side, impatience evident.

"Are you ready for some breakfast, Sprite?"

"Pancakes?"

"You know we save those for Sundays. How about an egg and piece of turkey bacon?"

Sighing dramatically, her dark curly hair bouncing as she does, she groans, "I guess but can you make them with extra love?"

Tapping the end of her nose I nod and go about scrambling her eggs and pouring them into the hot pan while she picks up her tablet and pulls up a cartoon to watch while I cook. When she was a baby and I would rock her back to sleep in the middle of the night, I made declarations to myself on all the things she wouldn't be allowed to do. No screen time during meals, no refined sugars, no dating until she's thirty. I've swayed in my resolutions on the first two but her dating is non-negotiable. Even if my own mother thinks I'm ridiculous. Little does she know what men are like these days. That would mean letting her in on some of my own escapades before Calypso came along. Hence, why I let my mother live in her state of ignorant bliss on that topic.

When the eggs are almost done, I sprinkle cheese on top and hit the start button on the microwave. The bacon snaps and pops a few times before the machine dings its completion. Scooping the eggs onto the plate, I slide it in front of Calypso. Without taking her eyes off the screen, she lifts her fork full of eggs to her mouth. Clearing my throat, I catch her attention. Brow raised, I take a sip from my protein shake and wait for her to dig deep for those manners I know she has.

"Thanks, Daddy. You're the best and so are your special eggs."

"You're welcome. Don't get too distracted by your show. We leave in fifteen minutes and you still need to brush your teeth."

Nodding her head, curls bouncing from side to side, she smiles and turns her attention back to the screen. Battles and wars is what my mom always says. Choose the battles but fight the wars. I have a strong suspicion the teenage years with my little girl are going to give the most epic wars a run for their money.

While she finishes her breakfast, I head outside to make sure Olaf has eaten some of his own breakfast. Calypso's birthday gift from my parents is running around the backyard chasing a bird that I think is winning whatever game they have going on. Glancing down to his food bowl under the covered patio, I note half the food is already gone and head back into the house. Plate and tablet abandoned, I hear the water running in the bathroom and thank God that my daughter is obsessed with brushing her teeth. It makes our mornings so much easier, and we're able to get out the door on time.

"Daddy, look!" Calypso squeals with excitement on our way to the truck. Excitement over the little things isn't unusual. The question is, what is she raving about today? A rolly polly? A broken rock? Ants eating a French fry? There are well over a million possibilities. And one I never expected.

"It's a fossil!"

Taking two steps toward her I look at the treasure in her hands. "Oh wow. That's really cool. But I don't think it's a fossil."

"Yes, it is. My teacher showed us a real one at school and it looked just like this. See the mark right there?"

Oh, I see it all right. "Honey, that indentation was left by rebar under the street."

She purses her cute and sassy little lips at me, because how would I know things? I'm not in first grade science class. "That wouldn't leave a fossil in a rock."

"Because that's not a rock. That's broken concrete probably from when the city dug up the sidewalk a couple months ago to fix a broken pipe."

Whipping her backpack off quickly, she unzips and carefully places her treasure inside. "I'm going to take it to show my friends. They'll be so excited I found a real fossil!"

I don't bother correcting her. I've met some of those kids. Calypso is the sharpest one in that class, which means there's no hope for them to figure out that's concrete.

Morning drop-off was surprisingly easy after our treasure hunt. I think everyone has finally settled back into their daily routines now that we've been back at it for a couple months. The long days of summer and no pick-up and drop-off lines a distant memory. Tapping the garage opener, I sit in my truck while the door rolls up, enjoying the air conditioning for as long as possible. Slipping out of the seat, I trek into my home gym and flip on the large fans and cue up my playlist before heading inside to drop my keys on the counter and fill my water bottle.

My gig as a part-time cover model requires me to work out daily, pushing myself just to the limit to keep my almost thirty-year-old body in prime condition. The competition is tough and the younger guys are slowly pushing us older guys out of the way. My mom has been teasing me that soon I'll be featured on a few covers dubbing me a "silver fox." I didn't have time to respond because my dad jumped into the conversation demanding the title for himself. As much as I hate to admit it, she has a point.

The calls from photographers still come, but the length between those calls is getting longer as the years ticks by. Thankfully, modeling isn't my primary source of income, it's just a way for me to build up my savings and Calypso's college fund.

And I do still have a small fan club of neighbor-hood women that strategically schedule their morning walks for this time of day and this path of the neigh-borhood. Strange how someone always has an untied shoelace directly in front of my garage.

Honestly, it doesn't bother me. A little ego boost never hurt anyone. Plus, having a few gawkers stroll by forces me to keep my focus. I don't want to look like a slacker for them.

Tugging my T-shirt over my head, I toss it in the washer before heading out to kick my own ass on the treadmill and weights before I have to shower and head to my day job. With each drop of sweat that falls from my head, I let my mind clear as I fall into the rhythm of my feet hitting the rubber surface. With five miles complete, I hit the free weights and wave when my fan club walks by. Finally, I crank out two hundred sit-ups as I close out my workout and hit the shower.

Dressed in a pair of dark gray shorts and collared

shirt, I slip on my flip-flops and head out to face the day. A day that will be full of telephone calls, estimates, and dodging questions about my love life. You know, the typical. The drive to work isn't long, and as I turn into the driveway of my childhood home, I smile at the nostalgia. The trees are bigger and the flowers more vibrant than when we were kids, but it's still the same brick home I spent my youth in, building memories.

The only thing that's really different is the size of the hill it sits on. I swear it shrunk. We used to do log rolls down the dip in the front yard. Now? Now it's one tiny dip I wouldn't even notice if I stepped over it. I asked my mom about it once, wondering if the house was somehow sinking or if it needed to be leveled. She laughed and told me it's always been that size. I just got taller.

Then she said there was a lesson in that—perspective is everything. I'm sure she's right, but so far I haven't had to put that into real life use.

I let myself in the front door and head straight for the kitchen where I know my mom is brewing up a fresh pot of coffee. One of the perks of working with my dad is spending my workdays in the home where I spent my childhood instead of a stuffy office. When my dad suggested we move the business into the home office, I thought he was crazy. Like everything else in my life, he was right and I was wrong for doubting him.

"Morning, Mom," I greet with a kiss to her cheek as she dries her hands on a towel.

"Hey, honey. How was my amazing granddaughter this morning?"

"Sassy as always. I swear every gray hair on my head is because of her. I imagine every hair on my head will be white as snow by the time she starts high school."

Laughing, Mom hands me a cup and slides the creamer over toward me. Leaning my hip against the counter, I take a tentative sip and nod toward the island.

"Are you ever going to get rid of that?" I ask, motioning to the kitchen island and the lopsided pot that she treats like it's coated in gold.

"Nope. Calypso made it, and it's important to her, therefore it's important to me."

"Well you may need to find a place to store it. Calypso found a new treasure this morning and chatted the entire drive to school about how she can't wait to put it on your table."

"Ooh!" Mom's eyes light up with delight, like only a grandmother's can. "What did she find?"

"Concrete." She cocks her head, the unspoken request to continue. "She thinks it's a fossil, Mom. Unless dinosaurs were made of rebar and had concrete poured over them, it's not."

Stepping toward me, my mom cups my cheek and smiles up at me. "Matthew, let the child believe. When you were her age, you insisted you were invisible. I never once disagreed. Imagination is a wonderful thing. Besides, you'll need ammunition when she hits those teen years and wants to date. A concrete fossil is a good place to start."

Barking out a laugh, I raise my cup to toast her before heading to the office and settling in for a day full of phone calls. The life of a financial advisor—still using my superpower of invisibility to help guide my clients toward financial security. One phone call at a time.

# Chapter 2

### Carrie

"**G**ood morning, Lukey Dukey," I singsong and carefully open the cage door.

My fur baby immediately climbs out of his nest of rags and flicks his tail at me, letting me know what a big man he is. He's not wrong. He's well into his adult years and by all accounts, should be back out in the wild. Unfortunately, nature doesn't always have the same plans I do.

And now I have a pet squirrel who can't survive in the wild.

"Don't make that face at me," I chide gently, also careful to make my moves smooth around him. I'm not worried he'll attack me or anything. I just don't like scaring him if I don't have to. Regardless of if he's been hand-raised, a squirrel still naturally falls on the "prey" side of the animal kingdom. Skittish is ingrained in him.

"I have some fresh pecans for you."

That gets his attention. He climbs through the opening and on to the top of the cage, balancing on his hind legs as he takes the nuts from my hand one by one and munches away. Pecans are his personal favorite. Followed closely by walnuts and acorns.

You know what he doesn't like? Peanuts. Of course he doesn't. Because they're cheap and I can afford them. But no. He'd prefer to starve to death than eat something that stays within our food budget. Leave it to me to end up permanently housing a rodent that has expensive tastes.

This is why I don't date much. I'm too much of a sucker. With my luck, I'd write my date's rent check if his story was sad enough.

I spend the next several minutes cleaning out the bottom of his cage and changing out nest rags while he jumps back and forth from the cage to my shoulder and back again. It's like I'm his personal tree. I don't mind. It's kind of cool to have a squirrel climb all over you. How many people can say that?

What I do mind is when my phone rings just as he lands on my shoulder, scaring him so he runs off.

"Dammit. Luke! Come back here!" I admonish while swiping the answer button. "Aren't you supposed to be on the road already?" I say to my other best friend and fellow blogger, Celeste.

She coughs, sniffles, and wheezes before answering me. That's not good. "Should be. But I have stupid luck and woke up this morning with a one hundred two fever and a body that won't stop shivering."

"Oh no!" I exclaim as I bend down and look for Luke under the couch. Where the hell is he? "So you can't go?"

"And infect my celebrity crush?" She takes a minute to power through another coughing fit. She sounds horrible. But I'm betting whatever virus she has is a cakewalk compared to the disappointment she feels.

Celeste is my blogging partner and focuses on the performance arts while I stick with word art—also known as books. Real name, Celeste Pumperkin, she's known as Celestial Starr by the theater community around the country. Well, those that follow us, anyway. She's built up quite a fan base with her reviews on various musicals and stage dramas, partially because she doesn't discriminate on the level of productions she sees. As a backstage manager by trade, she's heavily involved with bringing stories to life on stage, and that means taking in as many shows as she can, from Broadway productions to off-off-Broadway start-ups, even a few college plays.

Last year, she saw a tiny two-man show called, "Get Up" starring Hunter Stone. She was so enamored by his performance, she raved about him for weeks, telling me he was the future of theater and her new dream was to work alongside him. And then he did the unthinkable…

He joined the cast of a television series about vampires.

Which she now watches religiously.

Even though she didn't have a television until he joined the cast.

So imagine her excitement when she found out the show, which is wildly popular in the fifteen to twenty-five-year-old female demographic, was putting together a convention for fans to meet their favorite members of the cast.

Actually, don't imagine it. It included a whole lot of screaming, even more sobs of happiness, and general jumping up and down like the fangirl she is. It wasn't pretty. But it was so very Celeste.

That was close to nine months ago and she's slept with the printed tickets under her pillow ever since. I suspect that's where they are right now.

"I'm so sorry, honey." I try not to breathe heavy from the exertion of climbing under my kitchen table, trying to see if my squirrel is hanging underneath. He's still on the loose. "I know how much you were looking forward to this."

"I know you're trying to make me feel better about the fact that I'm dying without ever meeting the man I've been crushing on for so long, but I don't think you do know how I feel. Have you ever had your dreams shattered and stomped on while you lie in bed and cough up a lung?"

I would argue that we've all experienced our fair share of disappointment, but this is her moment of devastation. I need to be supportive of all the dramatics.

Plus I can't win if my mind is halfway on my runaway squirrel.

*Where the hell is he?*

"Where is who?" Celeste's raspy voice answers what I thought was an unspoken question.

"Did I say that out loud?"

"Yes you did. And the fact that you didn't even realize it means you're feeling frazzled. Tell me what's going on. Take my mind off the worst day of my life."

If missing a con is the worst day of her life, she's not doing half bad.

Looking around the room, I'm still halfway trying to figure out if I was a squirrel, where I would hide. "I can't find Luke."

Another cough. Another sniffle. "How did you lose him? He's got the longest, bushiest tail ever. It's probably sticking out from under the couch now."

"I already looked there," I say as I hightail it to my bedroom. "At first I thought he was hiding, but now I bet he's sleeping somewhere."

"You're the only person I know who would get stuck housing a squirrel who has narcolepsy."

I giggle because she's not wrong. I'm always finding the animals with the weirdest conditions. When I was a kid I had a three-legged dog. Then I had a rabbit that could only run in circles. Animals with life-altering issues always seem to gravitate my direction.

"At least he's healthy." I blow out a breath as I get on all fours to look under my bedroom furniture. If I don't find him soon, I'm going to be late for work. "Doc saw him yesterday and gave him a clean bill of health."

A garbled noise comes from the other end of the line, followed by an "ow." I suspect Celeste was trying to snort a laugh and instead got stuck with air in her clogged nose.

"You just better hope that thing doesn't turn on you when he realizes he's an adult, male squirrel and should be outside with the other rodents."

I roll my eyes as I stand up and walk toward the head of my bed. Maybe he decided to hide under the covers. I suppose it would feel nest like to him.

"If he was going to turn feral, he would have done it by now." I begin tossing my pillows on the floor. "Animals are smart. Some of them just know they'd never survive in the wild so they adapt to living with humans. Oh here he is!"

My furry friend is sound asleep, just as I suspected.

"Where was he?" Celeste asks, more out of curiosity than concern. She doesn't get my love of animals. But I don't get her love of vampires, so we're even.

"From the awkward position he's lying in, looks like he fell asleep trying to build a nest under my pillow."

"Eww. Yuck. He's on your pillow?" I can hear Celeste gagging, but I'm not sure if it's in response to

Luke's whereabouts or if throwing up is part of whatever ails her.

Lifting him gently, I cradle him to my chest, balance the phone on my shoulder, and stroke his fur while taking him back to his cage. He doesn't even stir. "He was not on my pillow, he was under it."

"Suuuure. It took you three hours to find him. I'm sure he was on top of it, rubbing his little squirrel butt all over it before you found him."

"Yes," I deadpan. "Because that's what they do. Rub their butts on things for fun. You're ridiculous, you know that?"

"Says the woman who lives with a rodent with a medical disability."

Taking one last quick look to make sure the cage is secure and he has everything he needs while I'm gone, I head toward the door.

"Are you sure you can't go to that con? You're sounding awfully sarcastic for someone who claims to be sick."

"My pending death is making me pissy! Leave me alone!" Yelling is apparently too hard on her lungs because she begins yet another coughing fit. I wait patiently while she catches her breath again.

Actually, I put the phone down on the passenger seat of my Honda Civic while I crank the engine and turn the air on. I can still hear her hacking up a lung, even before the Bluetooth connects, but it won't hurt her to believe I'm being a patient friend.

Finally, I've hit the road, and she's able to speak again.

"I think I need to go lie down. Sitting doesn't agree with me," she croaks, and I'm inclined to agree with her.

"I think that is a very smart idea. Take a nap, and text me when you get up. I wanna make sure you're not dead." Taking a right outside of my neighborhood, I head toward Critter Keepers and Wildlife Rescue, where I work with animals I don't get to take home.

"If you don't hear from me, tell my sister she owes my funeral a hundred bucks since she never paid me back for that pogo stick she bought."

*The what?*

Never mind. I don't even want to know.

"Will do. Love ya, friend."

"Back atcha."

We disconnect and not a moment too soon. I only have seventeen more minutes until I pull into the parking lot for work. That's seventeen minutes of the new Donna Moreno audiobook.

Hawk Weaver, here I come.

Fingers crossed he doesn't whistle again.

# Chapter 3

*Matthew*

I've always respected women. Actually I hold them in the highest regard. My mom is one of the greatest people I know. She's selfless and giving, always putting everyone's needs above her own while still remaining independent and pursuing her own happiness. I'll even admit to having a small amount of respect for the woman who gave me the greatest gift in the world. I never thought at twenty-two that a single hookup would have me reevaluating every life plan I had, but it did. Too young and immature to be a mother, she sacrificed her relationship with our daughter to pursue her dreams. I cannot imagine not having Calypso in my life, but her loss is my gain, a hundred times over.

My love for my daughter knows no bounds. This is never more evident than by the monstrosity I am currently trying to squeeze my body into. When my daughter begged me to dress up with her for Halloween, I mistakenly assumed we'd collaborate on the costumes. Maybe a pair of Storm Troopers or even a homage to the great duo of Wayne and Garth from *Wayne's World.* But no.

Instead, my petite little dictator advised me she had the perfect plan for us. I would be the Elsa to her Anna. This shouldn't have been a surprise since our dog is affectionately named Olaf and she loves to sing the soundtrack when she takes a bath. At the top of her tone-deaf lungs. Since I struggle to say no to her when she bats her long lashes at me and sticks out her bottom lip, I folded like a house of cards and am now trying not to tear the fabric as I tug the shimmery sleeve over my biceps. At least the ink on my shoulder is comprised mostly of blues and teals which matches this . . . outfit.

Once I manage to secure the flimsy mesh into place, I take in the horror show that is my reflection. The pink eye makeup that my mom applied thirty minutes ago seems to be brightening as the minutes tick by. Is that even possible? Does makeup grow? And who thought this itchy material was ever a good idea?

*The things we do for our children.*

"Daddy! You better hurry or everyone will run out of candy!"

Sighing, I pick up the blonde wig from the counter and secure it on top of my head. Nightmares. I'm going to give the kids in the neighborhood nightmares. Exiting my bedroom, I make my way to the living room where my mom is helping Calypso with the final touches to her Anna costume. My baby is growing up before my eyes and I hate that her mother is missing these moments. I know one day she'll have regrets and find a way to be a more constant fixture in our lives. Until that time, I'll do all that I can to be enough for her.

"Oh, Daddy," she sighs, bringing her hands to her chest dramatically. Good grief, it's time to monitor her screen time a little more closely. "You look so pretty."

My mom giggles and I shoot her a glare that clearly tells her to leave the comments to herself. Rising from the couch, she pulls her phone from her pocket and motions for us to stand together.

"Grandma we can't take a picture without Olaf!"

I let out a string of short whistles to call him inside but he never shows his face. In the distance the rumble of thunder fills the air and a gust of cool wind slices through the room.

"Oh dear, you two need to get a move on if you're going to get some trick-or-treating in before the rain starts. How about if I take a few pictures of you two now, and then we can do more with Olaf when you get back?" Mom asks, and my small sprite sighs in response.

Scooping Calypso up in my arms, I tickle her sides to draw out my favorite sound in the world. Her giggles are contagious, and I laugh alongside her as my mom orders us to settle down and look her way. After a few quick pictures, we're out the door, leaving my mom to pass out candy for any of our own trick or treaters.

The best part of living in a neighborhood full of kids is the way the families go all out for every occasion. Halloween is no exception with most homes decked out in spider webs, headstones, and spooky music. Since my daughter is not only sassy but fearless, she isn't swayed in the least by the efforts to make the homes creepy. Trotting up the steps of each house, she belts out her request for tricks or treats with a huge smile on her face.

Her pure joy at the attention we're getting is worth me wearing a costume I'm pretty certain is made of material I'm allergic to. Calypso is rambling on and on about how much fun she's having and the millions of candies she has in her pumpkin when a family of five dressed as *The Simpsons* steps up next to us. Sure. That lucky dad got to wear pants.

Pretend Lisa Simpson glances in Calypso's bucket and in perfect character tsks her trick-or-treating skills. "I have three trillion pieces," she quips with a flip of her hand.

"I bet my candies are better. Everyone loves Anna." I rest my hand on my daughter's shoulder, a warning to watch her tone, but there's no stopping a pair of little girls in a battle over candy.

"Well, my sister is too little for candy so I get hers and that's why I have *more*."

"Yeah well, millions are bigger than trillions so there." Her little hands cross over her chest as best as they can with her pumpkin in her hand. I don't have the heart to tell her it's more like thirty pieces and a box of raisins, but I'll let her have her moment. I also make a note to check her math homework more closely.

As I take her hand to cross the street, another rumble of thunder reminds us of the impending storm. Pretend Marge Simpson relays her concern about their animals being afraid of the storm which elicits a shriek of epic proportions from my little faux Anna, literally scaring a fart out of Pretend Bart. Or it was just good timing. Either way, what the hell are they feeding that kid?

"Daddy, what if Olaf is scared? We have to go home." Her little lip begins to tremble so I kneel down to her eye level and offer her a tentative smile.

"I'm sure he's fine but we can go home if you want."

"Excuse me, did you say Olaf?" the Pretend Homer asks.

Standing I nod before his wife interjects. "We saw animal control on the street earlier. Someone said there was a dog running down the street with a snowman costume on. I wasn't—"

"How long ago was this?" I know it's rude to cut someone off, but I can't imagine the level of chaos I'll be dealing with tonight at bedtime if Olaf is missing.

"Probably about thirty minutes ago? I don't really know."

Scooping up Calypso I start walking when I hear

the dad shout, "You better hurry, they're probably closing soon!"

Picking up the pace, I yell, "Thank you!" over my shoulder and take off in a short jog toward the house. When we reach the front door, I wait impatiently for the trio of kids on the porch to move before rushing through the door. Mom looks at me confused as I set Calypso down and whistle for Olaf again. I start rushing through the house calling him while my mom shouts after me.

"Mom, have you seen Olaf?"

"No. I assumed he was hiding from the doorbell and storm. What's wrong?"

I rush to the kitchen and grab my phone from the charger on the counter and start searching the internet for a telephone number to the local shelter. As the line begins to ring, I turn back to my mom, concern written all over her face.

"Someone said they saw a dog in a snowman costume picked up by Animal Control. Shit—"

"Language," my mom reminds me as she scoops my visibly distressed daughter up in her arms.

"Sorry. They closed at five. Dangit."

"What about Critter Keepers and Wildlife Rescue? I think they take animals there too."

Critter what? Confusion on my face, Mom chuckles and says, "It's that building down past the high school. They do wonderful things with local wildlife and pet adoptions. Your aunt—"

"Mom! Sorry to shout but I need to see if they have him. What's it called again?" I start pulling up the search engine on my phone when I note the time. Any business is probably closing within the next twenty minutes.

Picking up my keys and wallet, I turn to tell my mom the plan but she just nods in acknowledgement. I start to walk toward the door when a sweet voice calls me back. Her eyes are sad and the concern for her best friend is written all over her face. I hold my hands out for her and she leaps from my mom into my arms. I hardly hear Mom shouting that she'll lock up before she leaves as we rush through the garage and to my truck, strapping my now sniffling little girl into her booster seat.

Carefully so I don't run over any kids, I inch out of the driveway and down the street and hope the storm holds off a little longer and there's no traffic. Coming to a stop at a light, I look at the clock and send a little prayer up that we make it to our destination before they close. It's only then that I realize I'm still in costume.

# Chapter 4

*Carrie*

I hate Halloween. Mostly because I'm a weenie and don't do scary, but also because I think it's the most pointless holiday.

People spend way too much money on costumes to wear for one night so they can knock on random strangers' doors, like mine, and beg for candy I spent way too much money buying.

Then the kids all end up on a sugar high, probably puke half of what they ate all over themselves, and the candy and costumes that took so much time and money to pick out are ruined. Exactly what point does all of that serve?

I'm sure my strong feelings have nothing to do with Old Lady Ghesilin traumatizing my childhood. She lived across the street from my family for the entirety of my elementary school years and always decorated her yard with headstones, creepy mechanical hands that would move on the ground like they were digging their way out of a grave, and let's not forget the giant, hairy spider. Even the largest huntsman in the outback of Australia has nothing on that thing. I was the smallest in my class, so I just knew it was going to eat me alive.

But of course there was no avoiding the house at trick-or-treat time because some sadistic neighbor kid was always going to triple dog dare you to walk up to her front door. No one wants to lose face over a triple dog dare. Especially when you're the little one in the bunch.

I can't be positive, but I think Ghesilin must have found out about the challenge, because as the years went by the house would get scarier and scarier. Eventually you couldn't just shut your eyes and hope to feel your way back to the road once the challenge was complete. Oh no. You had to do that shit with your eyes wide open. It was almost as if her personal goal was to make me pee in my pants on her front porch.

She may or may not have succeeded in that quest my seventh-grade year when the stuffed scarecrow on her porch was actually her husband sitting really still until I rang the doorbell.

It's a memory I try not to think about and refuse to discuss.

On a side note, vinegar really does take the urine smell out of clothes.

Instead of putting myself through the misery of my least favorite holiday, I always work until closing on October thirty-first. In the good employee sense, it means I'm a team player. In a personal sense, it means I don't have to buy any candy and don't have to suffer through the doorbell ringing eight million times.

I don't tell anyone at work that my motives are selfish because I'm very strategic about it. I wait until the schedule comes out and as soon as I hear someone complain about working on a holiday, I pounce like Rocky, our resident feline. Except I don't jump from table to counter, and I have much more accurate precision so I don't fall into the gap in a humiliated heap.

No one said Rocky is the most graceful thing.

What I am, though, is an evil genius. I offer to switch shifts to help relieve the poor mom who wants to be with her children, give the obligatory "It's not a problem" when they tell me they owe me one.

And truly, I get it. If I lived closer to my family, who all still live in New Jersey, I'd want to take my cousins' kids trick-or-treating too. It's a family affair. But I made the choice to stay in Texas post college, and it's not in the budget to fly home for every holiday. Especially the one I hate in particular. So instead, I make the best of the situation by making a mental note of who I need to switch with should I get stuck working on Memorial Day. Because that's the holiday I love.

Sleeping in, maybe a boat ride on the lake, barbeque—way better than Steven King clowns and Freddy Krueger masks. I get tingly all over just thinking about the feel of the sun on my skin and the breeze through my hair.

It's a far cry from today's perfect Halloween weather. A roar of thunder rolls through and I walk toward the front window to see how bad it is. There's never anyone here on our extended hours days so I have a chance to really look at the sky. It's getting darker quickly, and not because of the time. The clouds are rolling in and fast.

"That's gonna suck when I walk to my car," I say out loud to myself as the first of many claps of thunder breaks, but I know it's going to suck even more for the animals here.

The Critter Keepers and Wildlife Rescue has two sides to it: the pet rescue and adoption side—where I don't normally work—and the wildlife rescue side where I spend most of my days. I love it. We take in all the orphaned and injured animals people find and do our best to raise them until they can be released into the wild. Most of the actual rehab happens in the home of one of our many volunteers. When eight litters of baby squirrels come in at the same time, it's hard for two employees to feed two dozen babies every three hours. Sending each set to a foster home ensures the babies get the round the clock care they need. Plus, release is a lot easier when it's in someone's front yard.

We also rehab raccoons, possums, and the occasional armadillo. We even had a baby deer one time. She wasn't here long before we found a specially trained person to raise her on their farm, but it was still a fun experience.

I don't normally work on the pet adoption side. It's more of an "as needed" basis, and Halloween is when it's needed. I don't mind, though. It's an easy way to make a buck and keep all that money I'd waste on candy safely in my bank account.

The downside is a day like today. When storms come in, the dog kennels can get loud. None of the dogs like thunder. I'm sure by the time I get back there to finish up for the night, I'll decide I need to stay late to comfort some poor baby with massive anxiety. That's nothing like the wildlife side. Those critters hear bad weather coming and they dig deep into their nests and sleep through it.

That's what I hope to do once I get home. No wonder I relate to squirrels so much. Hibernation during bad weather sounds amazing.

Glancing at the clock, I'm pleased to see it's finally closing time, and not a moment too soon. The wind is starting to pick up. That can only mean the rain is right behind it. If I'm lucky, I'll stay dry getting to my car.

But of course, my luck is about to run out. Just as I'm reaching for the lock, a big black truck comes to a screeching halt in front of the sidewalk. I've come to know only one type of person drives a vehicle like that. Young, cocky, and wearing a too tight T-shirt across his "I lift weights and here are my muscles" torso. Bonus points if he has blinged-out jeans too. Just great.

"Oh shit," I grumble to myself, cursing our policy to never kick someone out until they're done. "It's worth it for that one adopted animal," the boss always spouts. Yes, she's right, but I have yet to do an adoption at closing time on Halloween. After six years here, I think it's safe to say that pattern is pretty solid.

I don't have time to keep getting my feathers ruffled, though, because a very large Elsa and very little Anna jump out of the truck and start running toward the building as the first drops of rain fall. I snicker as the blond jogs like the man he very clearly is. It reminds me of when Channing Tatum did that lip sync. Man, that was funny.

Flinging the door open, the pair race in just as a total downpour begins. Not a nice little shower, but a complete and total soak. So much for staying dry in the parking lot.

"Phew! We made it just in time, Sprite," a familiar voice says behind me. I quickly lock the door, stalling because this can't be. There is no way the one person I was hoping to never see again just ran through my doors in a dress.

When I turn around, there's no denying it.

"Matthew?"

Very tall Elsa turns away from very short Anna and faces me. It takes a second for his eyes to widen in recognition, which isn't insulting at all, but when they do a huge grin crosses his face.

"Carrie? What are you doing here?"

My brain takes this exact moment to short out from

the shock and not understand what he's asking me. What am I doing in town? At the shelter? At this hour? In scrubs? The possibilities are endless, so I just pick an answer and go with it.

"Locking up."

"I can see that. But… you work here?"

"Yep. Not normally on this side of the shelter, but it's Halloween so I switched so someone else could have the night off, which is normally great but that rain is going to be a bitch to drive in. And… Oh shit, I said bitch." I throw my hand over my mouth, just now registering that I'm in the presence of a child.

Matthew chuckles and I hate that it sounds so, so… perfect coming out of his perfect mouth. It's so unfair that he can dress like a Disney princess and still be hot as hell.

"It's nothing she hasn't heard before." Gesturing to small Anna, he says, "Carrie, this is my daughter, Calypso."

I open my mouth to respond, but falter when her name registers. "After the siren who held Odysseus captive on an island before she was ordered to let him go?"

Matthew's lips quirk to the side, like he's trying not to laugh at how very obvious my book nerdiness is. "We call her Sprite."

"Okay," I say because I got nothin'. "Well it's nice to meet you."

Cue the longest, most awkward pause.

*Well done, Carrie. If you wanted the man to leave you alone, insulting his daughter's name should do the trick.*

It's probably a family name or something and I unknowingly made fun of a beloved grandma too. Fortunately, the smallest one of us turns out to be the most focused. And probably the most mature, if this whole scene is any indication.

"Dad. We're here for Olaf, remember?"

"Right." Matthew snaps back into focus like the man on a mission he is. I have no idea what that mission is, but I'm about to find out. "We need a dog."

I furrow my brow. What odd timing to decide to adopt. "Any breed in particular or are you just wanting to adopt a shelter mutt?"

"No, I mean, we're looking for *our* dog. The storm scared him and he ran off."

That makes so much more sense.

"Oh! Okay now I'm following. Come on." I gesture for them to follow me into the kennel area. "We always pick up a bunch of dogs when it storms like this. Although, with it being Halloween, we haven't processed many of them yet. What does your dog look like?"

"Like a snowman," the little girl blurts out as I swing open the door to the back.

As suspected, the noise is horrendous, and it goes

up a notch when all the dogs catch wind of us coming inside.

The girl, who I now refer to as Little Anna in my head because I just can't call her the name of a sex-nymph, immediately covers her ears. "They're so loud!"

"They always are," I shout back at her even though she probably can't hear me anyway. "It gets worse whenever there's a storm."

Noah, our canine resident, takes that moment to trot over on all fours, looking completely comfortable in this environment. I still don't know how he ended up being a permanent part of the shelter, but it happened before I got here. He doesn't even have a kennel, just roams around at will. It's surprising that no one has ever taken him home because he's actually a pretty good dog. Except when he lifts his leg and pees on people's dresses, which he's doing right now...

"Noah!" I admonish and shoo him away. "No peeing on princesses!" I glance up at Matthew sheepishly. "Sorry about that. I've never seen him do that before."

"Don't even worry about it." Matthew shakes the liquid that pooled at the bottom of his hem off quickly. "Gives me an excuse to throw this thing away. When I promised to dress up for trick-or-treating, I didn't expect it to be so damn itchy. Being a woman is hard."

That makes me smile. I love that he is one of those parents who dresses up with his kid. It's endearing.

Not that I care. Because… I don't. At all.

"Dad." Little Anna tugs on his lacy sleeve. "We have to find Olaf."

I jump in and answer before he can. "You're right. Let's go to the back kennels. That's where any new guys will be. You say he looks like a snowman?"

Little Anna nods vigorously. "He was wearing an Olaf costume. It even had sticks for his arms and a carrot nose."

"Hmm. Well I haven't seen any dogs matching that description. Maybe his costume fell off. Let's check."

After twenty minutes of looking in every kennel, a potty break, and one huge pitch for why a particularly cute puppy needed to go home with them (Little Anna lost that round, but I suspect it's only the beginning), we all come to the same conclusion—Olaf isn't here.

"I'm so sorry, guys." And I really am. Looking at Little Anna's sad face, I feel terrible that her beloved pet, which I now know is a beagle, has seemed to escape the clutches of the law at this point. "It's not over yet, though. He could be hiding somewhere, waiting out the rain to make his way home soon."

Matthew tucks his little girl into his side, blond wig beginning to slide off his head. "I hope so. With his nose, there's no telling how far away he is at this point."

"Well why don't you fill out our missing dog report," I suggest, making my way behind the counter and pulling out the form he needs. "I'll get it in the system and should Olaf show up, we'll call you."

"Really?" Little Anna's eyes brighten.

"Really." I hand a clipboard over to Matthew with everything he needs attached to it and wait while he fills it out.

I kind of hate myself for it, but while I wait, I watch. It's interesting seeing the way he interacts with his daughter. He's so patient with her, even when she bumps his arm making him draw a line across the page. Most people I know would reprimand their kid for not paying attention, but Matthew simply points to the line and explains why she needs to be careful.

When he takes off the wig, though, that's when I see him in a totally different light. Here is this physically beautiful man putting all his ego and looks aside to make his daughter happy. And not just trick-or-treating. He's actually in public dressed like that for her sake.

Dammit. I hate when the hot guy is awesome too.

It doesn't take long for Matthew to fill out the paperwork and bring it back to me.

"Done?" That was a dumb question, Carrie. He wouldn't give it to you if he wasn't.

"Yeah. So how does this work?"

I glance over the application quickly, making sure everything is filled in. "We'll put all your information into our system. When a new dog comes in, we scan for microchips first. If there isn't one, or we can't find information on it, we then cross reference your information with his to see if there are any matches. Fingers crossed, we'll find him really soon."

"I really appreciate it." He reaches down and picks up his little girl who lays her head on his shoulder. I'm sure between the candy, the dog hunt, and the weather, she's pooped by now. "And my number is on there. Maybe you can take it in case you happen to see him before he's processed."

"Um… yeah. Sure. I can text you if I see him." That's innocent, right? It doesn't mean I've changed my mind about his character when it comes to women, does it? He's just a guy.

A *hot* guy I don't have any interest in.

Pushing my very inappropriate thoughts aside, I walk them to the front door.

"Thanks for stopping by. Try to stay dry." I cringe because they're already wet and there's practically a hurricane out there. Way to not be awkward, Carrie.

"You too." Matthew smiles, perfectly confident in his ability to have a conversation. Unlike some of us. And by some of us I mean me. "And thanks again, Carrie."

He flashes me that megawatt smile that's made him a household name in the romance book community before ducking out into the now light rain, using the wig to shield his daughter's face from the drops.

I quickly lock the door, thankful for the break in the weather.

That doesn't mean I'm giving up my hibernation

though. A girl's still got to have some sort of pleasure in life, even if it's not of the male variety.

# Chapter 5

## Matthew

When I was in college, Friday nights were the high-light of my week. Not only did it kick off my weekend of partying but it was also the only weekday I didn't have classes. You better believe I scheduled it that way on purpose.

While my life today is nowhere near the shit show it was then, I still look forward to Fridays. Calypso and my parents have a standing sleepover date, one that has only been rescheduled a handful of times since she turned two. My parents would have been fine to start the tradition from almost day one but I wanted to be there for her. Hands on for every moment. Each mile-stone.

Then, after her second birthday, my parents all but locked me out of the house and demanded I get a social life and as my mother called it "some lady loving." According to her I was a grumpy asshole, except when

I was with my daughter, and it could only mean I was in need of female companionship. That was the first conversation we had about boundaries. Hers, not mine. One I know we'll have again tonight. It is Friday and our own sort of tradition.

"Daddy, what if Olaf comes home? I won't be here and he'll be so sad."

Sitting down on the couch, I pat my legs for Calypso to climb up on my lap. Her normally chipper and happy personality has been dampened by Olaf's still missing status. I was hopeful the first few days he was gone that we'd get a call from the shelter. Or, more truthfully that Carrie would call or text me herself and tell me she found him. By day three, I knew it was unlikely he'd come home.

"I promise, if Olaf comes home or someone calls about him I will call Grandma right away. You don't want to disappoint your Papa do you? He was excited to work on your puzzle tonight."

Sighing, she settles into my chest. I know her little heart is worried about her four-legged best friend but sitting around wallowing won't help. Besides, my dad really is looking forward to working on the jigsaw puzzle they're putting together. Somehow in the last few months, the two of them have become obsessed with puzzles. My mom says it's quite competitive and they get in very heated discussions over who found the puzzle piece first. I can only imagine my normally chill Dad sparring with my headstrong little Sprite.

"Oh Daddy, he's not excited. He's scared. I'm way

better at puzzles than Papa."

And just like that, the gloominess in her is gone and replaced with the normal sass. She hops off my lap and trots down the hall to her room for her little rolling suitcase. When she returns, I'm waiting by the door with the keys in my hand. Before we step into the garage, she stops and, leaving her suitcase behind, runs to the backyard and opens the slider.

"Olaf! Olaf!," she shouts and waits for a few seconds before closing the door again. When she catches my eye, she lifts one shoulder and returns to take her suitcase and walks out the door. Well, okay then.

Our drive to my parents' house is quick and only long enough for one song to be belted out from the backseat. Thank goodness. My daughter is many things but a singer she is not. Unbuckling herself, she waits for me to come around and help her down from the truck before she runs toward the front door.

"Don't worry, I'll get your bag!" I shout as the front door opens.

"Thanks, Daddy. Hi, Papa, are you ready for me? Do we have snacks?"

Laughing to myself, I grab her suitcase, and favorite blanket, and favorite pillow, and favorite stuffed animal, because why wouldn't she bring half her room for one night, and follow her path to the front door. Leaving her stuff by the entryway, I close the door just as she lets out a string of giggles. It's a welcome sound after the week we've had.

Pans clanking in the kitchen tell me where I'll find my mom and I head that way. Greeting her with a kiss on the cheek, I steal a carrot from the cutting board and settle in on one of the barstools. She doesn't say anything, not even about my thieving ways with her vegetables.

"Hi," I say and still nothing. "Mom?"

"Hmm?"

"Something wrong?"

Setting the knife down, she pauses, taking an audible breath before releasing it and turning to face me. I quickly run through the last few days, trying to figure out if I've done anything to earn the look on her face. Normally an expression she saves for my brother, her eyes are narrowed my direction, lips pierced in a fine line. Oh boy.

"Do you know what happened when I went on social media today, Matthew?"

"Uh… you saw spoilers for one of your shows?"

"Well, yes. Why do people do that? Not all of us watch in real time. Really, it's disgraceful how inconsiderate people can be about that. It's like with books. I mean, do I want to read a book after you've told me the entire story in your recommendation? Not really, Debbie."

"Who's Debbie?" I ask. I'm so confused.

Sighing, she mumbles something to herself and then picks up her phone. Tapping at the screen a few times she shoves it in my face. Oh yeah. That.

"And?"

"And? Matthew, do you think I want to be *tagged* by my friends on videos and screen shots of your bare ass. I mean, yes I wiped it until you were six but I don't need to see it now."

"I was wiping my own ass by the time I was six."

"Sorry to break it to you son, but you were not. Hell, you still had to strip naked to sit on the toilet and refused to poop in public until you were seven. That's not the point. The point is, your ass is all over the internet."

Barking out a laugh, I take her phone and start scrolling through her notifications. If she only knew how many of these same tags and messages I get daily. Not to mention on a cover reveal day. I won't bother sharing with her the very personal invitations I receive either. Today is a little more active since it was a video cover reveal, sexy music and all.

"This isn't even my ass, Mom. It's my hip."

"Don't sass me, Matthew." She snatches her phone back and grimaces as she sees what I'm looking at. "That is a hint of crack. Hence, ass."

"Mom, I've done more provocative covers than this before. Why is this one so bad? It's just the top of my ass and I'm wearing a towel. Also, for the record I had on boxer briefs too."

"Yes well, it's still weird, and I may have to unfollow you. I hate to be unsupportive but it's very awkward."

I don't bother pointing out she reads the books I'm on the covers for and insists on telling me all about them. There are no boundaries when it comes to those conversations. Hearing my mother recap a story about two men and the coed they both fell in love and, ultimately, into bed with, was not my favorite conversation. Nor was the one about the alien dragon or whatever it was that fell in love with a shape-shifting lumberjack. I still don't know how something like that works, but that's not my job. My job is to pose and give my most smoldering look, usually while half naked. The story inside the pages of whatever cover I grace is for the author to handle. I will continue to happily collect the paycheck and invest the money with the single goal of sending Calypso to college.

"Can we talk about something else?" I ask.

Nodding she says, "Any word on Olaf?"

Shaking my head she frowns and begins tossing the vegetables she was cutting in oil and seasoning before dumping them in a pan and sliding it in the oven. While I may not be staying for dinner, I know what will be in a Tupperware container with my name on it when I pick up Calypso tomorrow.

"What are you doing tonight?" she finally asks.

"Just the usual. Meeting a few of the guys for drinks and maybe some pool."

"I wish you'd find yourself a sweet girl to spend

your time with. Both you and Sprite need a lady in your lives."

"And that's my cue to leave." Rising from the chair, I grab my keys and round the counter to kiss her on the cheek. "I'm outta here. Love you, Mom."

"Love you too, son. Make sure you wear a condom this time."

Chuckling, I stop by the two puzzle masters and say my goodbyes before heading out the door. While all I want to do is go home, order a pizza, and watch a college game, I turn my truck toward the sports bar across town. It's one night a week, and I need to suck it up like a big boy.

When I pull in the parking lot I see it's a little busier than it was last weekend. My mom's words rattle around in my head as I park and make my way inside. I wonder for a minute how many other single parents are here. Statistically speaking, probably quite a few. Heading toward the corner we commandeer each week I see the guys are already in a game of pool so I sit down and pour a beer into the empty glass waiting for me.

Taking a sip, I look around the room. It's your run-of-the-mill sports bar with large televisions mounted on the walls, a different game or sporting event on each. A large oval bar in the middle of the space takes up a large portion of the room while the far side of the establishment is lined with booths and tables. I spot a few familiar faces and return the smile of a blonde I met about eight months back. Lisa? Lana? Lori. That's it.

Lori with the fondness for pink, glitter, and handcuffs. My initial thought when she pulled those out was more on the kinky side than scared. Then she started saying random things that made no sense. Each statement with a sexy purr of a voice and lustful look in her eyes. I was this close to calling an ambulance, thinking she was having some sort of psychotic break because none of what she said made sense. But then I realized they were lines from books.

Books I had been on the cover of. She wasn't just anyone, she was a fan. Or, more accurately, a bit of a stalker. So not 5150 crazy, but batshit, nonetheless. Her admission that she'd been coming to the bar for weeks, watching and waiting for the right opportunity to approach me freaked me out. When she stopped quoting romance novels, she began telling me the name of our future children, and I quickly feigned gastrointestinal issues and ran like the house was on fire. After she reached out to me via social media a few days later, I tactfully told her I didn't think it would be fair to see each other again for fear of what it would do to my career if I had to give up modeling for her. She seemed to buy that and swore she'd never want to keep me from my passion.

Interesting that someone would think eating a strict diet, working out seven days a week, and posing almost naked was a passion, but I went with it and managed to let her down easy, and without having to buy thicker blinds. Last thing I needed was to give in to her full lips, sexy come-ons, and end up with another unplanned pregnancy. Something about Lori screamed "hole in the condom."

The realization of the thoughts that I'm having and what my passions really are, hit me hard. Mom's right. I do need to find someone. I'm almost thirty years old and the only semblance of a romantic relationship I've had in six years is seeing the same girl more than twice in a six-month time frame.

Tossing back the rest of the beer, I pull a twenty from my wallet and slide it under the empty pitcher. My buddy Kevin looks over, eyebrow raised, and I say, "Next one's on me. I'm going to head home. Call you next week."

Before he can respond, I walk away and head home. Not that there will be any romantic possibilities there either. But, at least at my house, nobody is poking holes in condoms.

# Chapter 6

## Carrie

All weekend, I thought about Matthew and his daughter, whose name I still can't even think without wondering who the hell named the poor child. My weird thoughts kind of pissed me off. Not just that I couldn't get over seeing Matthew as something other than the cover model who sleeps with readers at events, but that I couldn't stop wondering why, of all the mythological characters you could name your kid after, you would choose the worst one ever. Well, her name isn't Medusa so I guess it's not the worst one ever.

Even my weekly phone call with my mother didn't distract me from the topic at hand. Finally, after too many minutes of responding to all the updates on family and friends with a half-hearted "Uh huh," my mom called me out and told me to call her back when I could give her my undivided attention on something more important than my book boyfriends.

Normally I'd say she has me pegged. I do spend too much time in my head thinking about my perfect version of a man. I admit, my ideals are pretty high and much to my mother's dismay, it makes marrying me off to "a good man who has a good job damn near impossible." Yes, she used those exact words. And yes, that's what her goal has been for me my entire life. Marriage and babies. Every little girl's dream.

Except mine, apparently. My dreams include a solid friend turned lover who understands my passion for animals and stories and maybe brings some humor into my life.

Instead, I suddenly have Matthew showing up. Matthew, whose daughter has the strangest name ever. I bet it's so unpopular it doesn't even make it in the top one thousand most popular baby names for the last hundred years. Or, it's so original by the time she's in high school, four other classmates will have the same name.

I have got to stop overthinking this. Maybe if I just say her name out loud a few times it'll stop sounding so strange to me.

"Calypso," I say once. "Calypso." This time with an emphasis on the "lip." "Calypso." And now a sing-song voice. "Nope. Still weird."

Not that it matters. The likelihood that I'll see either of them again is pretty low. Of course, I said that after the last author event we both ended up at, so my track record isn't looking great.

No time to think about that now, though. I've got some raccoons to pick up from our intake area.

Late fall and early winter babies are unusual, but not unheard of. What makes it hard is not many people are spending time outdoors, so we don't usually find them when they fall out of the nest until it's too late. I'm curious what shape these guys are in and how much work they're going to take. The rescue has a couple of really solid volunteers we call on, but the age difference between the little guys they're already raising and the newbies might make it difficult.

Pushing the door to the back open, I see my favorite doctor gently stroking a frightened kitten and talking softly to it. He looks up at me behind his thick rimmed glasses and smiles.

"Bottom left." He gestures with his head to the cage where my little ones are waiting for me.

"Who's that little guy?" I ask referring to the black and white furball he's still petting as he places it on some blankets.

"There's a feral mama out near the new strip mall. Someone's been trying to catch her babies for a while so we can get them off the street." He shuts the cage door quietly and picks up a clipboard to make notes. "I think this might be the last one."

Doctor Richards retired from his practice a couple years ago after four decades on the job. From what he tells us, he was hoping to travel the world, seeing as much as possible. Then he went on one trip to Europe and decided he liked the idea of traveling more than actually doing it. So he sticks to reading books about his favorite places and working for the shelter in the mornings to stay busy. As an office, we never let him forget how grateful we are for him. It's hard finding a vet who is willing to come in every day. It's even harder to find one who will work within the constraints of a non-profit's tiny budget.

"That's great. Did they catch the mama too?"

"Yep. Spayed her last week and sent her back on her way."

"Good," I say absentmindedly as I wash my hands to pick up my newest charges. Once an adult cat is feral, it's almost impossible to acclimate them into a pet situation. It's best to just make sure they can't have any more litters and let them live their lives out in the world on their own terms.

Not unlike these babies who will turn on me in a matter of months before making their new life in a random tree somewhere. Drying my hands and reaching into the cage, I search the blankets for a warm body.

"There you are," I say quietly when I find one. Pulling it to me, I begin my inspection. "Look at you, sweet one. You've got lots of fur. That's so good." It's likely what helped him survive until he was found. When they're brand new, there's almost no way to keep them from freezing to death within minutes. "And you're so noisy," I coo, listening to his strong purr. It's not the same kind you'd hear from a cat. It's much louder and demanding. "Let me look at you. Oh, your eyes are still closed. You don't appear to have any injuries. And you are a…" I flip him over carefully. "A boy! Yep. Definitely a boy. Just pooped on me and have no regrets about it, huh?" I fuss at him as I stroke his soft body. "At least I know you ate recently."

Feeling confident that he doesn't need any specialized treatment, I put him back inside and pull out the second raccoon. Although this one is a bit smaller, she's still the size of my palm. She has a few different markings but they look almost identical, which means they're probably from the same litter. That means either the entire nest fell down and we need to monitor for potential internal injuries, or their mama never came home to feed them, and they went rooting around for food. My money is on the food search. I love raccoons but they have a bad habit of crossing the street in the middle of the night. Chances are, she's squished on a road somewhere. Fingers crossed, it's not on my drive home.

"So I've got a boy and a girl," I announce to no one in particular, although I have no doubt Doc is paying attention. "About four weeks old. They look great." I begin gathering a small transportation cage so I can take them back to the wildlife center and get them settled in.

Just as I turn, I see Doc picking up a dog I didn't notice before and placing him on the examination table. Not such an unusual task, but what stops me in my tracks is the dirty, torn fabric carrot dangling from his collar.

No way.

I consider my options and what I should do. There's no doubt in my mind this is the beagle I've been thinking about all weekend, and I know who he belongs to. The question is do I let Olaf go through processing and hope for the best? Do I alert Jamie that this one has an owner and I know who it is? Or do I just text Matthew myself?

I'm ashamed to admit, I plugged his number into my phone last week when they were here. It was less about having his digits and more about not having to go back up front to find it later if the dog turned up.

Which is exactly what's happening here, and that means my planning ahead was spot on. Right? Right. It had nothing to do with the fact that Matthew was actually nice. And charming. And melted my heart with the way he talks to his daughter—

Fine! It's all those things. But it worked for everyone's benefit, so I decide to take a picture and send it to Matthew myself. Because I'm a good person. Who may need a little medication to keep me focused.

Whatever. Caffeine works on the brain the same way Ritalin does and is much tastier.

Grabbing my phone from my back pocket, I decide to try and build a little excitement first. This is important news! The prodigal pet is about to return home.

Biting my lip, I'm proud of myself for doing my best to make amends with Matthew in a fun and interesting way.

Me: I have a surprise for you!

I'm surprisingly nervous as I wait for those three little dots to populate into something I can read.

M: Who is this?

I should have expected that. We didn't exactly exchange numbers. I'm just being a stalker. Let's back up and start again.

Me: Sorry. It's Carrie.

M: Oh hey

Well that was disappointing. So much for witty banter and fun conversation. Forget it. I might as well just cut to the chase. I don't even respond just attach the picture I took of Olaf and press send.

*M:* Oh wow! You found him!!!!!

"Hmm. Five exclamation points for the dog but no punctuation at all for me. Figures."

"What was that?" Doc asks as I shove my phone back into my pocket.

"Nothing. I think I know that dog."

"Oh yeah?" Doc concentrates on listening to Olaf's heart with his stethoscope. "It would make it a lot easier if we didn't have to go through the whole rigmarole of tests with him. What did you say his name is?"

"Olaf." The dog's head immediately whips over to look at me, floppy ears perked up at his name.

"Based on his reaction, I'd say you're right." Flipping the stethoscope over his head and around his shoulders, Doc strokes Olaf's fur. "And the carrot. If you know his family, you might as well message them. The sooner he can go home, the happier he'll be."

"Already did." I pull the phone out again and sure enough, Matthew sent another text.

*M:* We'll be there as soon as school is over. And thank you!

Settling my raccoons in the travel carrier and heading back down the hall, I do my best to stop thinking about Matthew, Olaf, and, and… "Calypso."

There. I said it without breaking out into a laugh. I mentally pat myself on the back and get back to work. One dog may be going home, but these racoons are still in limbo.

Time to get them fed.

"Hey!"

I startle and throw my hand over my heart, trying to get it back under control.

"Jeez, Jamie. I know you love our new phone system but do you have to keep doing that?"

Her shrill laughter blares through the intercom. "I have little entertainment in my life these days now that Chris is on the nightshift. Making you pee your pants is my latest goal."

"It's like Old Lady Ghesilin all over again," I grumble and finish shaking the small container of squirrel milk I just mixed. Thank God the top was already sealed. I should find out when her husband ends this series of night shifts at the firehouse. He needs to take some of the heat off me and keep her entertained.

"What? You know you have to talk louder over this thing."

"Nothing, honey!" I yell a little too loud on purpose. "Do you need something from me or just felt like calling an ambulance after giving me a heart attack."

"As much as I love a man in uniform, I actually need you to come to the front."

I crinkle my brow. Why would she need me at the front? "Did someone drop off at the wrong side again?"

"Sort of."

What does that mean?

"Just move your tush and come up here." She clicks off without another word or the opportunity for me to ask more questions.

I pop the milk in the fridge and clean up the mess quickly. I'll be back in a second, I'm sure, but I still don't like leaving powdered milk on the counter. Nothing invites roaches faster than tiny particles of animal food.

Looking down at myself as I walk the halls to the front reception area, I realize what a mess I am. You wouldn't think tiny animals could make such a mess, but they do. I'm covered in squirrel milk, probably drops of pee because they're not that big, and, oh look.

A poop pellet. Awesome.

I'm never more aware of how dirty I am until I turn the corner and the most precious family is standing in the lobby. Matthew has a huge smile on his face as he watches... Calypso... nuzzle into Olaf's neck. It's no wonder this man is a model. If it wouldn't make me look like a creeper, I'd whip out my phone right now and capture this picture-perfect moment. I bet I could make some money off a stock photo like this.

"Matthew?"

He looks up, that smile unchanging as I approach.

"Carrie, I'm so sorry to interrupt your workday."

"No, it's fine," I say with a dismissive wave that morphs into a stealthy flick of my middle finger at Jamie for setting me up. She just cackles a laugh and answers the phone when it rings. "I'm just glad we were able to find Olaf for you."

"I can't thank you enough for texting me." He bends down and rubs Olaf's back. "I was about to give up hope that he'd ever return. Someone's really good at hiding, aren't ya boy? Huh? You have fun out there chasing squirrels?"

I bristle. Olaf better not have been chasing my squirrel or next time he shows up, I'll wait until after he gets his ringworm check to mention I know him. That little hooky thing in his bum will show him who's boss.

"Anyway." Matthew startles me out of my premeditated thoughts. "I just wanted to say it in person.

Thank you for everything. Sprite." He nudges the little girl gently. "Do you have something you'd like to say to Carrie?"

She pats Olaf one more time and stands up, looking me dead in the eye. "Would you like to come over for dinner tonight?"

Well, that was unexpected. Based on Matthew's uncomfortable body language, I don't think he was expecting it either.

"Um"—he chuckles uncomfortably—"close, but I was thinking more of a thank you."

But Calypso is determined and stands up even taller if that's possible, looking him dead in the eye. "But Daddy, Grandma says it's always nice to include our friends. And Carrie found Olaf so she's our friend now, right?"

I really should jump in here and say I'm busy, but honestly, it's fun watching Matthew squirm. He's got this blush running up his neck and his hand keeps running through his hair, like he doesn't know what to do. It probably makes me a horrible person that I'm so entertained. Actually, no. Of all the thoughts I've had about this family the last few days, Matthew squirming is on the mild side.

"Well yes, that is true," he says with a nervous laugh. "But it's a school night, Sprite."

She turns back to me, and I know what she's about to say. "Okay. Then we'll do it Friday."

Matthew sort of makes a choking, laughing sound,

realizing he just keeps letting this kid dig him into a deeper hole. I haven't had this much fun in a while and I haven't even said anything yet.

But of course, Matthew has yet another excuse. "Friday is your sleepover night with Grandma and Papa."

Calypso sighs and rolls her eyes, hands settled on her little hips. This one has some serious gumption. I love it. "Then Saturday. And that's my final offer."

Calypso's staring at me and I'm staring at her. Matthew is still fumbling around trying to figure out how to get out of this, but something about this girl has me wanting to play along with whatever her game is. If there even is one.

That's actually probably a little conspiracy theory on my part. But I don't care. Now I'm intrigued, so before Matthew can find another excuse, I blurt out, "Saturday it is."

Calypso smiles and leans down to pet Olaf again. Matthew is frozen in place, probably still trying to figure out what just happened. And Jamie is silently celebrating behind him where he can't see her ridiculousness.

She and I are going to have words later. I know she was trying to set me up and she thinks I just fell for it. She has no idea Matthew is the one who got duped this time.

Before anyone can move, except Jamie, who is now twerking for some reason, I smile brightly at Matthew.

"I need to get back to work, but I'm glad you got Olaf back. Text me the details for Saturday. Bye Calypso."

"Bye!" she calls out after me as I turn and walk away.

It isn't until I'm back at the counter feeding a raccoon that it hits me. I just allowed a six-year-old to invite me to dinner. With Matthew. Who I don't like.

I just got snowed by a kid.

# Chapter 7

*Matthew*

Saturday mornings growing up were spent sitting in front of the television with my brother, eating pancakes, and debating which Power Ranger was the best. Red. It's the Red Power Ranger.

Over the years, my weekend mornings went from pancakes to hangover cures in college before morphing into early morning feedings. Now that my little girl is older and spends her Friday nights with my folks, I spend my Saturdays catching up on laundry, paying bills, and squeezing a workout in before I pick her up for a day at the movies or park, weather permitting.

Not today though. No, today I'm adding a trip to the grocery store to the list of to-dos instead of the park or movies. My little Sprite will not be too happy with the change of plans but hopefully she'll remember the sacrifice the next time she thinks of inviting virtual strangers over to our house for dinner.

Dinner. I'm still not certain how she managed to bamboozle me into this, but here we sit. Me making a shopping list on my phone while Olaf chases a bird in the backyard. Lucky guy, he doesn't have to entertain a woman who until last week has only ignored me or made me feel like a complete idiot.

Seeing Carrie in her own world has reminded me how different most of us in the book community are in real life. Sure, we dress up and put on a smile at the industry events and signings, putting our personal lives and problems to the side to give readers a great experience. As a cover model, I've spent enough time sitting to the right of Donna Moreno to see how excited the readers are to meet their favorite authors. The first time I saw Carrie at a signing, she looked at me like I was a nuisance. Granted, I was trying to make a point by hitting on her, but she still gave me the evil eye. Then at the NANA's earlier this year, she reluctantly allowed me to buy her a drink but not before she warned me of her intentions. Or lack thereof.

I think her attitude toward me in the past and the way she's been the last two times I've seen her at Critter Keepers is what interests me most. I never know which version of her I'll encounter, but as long as she grants me her megawatt smile at least once, it's worth whatever snide comment I may have to endure.

My phone chimes a reminder for me to leave and pick up Calypso from my parents' house so I flip off the Bluetooth and lock up the house. The storm we had last week is a distant memory as I slip my shades on and drive with the window down. The sun is bright, warming my skin as I make the quick drive across town. Slowing as I turn onto my parents' street, I see my dad walking a little behind my daughter who is pedaling her little legs like her life depends on it. She's laughing, her curls sticking out beneath the bright purple helmet on her head.

I pull up to the curb about a house distance from where she's riding. When she spots me, a huge grin spreads across her face.

"Daddy! Look at the cool bell Papa put on my bike," she announces as she flips a little switch on her handle bar setting off a high-pitched whistling sound with each flick of her finger.

"Oh wow. That's really awesome. Pretty cool of Papa to put that on your bike at his house." I look at my dad who smiles wide, a mischievous twinkle in his eye.

He wouldn't.

"Don't worry, he got me two. Can you believe that? One for my bike at home too. Papa is the best. Do I have to go home now?"

Shooting a look to my dad that clearly conveys my appreciation for his kind gift for her bike at home, I shake my head before answering my daughter. "You finish your ride but make it quick, we have to go to the grocery store. I'll go say hi to Grandma and grab your things."

With another flick of her thumb, she triggers her bell and then takes off again with my dad in tow. I make my way to my parents' house and park in the driveway before letting myself inside. My mom is nowhere to be found so I start walking around, looking for her. As I turn toward the hallway that leads to the bedrooms Darryl and I used to occupy as kids, she steps out of the bathroom and screams, her hand grasping her non-existent pearls.

"Dear Lord, Matthew. You scared the shit out of me."

"Language, Mother," I tease. Her response is a smack to my arm as she pushes me out of her way and back into the main living area.

"I'm buying Dad a cuckoo clock for Christmas. I don't care what you say. He's getting paid back for that damn bell he's sending home with Sprite."

Laughing, she opens the refrigerator door and begins pulling a few Tupperware containers from the fridge. As expected, my name is written across the top.

"So, I hear you have a date tonight."

"It's not a date."

"Well, from what I hear a very pretty woman with princess hair who saves animals is going to be your guest for dinner. And, if memory serves, you haven't entertained a woman in your home since… well, since I was over for tea with Sprite on Mother's Day."

Choosing not to answer right away, I walk to the cupboard and pull a glass from the shelf and push the water dispenser from the refrigerator door. As I take a large drink for my suddenly parched mouth, I toss around what she said. I have always tried to keep any woman I've taken out separate from my life with Calypso. That's why I don't bring women home and I don't do relationships. My primary focus is on my daughter and being the best parent I can. She only has one in her life full-time, and I'll be damned if I'm going to let her feel like she's missing out.

"It's not a date. Carrie was kind enough to let us know about finding Olaf and keeping him out of the system so we didn't have to do a bunch of paperwork. We're thanking her. Plus, it was Sprite's idea, and she kind of steamrolled us both into it without asking first."

"Mm hmm. Well, I'm just happy to hear you're doing something social that doesn't involve a sports bar. I assume you're making your famous chili and cornbread?"

"Obviously."

"Just remember to take some Beano first."

The afternoon flew by and suddenly I'm rushing around the house like a chicken with its head cut off, trying to shower and get dressed before Carrie arrives. The chili is simmering on the stove, and Sprite is cleaning up her room, so I have just enough time to wash the day off of me before our dinner guest arrives.

We've exchanged a few texts today, mostly her making sure neither Calypso nor I have any food allergies. When I reminded her I was the one cooking, she said her mother would kill her if she showed up without something for her hosts. I hope whatever she brings, it isn't a fruitcake or jello mold. Just thinking of either one makes me cringe as I slip a long-sleeved shirt over my head.

I'm keeping it casual tonight with a pair of dark wash jeans, a black long-sleeved Henley, and no shoes. We rarely wear shoes in the house, and I figure this keeps it from looking like I put too much thought into the night. Adding a little product to my hair, I run my fingers through it, letting the strands do what they naturally want but always looking like I made an effort.

Stopping by Calypso's room, I see her small bedside lamp is on but she's not in there. Then I hear it. A pair of giggles coming from the living room. One I recognize as my little girl while the other is that of a woman. Giggles mean smiles. Dammit. I'm a little too excited at the thought of Carrie smiling.

Rounding the corner to the living room, I watch as my little girl drags Carrie by the hand, showing her each piece of furniture and where we keep everything. Maybe I should entertain more often. It's clear my daughter doesn't understand boundaries.

"And this is where my daddy keeps his big thing of powder. He says it helps him make muscles. I think it smells like Olaf's farts after he digs in the trash."

Carrie laughs, and because I'm afraid she'll take her on a tour of my bathroom and show her where my waxing kit is stored, I clear my throat. Both ladies turn to face me, the taller one smiling while the little one scowls.

"Hey."

"Hi. Calypso was just giving me a tour."

"I see that. Hey, Sprite, why don't you check and see if Olaf needs water and give him a biscuit."

She hesitates for only a beat before dropping Carrie's hand and skipping to the mudroom where we keep the bin of dog treats. Fiddling with her hands, Carrie shifts on her feet. Awkwardness rolls off both of us, neither of us speaking a word and then we hear it.

"Olaf! Where are you? I have your biscuit. You better not be drinking toilet water, I'm not sure I flushed!"

Covering my face with my hand, I let out a groan at the same time Carrie starts laughing. It isn't a quiet laugh. Or even very ladylike. This is more of a cackle with a weird honking sound. Is she part goose? When she snorts, I lose it and join her hysterics.

"She says whatever comes to her mind, doesn't she?"

"You have no idea. Can I get you something to drink? Glass of wine? Water?" I ask, turning into the kitchen and stirring the chili.

"Water is fine. I brought dessert. Just some cupcakes from my favorite bakery. I hope you like bacon and maple syrup."

Eyes wide, I fill her glass of water and slide it over before asking, "On a cupcake?"

Nodding her head, she takes a sip from her glass as

a small smile appears over the rim. I'm glad she told me now so I can avoid that second bowl of chili and save room for cupcakes.

"You have a beautiful home. It's not what I expected at all."

"Thanks, I think. It took me a few years but I can officially say it's complete."

"You did the work yourself?"

Before I can respond, Olaf runs through the room barking with Sprite hot on his heels. She's scolding him about messing with her socks as she chases him into the backyard. We watch their antics in silence before I turn my attention back to my house guest.

"I had some help but a majority of the remodel I did myself."

"Wow. That's cool. I can't even hang a picture with tape let alone practically build a new house. Are you some sort of construction guy? A house flipper?"

Shaking my head, I tell her the one thing I don't let anyone in the book world know about me outside of a few authors.

"Nah, I'm a financial advisor."

Her eyes are as big as saucers as Calypso bounds back into the room and lets loose a belch that would make any fraternity member proud.

I guess Carrie's laugh isn't the only unladylike thing around here.

# Chapter 8

## *Carrie*

I considered cancelling a few times this week. Okay, many times. I considered cancelling many times. But whenever I picked up the phone to text Matthew an excuse, I was reminded of Calypso's determination for me to break bread with them.

I'm probably reading into her behavior way more than necessary, but I was intrigued by what made this dinner so important to her. Is it because in her mind I found Olaf, so she really is trying to be polite like her grandma taught her? Is it because she doesn't have a mom and she is craving the attention of a woman? Is it because I'm the nice animal lady and she's an animal lover? I get that a lot, especially when school field trips roll through the facility.

And that, ladies and gentlemen, is what goes through the mind of an overthinker. No wonder I'm always tired. The gerbils never stop running on the wheel inside this brain. Sometimes they run really fast and hit me with a great idea. Some of my best blog posts come with the rapid thoughts after I finish an amazing book. But mostly, they're just huffing and puffing and trying not to fall off.

It's been suggested over the years that I may need a tiny bit of medicinal help to keep my scatterbrained thoughts under control. Those who have suggested, namely my mother and Jamie, are probably not wrong. I am scatterbrained and have all the classical characteristics of some form of attention deficit. But until I burn my house down or forget to pay all my bills, I'm too lazy to pursue that avenue. There are better things to do with my time. Like read all the books. And save all the animals. *And* figure out why a six-year-old child wants me over for dinner.

So I'm glad I didn't cancel. Not only will it satisfy some of my curiosity about this man who is very different than what the rumors would suggest, but it's oddly relaxing around here. Not that I expected chaos. I just didn't expect to feel so comfortable. Maybe it's because Matthew is barefoot. That simple gesture makes this entire scenario feel more casual. It's just a couple people making chili and hoping it takes long enough to digest for me to get home to my own bathroom. Really, I know chili is easy to make, but it seems like that might put all of us in a bad predicament if we aren't careful.

Matthew is putting the final touches on dinner while Calypso is off somewhere washing her hands. I'm taking advantage of the moment and perusing the framed pictures scattered across the small built-in bookshelf. One of them catches my eye.

"Is that"—I point to a picture—"the Sydney Opera House behind you?"

He places the pot of steaming chili on the table and takes off his oven mitts. "Yeah. I'm standing on top of Harbour Bridge there."

I turn back around to take a closer look and sure enough, he has a harness around his waist and is wearing a blue jumpsuit.

"Oh man, that's awesome. I've always wanted to go there." Lifting the frame from the shelf, I study the picture closer. The blue of the harbor always blows my mind. But the Opera House is just stunning. "I find the Opera House fascinating."

"I was shocked to discover it's actually not very attractive."

"Really?" I've never heard anyone say that before.

"Don't get me wrong, it's cool looking from that angle and they do some really neat things with lighting. But it's made of wood and concrete so from the front or back it's… not what you'd expect."

I look back at the picture of what I'm sure is my favorite place in the world. "That's so weird. I wonder why it's so famous, then. It's in every action flick set in Sydney."

"That's easy. The acoustics. I had a chance to hear

Adele there and the experience blew my mind. Made every other concert hall I've ever been to sound like an elementary school stage."

I quirk an eyebrow at him. "Do you frequent concert halls?"

A wide grin covers his face. "I've been known to take in a concert or two. I like exploring different kinds of music. I don't always find something I want to hear again, but I enjoy the experience. I'll be right back. I'm gonna check on Sprite."

I'm surprised by what I've learned tonight and I haven't even been here an hour. Matthew isn't just a pretty face and a set of washboard abs. He's smart. Anyone who works with numbers like he does has to be. Based on these pictures I'm looking at, Mr. Cover Model is also well traveled. He's a good dad, and he can do his own handyman work.

What the hell is wrong with this man?

He's literally the cream of the crop and he's still single? I don't get how one of his one-night stands hasn't snatched him up yet. Not that I'm interested.

"Just keep telling yourself that, Carrie," I murmur to myself.

"She's just going to be a few more minutes," Matthew states, coming back into the open room. "There was a mishap with the soap." I furrow my brow in question. "Let's just say it's easier to make bubbles than it is to get them to go down the drain and trying to help only makes more."

"Ah," I say and turn back to the one picture that keeps catching my eye. Probably because it's on my bucket list. "Did you know they have to continually paint Harbour Bridge? It takes a year to get from one end to the other and then they start all over again."

Matthew comes up behind me as I keep looking around. He isn't close, but I can still feel him. Smell him. As much as it pains me to say it, he smells amazing and his proximity makes my heartrate pick up a little speed. Not because he's hot and talking to him is no longer a chore. It's just because we're talking about a place I've dreamt about most of my adult life. That's my story and I'm sticking to it.

Other than photos of his travels, there are an overwhelming number of pictures of Calypso in all stages of her young life. She's always been a beautiful little girl, her curls evident very early on. She shares many features with her father but still, I wonder what her mother looks like.

"That's actually not true."

"What's not?"

"About Harbour Bridge."

I scrunch my nose in confusion. Wow, he is standing really close. "Painting it? Of course it is. I read it on the internet."

As soon as the words are out of my mouth, I recognize how ridiculous I sound. Matthew's knowing smile means he caught it too.

"While the internet is a valid source of

information"—I cock an eyebrow at him playfully, making him chuckle—"it's not always correct. But in your defense, I thought that too, until I did the bridge climb."

"Really?"

"Yeah." He reaches around me to pick up the picture and looks at it while he talks. "It's one of the things they addressed in the information portion of our climb. No one really knows where that rumor started. Maybe it took them a year when they first built it or something. But they only do the painting and repairs as needed. Now that I think about it, we didn't see anyone working on the bridge when we did the climb, and the entire excursion was about three hours."

Three hours? That's a lot more climbing than I'd ever want to do. Maybe I need to reconsider that as a goal for my far-in-the-future trip. "Was it worth it?"

"Totally," Matthew says without hesitation. "The view was stunning no matter where you looked. It was like being on top of the world." He places the picture back down on the shelf. "Come sit down. Calypso should be almost done by now."

I follow him to the table with four seats and choose the place setting that doesn't have an Elsa spoon sitting next to the bowl. I'm oddly disappointed I have to use big people silverware. Where was all this character stuff when I was a child? And why do the manufacturers assume adults aren't fans of animation? I'd eat my ice cream out of a Moana bowl any day. Kids these days are so lucky.

"So did you spend a lot of time Down Under?" I ask, unable to change the subject. The flight alone is close to twenty-four hours so when I go, I plan to stay a while. It takes a whole lot of money and even more co-ordination for a trip like that, which is why I've never been.

"Sprite! Dinner!" Matthew calls and sits down at the chair next to mine. "A couple weeks."

"A couple weeks!" I exclaim. "That's awesome! How was Sydney? Did you love it?"

He takes a drink of his water, trying to cover this weird look on his face. Maybe I'm imagining it, but it almost seems like he's stalling. Why, I have no idea. Did I trigger bad memories or something? Was he assaulted by a kangaroo?

And there's that overactive imagination again.

Finally, he's done hydrating and puts his glass down. "Sydney is… not what I expected it to be."

Hmm. Not the answer I thought I'd get.

"How so?"

He rubs his bottom lip and I can tell he's really contemplating his words. It's the exact opposite of me, who just blurts out whatever comes to mind. This is probably why people love him and half my friends only tolerate me. Not that Jamie is one to talk. One of these days, she's going to get caught when she imitates the boss behind her back. And I mean literally right behind the boss's back when she's talking to me. I look forward to that day and the entertainment it's going to give me.

Matthew, on the other hand, seems to be figuring out how best to describe his thoughts. I should try to be more like that.

"One of the things I like about traveling is learning how other cultures live. It's interesting to me." I nod because I can understand that. "When I went to London, it was this huge culture difference. The entire feel of the city was different than what I was used to. Everything from transportation to etiquette to lifestyle. It was all different. I expected that same thing when I went to Sydney, but with the exception of some subtle differences, it felt like I was still in the States. Just maybe in a place like New York City."

"Really?" That's not what I expected him to say at all. "The accent wasn't a dead giveaway?"

He smirks. "That was the least subtle difference. Like driving on the other side of the road. Actually, now that I think about it, it sort of reminded me of San Francisco. A lot of people. A lot of interesting character in the different parts of town. A lot of hills that you end up walking up and down. And they're very proud of their bridge."

I giggle. "Well, yeah. Both bridges are amazing."

He smiles and nods. "I totally agree with you. It wasn't that I didn't enjoy Sydney. I did. Very much. It was just a different kind of enjoyment than I expected." Leaning back, he calls out again. "Sprite! Let's go! I have no idea what's taking her so long."

"It's okay. I'm enjoying hearing about Australia anyway. So if Sydney wasn't your favorite part, what was?"

"The beaches," he blurts out without hesitation. "Without a doubt, Australia has the most incredible coast line, unlike anything I've ever seen in my life. Even the colors were different."

"What do you mean?" I lean onto the table, completely engaged in his tales. He's animated and excited about it, and I find myself hanging on his every word.

"It's hard to describe but the hues of the blues and greens were something I had never seen before. Like I knew the trees were green, but it was an entirely new shade."

"Really?"

He settles back in his chair, very clearly lost in whatever visual images are in his brain right now.

"Yeah. A buddy of mine and I were talking about it while we were there. I don't know if it's because it's south of the equator and the sunlight reflects differently, or maybe because the vegetation is different and the eucalyptus trees give everything a sort of blue hue, but I've never seen those colors again."

I open my mouth to ask more questions about the places he visited and things he's seen, but I'm suddenly distracted by a pint-sized princess.

The second Matthew looks over, I see the shock on his face. Being the good dad he is, though, he schools his features immediately. "Um… what took you so long, Sprite?"

She quietly sits down at the table and clasps her hands together. I'm pretty sure she's going for demure, but the bright blue eye shadow and very red cheeks sort of throw the whole thing off. Talk about color hues I've never seen before.

"Grandma says you should always look your best for company," Calypso says matter-of-factly.

I'm not sure grandma meant to dress up like The Joker for dinner, but I appreciate the thought she put into her... umm... outfit.

I look over at Matthew, who seems to be mulling over how best to handle the situation. Catching his eye I shrug my shoulders and say, "Then I guess it's time to eat."

# Chapter 9

## Matthew

I've had bacon and maple syrup in the past. Like most kids, my brother and I used slices of bacon to scoop up the leftover syrup from our plates. Never had I considered making cupcakes with both flavors swirled through the center and then prominently sprinkled and drizzled over the frosting. The cupcakes Carrie brought for dessert are worth every extra sit-up and pull-up I'll be doing this week. Calypso was equally happy with the bright pink strawberry cupcake with glitter on top.

While I clean up the kitchen from dinner and dessert, Carrie is helping my little princess remove the war paint from her face. I knew that makeup kit my brother gave her last year for Christmas was going to resurface one day. I just didn't expect it to be so... bright. And thick. I tried wiping it with a wet paper towel and I swear it was six inches thick and starting to stain her skin. Carrie assured me she could help her get it off with a little soap and a lot of patience. Something I'm lacking when it comes to things like this.

A string of giggles from both ladies wafts down the hall, making me smile. I hadn't realized how quiet the house is with only two of us living here. Usually, our school nights are filled with homework, arguing over ending bath time, and bedtime stories. Once my pint-sized wonder is fast asleep, I throw myself on the couch, hit my social media accounts, respond to emails, and if I'm lucky, watch a few hours of television before crashing.

Tonight, with Carrie here, it's different. I'm uncertain if it's because we aren't home alone or because Carrie's laughter is so prominent. And loud. No, infectious. It's infectious. Okay, and loud.

Another string of giggles from my little girl fills the space, and while I'm curious what Carrie is saying to make her laugh, I refuse to listen. I have a feeling whatever female insight she's sharing with Calypso will be relayed to me. For days. And in great detail.

Cuing up my favorite playlist marked "chill," I let the music fill the space and drown out the laughs while I stand here. Since I haven't entertained or had many guests in the last few years, I'm not quite sure what to do now. The kitchen is clean, the music is playing at a reasonable volume, and I'm standing here like an idiot. Turning on the television doesn't feel right and yet, I can't keep wiping down the counters.

This is ridiculous. I'm a grown man in my own home. There is absolutely no reason for me to feel awkward. I'll just turn on the television and watch some sports highlights. That's normal and since it's taking half a lifetime to scrub the gunk off my kid's face, I may be completely caught up on every current sporting event happening in the world, not just the U.S.

The moment I pick up the remote control, I hear from behind me, "She's back to her natural self." Turning to look at Carrie over my shoulder, I double blink at her. How she looks so relaxed and at home here. Like she fits. Gone are her shoes, set near the front door before dessert. Her "princess hair" as Calypso called it is now atop her head in a messy bun. But, what's most noticeable is the fact that her makeup is gone. She's scrubbed her face too.

I knew Carrie was pretty. That much is evident to anyone who meets her. This version of her, casual and natural, is more. She looks young, much younger than I think she is.

"You're back to your natural self too."

Smiling she nods. "Yeah. I took her first layer off but then she asked me about my makeup. I felt kind of like a hypocrite scrubbing her face and leaving mine made up. So, I had her copy me and we did it together. Unfortunately, she' s a little overzealous with water and was bordering on soaked to the bone. I sent her to change."

"Thank you." It doesn't seem like enough, but I also can't seem to form any more words.

"So—"

"Daddy!"

Carrie is cut-off by a now fresh faced six-year-old who leaps up on the couch and bounces. Maybe the cupcake was a bad idea. Sugar and my little sprite are not always the best combination.

"Daddy! Carrie! We should play a game. I vote Candyland. Oh! Or Connect Four. Daddy is not good at that one."

I start to tell Calypso that we should let Carrie go home but she beats me to it with a challenge for us both.

"I am the reigning Connect Four champ in my family. Do you think you can beat me?"

I look to Calypso, assuming that's who she's directed the question at when I see her looking at me. Shifting my gaze to our guest, I find her eyes on me, a smirk on her face. When I don't immediately respond, she raises a single brow and instantly triggers my competitive streak.

"Bring it on."

That crazy laugh of hers fills the air as Sprite jumps down from the couch and starts singsonging, "You're going down, Daddy."

Groaning, I run my hand down my face and peek at Carrie through my fingers. Her bright smile is irresistible, and I return it with my own. She winks at me before turning her attention to Calypso and helping her set up the game on the coffee table. I watch for a few minutes as they chatter away like this is something we do together all the time.

The battle for the most superior Connect Four player is one for the books. Calypso gave up trying to mediate Carrie and me after game two and turned her attention to my phone and her own playlist. Somewhere between Disney soundtracks and my fourth victory, she settled on Carrie's lap where she still sits as I swap out the Connect Four game with Chutes and Ladders.

Her eyes light up as she watches me flick the spinner with my finger. I know that look.

"Okay, everyone remember the rules?" I ask, and my little sprite looks up at Carrie, hero—or heroine—worship evident. When Carrie nods she turns back around to face me.

"Yep. Let's do this!"

The feistiness I witnessed from Carrie in the past has been out in full force with each game we've played but I think she's about to meet her match in Calypso. Our family is a little competitive and that includes the youngest member.

I flick the spinner first, landing on a three. Carrie is next with a two. With better hand-eye coordination than other kids I know, Calypso takes her turn and the little plastic arrow spins so fast it looks as if it's going to take off like a jet plane. When it lands on five she hoots and hollers like we're cheering for our favorite sports team.

The upside to these children's games is how quickly they can go. I am not looking forward to the day Calypso outgrows these games and we're sitting on the floor for hours buying houses and hotels. Of course, hopefully by then she'll see the benefits of playing at the dining table.

"Okay ladies, how about you let the old man get a win in?"

Both of them giggle and shake their head at me. Rolling my eyes, I look down at the spinner and notice it's on a three. Wait a minute.

"Sprite, how many spaces did you move on your last turn?"

"Umm . . ." she begins, eyes cast downward.

"What's—?" Carrie begins, but I raise my hand to cut her off.

"Calypso Annabeth Roberts. Are you *cheating*?"

Attempting to roll her eyes but only looking like she has some sort of weird tick, my little girl huffs and straightens her back while looking me straight in the eye. Clasping her hands on the table in front of her, I hold back a smile at her attempt to look serious.

"Daddy, Papa says it's not cheating. It's creative play."

Carrie poorly disguises a laugh with a fake cough, and I just shake my head.

"Well, you're only allowed to play creatively with your Papa from now on. Okay?"

Smiling wide, she nods her head and reaches for

the spinner. Snatching the cardboard it sits on from her reach I say, "Not on your life. Move your space back so it's only three spots. It's my turn."

The rest of the game goes without any further creative play, and I manage to squeeze out a victory. It's only one but at least I don't have a big zero next to my name. It's only when Calypso and Carrie are deciding what game we should play next that I realize tonight is quite possibly the most fun I've had in years. Sitting on the floor strategizing, teasing one another, and laughing until we cry reminds me of simpler times. Before late night feedings, potty training, and Disney princesses. There's no expectation and no promise for anything more than a new friendship and that's freeing.

# Chapter 10

*Carrie*

Stroking Calypso's hair, I now understand why people have kids. This is really nice, having her snuggled up against me, looking like a peaceful little angel. It took a whole lot of obnoxious bouncing around for her to get to this point, but the sugar crash more than made up for it.

"How'd you get into wildlife rescue, anyway?"

I look up at Matthew, whose relaxing in the chair across from us, feet propped up on the table. He looks tired from the day, and yet very alert to our conversation.

"Well," I begin, thinking back on my childhood. "I grew up in New Jersey."

"Ah, I thought I detected a small accent," he says, his eyes seemingly twinkling.

"It's not much but it's there. I tend to pick up whatever accent is prominent wherever I go. It's like a cha-meleon-effect thing."

Matthew chuckles. "So when you finally get to Australia, you're going to come back sounding like Crocodile Dundee."

I smile that he's so sure I'll ever make it on my bucket list trip. "Quite possibly."

"Anyway, you were saying?"

"Oh. Yeah." I settle into the couch more, continu-ing to stroke Calypso's hair. "We lived kind of in a woodsy area. It wasn't uncommon to see all kinds of critters, especially at night. I don't remember when it began but I was always rescuing baby animals. It used to drive my mother bonkers."

"I take it she's not an animal person?"

"Oh no." I shake my head vehemently. "Not at all. She allowed me to do it, but there was no way she would help. I will give her a little bit of credit though. She did allow me to use the garage as a raccoon shelter for a little while."

Matthew's eyes bug out of his head. "A raccoon shelter."

I laugh lightly. People are always so afraid of rac-coons but really they're my favorite. "Oh yeah, I love raccoons. They have the personalities of dogs with the mannerisms of cats. They're fun."

"They're dumpster divers."

"Only when they're hungry," I say with a shrug.

"And they're actually really clean. If they have the means to do it, they always wash their food before eating it. But they're also really inquisitive."

"You mean destructive."

"My mom would agree with you on that. They did a number on the garage." I laugh at the memory of us pulling the built-in wood cabinets away from the wall and discovering they had ripped a hole in the sheetrock and made a nest. And that was just one part of the damage they did. It took months for me to clean it all up. Needless to say, the garage was off limits for my rehab efforts from that point on.

Matthew shifts in his chair, drawing my attention back to him. I try not to notice how his jeans pull in all the right places but, come on. I'm tired. I'm stuffed. And I've laughed all night long. A little attraction is normal at this point, right?

"That explains the career. How did the blogging come about?"

I shrug. "Hobby. I like romance. I like stories. I like the idea of fate and pushing through problems for your one and only. It keeps me grounded in a weird way while keeping me from settling for what I don't want." Suddenly feeling uncomfortable with how much I'm sharing; I act quickly to turn the tables. "What about you? Financial advising? How did that happen?"

"Family business." He begins absentmindedly picking at the label of his beer. "The pay is steady, I don't mind the work, and as long as I don't take advantage of the obvious nepotism, it's almost impossible to get fired."

"And the modeling?"

"A dare."

I didn't see that answer coming. "Really?"

He nods, a grin on his face. "A buddy of mine in college dared me to try out when this agency was scouting on our campus. I'm pretty sure he was trying to set me up for some humiliation. It sort of backfired on him."

I can't help but laugh. "I can see that."

The conversation lulls and we sit in comfortable silence for a few minutes. It's odd because I should feel like I'm imposing, but I don't. I feel like I'm right where I'm meant to be.

Gesturing to his daughter, Matthew says, "I should feel bad that I beat her so many times at checkers, but I don't. This was too much fun."

A small smile graces my lips because he's right. I haven't done a game night in I don't know how long. I had almost forgotten the appeal.

"Next time, I will crush you with Scrabble," I tease quietly, not wanting to ruin this moment.

"Oh you will, huh?" Matthew puts his beer bottle down on the side table and stretches his long legs out on the floor. He doesn't look like a model in this mo-ment. He looks like a normal, everyday guy. Still hot. But much more approachable. "I'll have you know my

English teachers always complimented me on my vocabulary."

I blow out an unimpressed breath through my lips. "Knowing what a word means for a state test is different than knowing how to use the letters "x" and "q" to maximize your points. Besides, your English teachers were just impressed that such a hot guy knew how to spell."

His very hot eyebrow quirks on his very hot forehead. Who knew a forehead could be sexy? But his is. Even making playful expressions, there are no lines or wrinkles there. If I move my eyebrows, I have so many lines you could wash clothes on my face.

What a coincidence. He has washboard abs. I have a washboard forehead. It's a match made in Maytag heaven.

"I'm not afraid," he says. Suddenly, the air changes in the room. It's gone from light and fun to sultry. Or it might be steam coming from the dishwasher. Either way, we hold each other's gazes for a few seconds too long before realizing what we're doing and looking away. Clearing his throat, Matthew adds, "But, I should put her to bed."

Standing, he stretches his arms over his head before leaning down to scoop up Calypso. He gets close, but then stands back up.

"Problem?" I ask, because he's clearly thinking through how to do this.

"It's just…" He cocks his head, looking at us from

a different angle. "She's so high up on your lap and draped across you. She's such a light sleeper, if I try to turn her around she's gonna wake up and that never goes well."

Looking down at our position, I see what he's talking about. "Hmm. Let me see if I can…" Slowly scooting my butt down the couch, I try to get my body underneath Calypso more. "Maybe if I can… hang on," I grunt and keep moving. Matthew seems to figure out what I'm doing and moves spare arms and legs out of my way. I have no idea how Calypso has more than two each, but I swear kids turn into rubber octopuses when they sleep.

Finally, Calypso is completely draped over me, her head on my shoulder, but I've somehow ended up squatting on the floor. I'm no stranger to lifting heavy creatures—Golden Retrievers are a popular breed and they aren't small—but there is no way I can power lift my way to a standing position.

Looking up at Matthew, I gesture to my predicament. "Can you um… give me a little help here?"

"Oh! Yes!" He hops into action and somehow maneuvers himself until he's standing behind me. In one smooth movement, he bends down and lifts me up from under my arms.

Wow. He's strong. And sexy. That's the first time a man has held me that close in at least a couple years so it's having more of an effect on me than it should. Clearly I need to get out more if picking me up off the floor makes me swoon.

Matthew is still moving his arms around to try and figure out how to get Calypso off me. It's cute, but unnecessary.

"Matthew," I whisper yell and blow some of Calypso's hair out of my face. "Just show me where her room is. It'll be faster."

"Right. Yes."

It's kind of cute how he's not sure what to do in a situation like this. It's as if he's never had a woman around his kid before. Now that I think about it, that kind of makes sense. He's a super huge flirt at all the book events we've been at together, but I've never heard him talk about a girlfriend. And he's never posted pictures of a woman except his mother, not that I've been paying attention.

Fine. I pay attention. It's called research. I am a blogger, after all. It's kind of my job to know what's going on with the much sought-after models and authors. Matthew happens to be much sought after and not just by talented authors whose covers he graces. Readers practically worship him. And his live videos.

But he was also uncomfortable when Calypso invited me over and kept trying to get out of it. It never occurred to me that he doesn't like introducing women to his daughter. I'm not sure if I should feel flattered that he's allowing me to follow him down the hall to her bedroom, or embarrassed that Calypso and I have pushed him into an evening that made him uncomfortable.

Oh well. If he was really concerned he'd have stopped me by now, right?

Matthew pushes the bedroom door open, and I feel like I've died and gone to fairy-land heaven. This room is everything little Carrie's heart would have desired if she knew such magic existed. The full-sized bed is covered in fluffy pink and purple blankets and pillows. A huge set of fairy wings is attached to one wall with a full-length mirror right in the middle so you always know how beautiful you are, no matter what you're wearing. And what appears to be small twinkly lights are dangling from the ceiling. When you look closer, though, they're tiny little fairies that light up instead of a nightlight. Suddenly, I want to redecorate my room so it can look like this one. I'm still a kid at heart. It wouldn't be weird at all.

Well, until Luke attacked one of the fairies and ended up dangling from the ceiling himself. That might not go over well.

Working in tandem, I wait for Matthew to pull the blankets down before laying Calypso on her bed. I have to be strategic about this, though. If she's a light sleeper, the alternate pressure will wake her up. So instead of just plopping her down and tucking her in, I sort of lay on top of her until I feel her entire body go lax. Then I slowly, carefully pull my body away, simultaneously pulling the blankets up to try and offset my movements.

When I'm finally free of her grip without so much as a groan of protest out of her, I turn around ready to fist pump the air at my victory. But Matthew is standing there, a strange look on his face.

"What?"

"It's just…" He looks back and forth between me and Calypso a couple times. "That's the move I have to use to keep her asleep. How'd you know to do it?"

Pointing at myself, I make sure to keep whispering. "Light sleeper. My mom used to use it on me. Worked like a charm until I was about nine, so you only have a few years left to maximize it. You've been warned."

We creep out of the room, Matthew shutting the door soundlessly behind us. Waving me down the hall, I follow him back into the open concept living area where it's safe to make noise again.

"Those fairy wings are awesome," I say, blinking my eyes as they adjust to the light. "You have an amazing eye for decorating. Her room is so cool."

He saunters over to the coffee table and begins picking up the game. "I wish I could take credit for any of that, but it's all her mother's doing."

*She has a mother?*

It's weird how my brain completely bypassed that part of their lives. Obviously Calypso has a mother. It's not like Matthew could have made her without one. Still, it feels weird thinking about some woman out there having a relationship with this little girl. It feels weird knowing that woman has a relationship with *Matthew*. I'll just ignore all the reasons why that is.

I want to ask about her, I really do. But I'm trying to be polite. One dinner he was forced into doesn't make us friends. It makes us tricked into dinner by a child. I don't really feel it's my place to ask. Even though I really, really want to. Oh, what the hell.

"Well then I stand corrected. Her mom has got a real knack for design."

Matthew doesn't seem to notice my inner turmoil or even mind the conversation. "She's a real creative type. Very artsy."

"Oh. So, um… does she do interior design for a living or something?"

I'm pushing for information. I know I am. And I'm pretty sure that smirk means he knows it too. "Is that your sly way of asking if she's still around?"

Busted.

I roll my eyes playfully, not as much annoyed as trying to not feel embarrassed by my curiosity. "You can't blame me for wondering. It's not like I know a ton of single dads out there who have custody of their kids."

"There are more of us than you think."

"No doubt. I just don't know any of them, I guess," I say with a shrug. "It just had me wondering. But you don't have to tell me anything. I know it's not my business."

His eyes flicker toward the kitchen, and I'm sure he's looking at the time. While one of our trio is tucked into bed, it's not too late and I'm not ready for the night to end.

"How about some coffee?" he asks.

"Do you have any tea?"

Smiling, he nods and walks to the kitchen to fill a kettle. It's not one of those Americanized ones you find at Target. This is a heavy-duty thing that he probably ordered online from some British company to make sure it was the best of the best.

Setting the kettle on the burner, he turns to the cabinets where he begins gathering various teas and cups onto a tray. Wow. This is the fanciest tea I think I've ever had. I wonder if he'll present me with some crumpets too.

"I didn't know Calypso was coming into my life until she was already here."

His admission stuns me so much, my eyebrows shoot up, giving me that washboard forehead again. If he keeps this up, I'm going to need some Botox and fast.

"You didn't?"

He shakes his head and leans against the counter, crossing his arms as he tells me the story. His body language isn't lost on me, and it makes me wonder if he's in a sort of self-protection mode. Maybe from what he thinks will be my judgement. Makes sense. I have been sort of a judgmental bitch to him.

"I met Calypso's mom at a club. She was this

amazing dancer so of course all the men gravitated to her. But for whatever reason she wanted to dance with me that night."

I scoff. "Because you're hot. How many times do I need to tell you that?"

He smiles at my outburst but doesn't respond. "Anyway, you know how it goes. We had a one-night stand, didn't exchange numbers, and I never heard from her again." Actually, I don't know how that goes, being that I've never had a one-night stand, but I'll take his word for it. "Close to a year later, she tracked me down somehow, probably from the few gigs I had started booking at that point, and she showed up on my parents' doorstep with a six-week-old baby."

I gasp. "Oh man. I bet that caused some drama."

"You have no idea. My mother was at the grocery store, and when she came home I was holding a screaming newborn. I can't even tell you how much my mother lectured me about being a twenty-three-year-old single dad. She got over it, but yeah. It was rough."

"Wait, single dad? So she just left Calypso with you?"

He nods and turns to check on the kettle which is starting to make some noises. "She says she tried really hard to be a good mom, and I believe her. But she was eighteen years old… and…"

"Holy shit, she was eighteen?" I exclaim. "You're a dirty old man!"

Matthew looks at me like I've lost my mind. Which I may have. "I was twenty-two when I slept with her. It's not a huge age difference."

"No, but it seems like a huge life experience difference," I blurt out as I lean back, hands on the counter. "At twenty-two you've been through college and can drink and stuff. At eighteen, you're just… not even really adulting yet."

He licks his lips and I can tell he's amused by my thoughts. "Well, in my defense, I didn't know she was eighteen until I got a copy of Calypso's birth certificate."

"The pigtails and lollipop weren't a giveaway?"

Matthew chuckles and pulls his phone out of his pocket, clicking open an app. He scrolls for a second before turning it to face me. "Here. This is Delilah."

"Delilah? I assume she's the one who named Calypso?"

"Yep."

"Makes so much more sense now." I take the phone from him and stare at the picture of a beautiful brunette with a tiny little baby. "Is this Calypso?"

"When she was just a week old."

"Okay, you win." I hand him the phone back. "No way I would have guessed she was eighteen. My first guess would have been twenty-five at least."

He clicks his phone off and puts it in his back pocket. "Me too. But anyway, Delilah tried to be a good mom but she was so young and had a lot of dreams. Dreams she couldn't keep up with as long as she had a kid. From what I gather, as soon as her doctor cleared her for normal activity post-partum, she realized pretty quick that a baby was going to create a lot of inconvenience in her life."

"So she just dropped Calypso off and left?"

He bobbles his head back and forth. "It's not as simple as that, but sort of. For the first year, she didn't come around at all. I filed for full custody and as soon as the DNA test was processed, I had it. Mostly because she never came to a hearing."

"DNA test? You didn't know she was yours?"

"Oh, I knew," he says with a smile. "She looked identical to some of my mom's baby pictures. It was more a formality, so all our ducks were in a row for court. But I guess it was about a year after that when Delilah called to check on the baby. She was really sad about everything she'd missed out on."

My heart sinks. "Please tell me she didn't file for custody."

"Nope. I think she's always known she would do Calypso more harm by trying to force herself into the role of full-time parent, and it's more emotionally balanced to spend some good quality time with her when she's here."

"And to bring her some amazing decorations for her room."

Matthew smiles. "Yep. She only comes around a

couple times a year, and I never know when she's going to pop in. She's a semi-professional dancer, still chasing the dream. But when she's here they have a great time. They'll play dress-up and then Delilah will tell her some magical mystical stories. Or they'll go in the back and look at the stars and talk about the constellations. She can weave a really good tale, that's for sure."

"Sounds like she's a free spirit."

"Very much so. She's not a bad person. A little odd in some ways, but as long as she's good to my daughter, I don't mind her stopping by and hanging fairy lights. It's their thing."

I nod, absorbing all the information he's told me. It seems I have misjudged Matthew from the beginning. He isn't just a pretty, flirty face. He's a father. And one of the best I've ever known.

Before I can respond, the kettle starts shrieking.

"Anyway, enough of that," Matthew says, taking the kettle off the stove and setting in on top of a hot pad on the tray. "I've actually got a Scrabble board and the sudden desire to kick your ass."

I smirk at him playfully because it feels like I should. But secretly, I kind of want to let him win, just because he deserves the best life can give him because of the person he is.

What is it with this family manipulating me and my emotions?

# Chapter 11

*Matthew*

The last thing I want to do after this long week is work out. Just the idea of lacing up my running shoes for a five-mile run or throwing around some weights makes me want to call the photographers I work with and tell them all I'm heading into early retirement. That's believable, right? I'm almost thirty years old and already I'm getting pushed aside for the younger, hotter, baby-faced guys coming up the ranks.

I won't do it though. Calypso may only be six years old but I know there will be driving lessons, a car, proms, and as much as it pains me to say it, college tuition in our future. Of course, this morning when she put her shoes on the wrong feet and attempted to make her way out of the house without changing them, I wondered for a brief moment if college was a pipe dream.

It's those realizations that drive me to workout. To

keep my body in the best shape possible to make extra money for her future. Accepting my fate, I grab my phone and water before heading out to the garage gym.

I set up my camera to take some video I'll need to post later on my social media accounts. Yet another detail of my side job—keeping up interest from my fans. Posting shirtless videos of myself working out isn't my favorite part but is a necessary evil.

As I press the record button and wrap my hand around the handle, Olaf lets out a string of barks that I'm going to have to edit out of my video. These aren't his normal playful barks nor are they his attempt at sounding vicious, though. He tends to save that particular growl-bark combo for the neighbor's gardener. Which happens on Friday. I know for a fact it is only Wednesday.

Hump Day. Wine Wednesday. Woman Crush Wednesday.

Everything that isn't Friday.

"Olaf, give it a rest!" I shout over my shoulder. He doesn't listen. Instead, he seems to only get louder.

Ditching the video and tossing my phone and bottle on the counter, I make my way to the slider. Peering out the screen door, I look for Olaf and whatever has him going nuts. Not seeing him at first glance, I step outside and begin walking around.

"Dammit, Olaf. What has you going nuts?"

With his front paws on the tree, he's stretched up as high as he can get as he begins howling. Great. Get a beagle they said. It'll be great they said.

"Olaf, I swear. The neighbors are going to call animal control. I know Carrie would tell me when they picked you up but seriously, I do not want to explain this to Sprite. Come on," I implore him, clapping my hands. Nothing.

Leaning down, I tug on his collar and nudge him toward the house.

"How about a cookie?"

That gets his attention and he abandons his post, instead taking off running toward the open screen door and into the house. Closing the door, I make my way to the container and toss a biscuit on the floor for Olaf to snack on while I escape to the garage. I really need to work off some of this newly discovered tension that seems to have found its way to my shoulders.

Powering up my most aggressive playlist, I decide weights can wait. I insert my earbuds, strap my phone on my arm before closing the garage door and taking off down the street for a run. I'm only two houses down when I see three of the ladies from the neighborhood congregating on the lawn. It's barely eight in the morning and all three look like they're dressed for the club. Or walk of shame. Who am I to judge?

Offering a small smile to them I watch as each turns her body toward me and waves. Fingers only. I see their mouths moving but thanks to the guitar solo currently pounding in my ears, I can't hear what they're saying. Picking up the pace, I let the rhythm of my feet fall in tempo with the music and regulate my breathing.

It's going to be a long day.

A very long day.

Leaning back in my chair, I slip the pen between my fingers, not really listening to the rant my client is currently on. While I empathize with his current situation, I am not his friend nor do I want to be. The guy is an asshole and his wife figured that out after affair number six and child number four. The child she is not carrying. Why he thinks calling his financial advisor to vent is how he should spend his—and my—dinner hour is beyond me.

"Peter, I understand your frustration. I promise we have maintained meticulous records and will be able to provide everything to your attorney when the time comes."

"You're absolutely sure we have to disclose everything? I mean, it's my money. I'm the one who busts my ass and hired you to build my portfolio not my wife."

Sighing, I toss the pen on the desk as Mom pops her head in the door to check on me. I hold a finger up to indicate I'll be just a minute before turning my attention back to the call.

"As I said earlier, we will do what we are legally required to. I have no idea what divorce laws are like, but I'm sure you've hired yourself a good attorney.

But, can I make a suggestion? Not as your financial advisor but from one father to another?"

"Sure."

"Put the kids first. Your children are innocent in all of this and shouldn't take on any of the stress. Take it from someone who has to co-parent. When you want to rant and rave about your ex-wife, stop and look at a picture of your kids. Remember how your words and actions affect them."

The line is silent. I'm sure I've overstepped, but I hate guys like this. I can tell already he's going to try and get out of his financial obligations to his wife. I only hope that choice doesn't hurt his children.

"Anyway, I'm going to get going. I have a little girl waiting to tell me about her day. You take care and I'll talk to you later. Have a good night."

Before he can respond, I click the end call button and remove my headset, tossing it on the desk. With a few clicks, I begin the process of engaging the backup system before shutting down my computer. When everything is powered down, I flip the light switch and exit the office. My dad's booming laugh guides me to the kitchen where my family sits, spouting off made up fortunes that may be in our cookies later.

When Mom sees me, she smiles and slides a white box with red writing across the table to my seat. I know the best Kung Pao Chicken sits in that container. My weakness. Since I'm the only one who likes the spicy goodness, my mom always gets a small side for only me.

As I settle into the chair, the same seat I've eaten hundreds, probably thousands, of meals at over the years, I roll my neck, letting the tension of the day go. While the table and chairs have been upgraded over the years, we still sit in the same seats as when I was a kid. Only now, Sprite sits to my right, naming the broccoli on her plate. Each "tree" as she refers to them has a name and she always says goodbye to it before stuffing it in her mouth.

"Sprite, honey, you need to take bites. I don't want you choking," Mom says.

"Ih ohay gwammuh."

"Baby, slow down and eat correctly, please." My tone gives no room for argument.

No sooner do the words leave my mouth than she leans over, mouth open above her plate as the chewed up green vegetable falls from her lips. Three different responses from the adults at the table catch her attention. A sly grin takes over her face as my dad barks out a choking laugh, Mom mumbles under her breath, and I groan.

"I'm all done!" The pint-sized one announces and stands from the table, taking her plate to the kitchen.

While she's off playing with her toys, my parents and I go about finishing our dinner and confirming plans for Thanksgiving and, in code to avoid tiny ears, coordinating Calypso's Christmas gifts. Then it happens. The same topic my mom brings up every few months. Only this time, she has a partner in crime.

"So, any dating prospects? You know you aren't getting any younger, Matthew."

"Thanks, Mother."

"Oh Daddy, you should take Carrie on a date. I bet she'd say yes if you were really nice and gave her flowers," Calypso says excitedly, her little eyes wide and her hands clasped to her chest.

"Why, I think that's a wonderful idea. Sprite has told me all about how fun game night was and how pretty this Carrie is. I think a date sounds perfect."

Calypso climbs up on Mom's lap like the little traitor she is. I thought we were a team. The two of us taking on the world. Turns out she's in cahoots with my mom to set me up.

"And on that note, we need to get home. It's a school night for someone," I retort and stand from the table, taking my plate and a few empty containers to the kitchen. With the topic clearly not up for discussion, my mom and I go about cleaning up our dinner while my daughter and Dad work on their puzzle before I really call it a night and usher Calypso out the door.

She chatters all the way home, talking about all her favorite "trees" and which bubbles she wants to use tonight for her bath. I wish I could switch from topic to topic like her. The mind of a six-year-old is amazing and a little chaotic. When we pull up to the house, she's moved from bath time to why girls can do anything boys can do, even fly to the moon.

The minute I kill the engine, I hear it. The incessant barking from earlier but at an epic level. Great, I just know I'm going to be on my hands and knees digging around a bush with a flashlight to save Olaf from whatever has him freaking out.

"Let's go, Sprite. I need to see what has Olaf making such a racket."

"Daddy! What if it's a zombie?"

"A what? Never mind. I need your tablet before bath time. Time to check the parental controls."

Making our way into the house, I flip the light in the kitchen before pulling the flashlight from the drawer and heading straight out the door to where Olaf is standing, butt up in the air, his nose in the bushes along the fence.

Now I know where the term "downward dog" came from. This dog is going down.

"What is it, buddy? Let me in there," I say, nudging him out of the way and dropping to my knees. It's then that I see it. A tiny little pink… what is that? An alien baby? Maybe Sprite wasn't too far off with the zombie thing.

"Olaf, I swear, get out of the way," I groan as I push him farther to the side and scoop the little creature up into my hands.

A high pitch screech behind me startles me and Olaf both. He runs away whimpering while I shift, barely avoiding dropping the critter.

"Calypso! You scared me."

"What is that? A baby? Oh! Daddy, is it for me? Do I get to keep it?"

"No, you don't. But I think we need to get it inside and warm it up. I don't even know what it is."

Rising from the ground, I motion for her to pick up the flashlight and head toward the house. Wrapping the small thing in a kitchen towel, I do the only thing I can think of. I pull my phone, snap a picture, and text it to Carrie. If anyone knows what to do with a random pink critter in my yard, it's her.

# Chapter 12

*Carrie*

The house is a mess, I'm in my jammies, and Luke has disappeared on me again. It's not that I mind him running around a bit. He's the only animal who lives here so there's no danger. Except, I wasn't expecting to have company tonight.

Not that Matthew bringing over a baby squirrel is considered company. It's more of an urgent animal rescue situation. Our focus will be on the tiny newborn, not on my small duplex and how it looks like a tornado hit recently.

Oh who am I kidding? Matthew may not care, but I do. And that just pisses me off. I shouldn't care what he thinks about my housekeeping skills or my giant nightshirt and ratty sweatpants. But I do.

After spending the evening with him and Calypso, he just seems so much—more. So much more than just a pretty face who loves to flirt and keep his bed warm with a random body. Which I realized the other day I don't actually know if that's true. The rumor mill amongst bloggers and his flirty pickup lines only confirmed that impression I had of him. Until now.

Now he's this amazing guy who is a good cook, a great housekeeper, and a fantastic father of the most amazing little girl. She's witty, smart, and one heck of a "creative player."

And I'm the crazy lady with a squirrel for a pet.

"Come on, Luke," I call out as I get on my hands and knees to look under the couch. "At least humor me and get in your cage until they get here, will you?"

Of course, now is when the doorbell rings. I should know better than to hope the lone man in my life will help me out at a time like this.

"I hope you fell asleep in the sink again," I grumble as I make my way to the door. "It'd serve you right if I didn't see you before washing my hands."

I pull the door open, expecting to find Matthew in all his cover model glory standing on my front porch. Instead, it looks like he and Calypso have been digging in a mud puddle.

"Rough day?" I ask, gesturing them in. Matthew looks down at both of them and it's as if he's just now realizing that they're both covered in dirt.

"Oh. Yeah. I had to manhandle Olaf out of the way to figure out what was making him go ballistic."

"And I thought Daddy was fighting a zombie and was saving him," Calypso tosses out proudly. I raise my eyebrows at her in question, so she leans in and quietly adds, "Always go for the head. It's the only way to kill them."

"Seriously. No more iPad at Grandma's house until Papa stops unblocking websites." Matthew's frustration is evident, and I suspect this isn't the first time they've had this discussion. But we don't have time for this. I've seen a picture of this new baby, and he's probably on borrowed time.

"Okay, well come in and let me see this little one you have for me."

Matthew holds out a dishrag which I take gently, pulling it to my chest. Moving quickling, I head toward my dining room, currently also a squirrel bedroom, when I hear the front door close. Gently, I set the towel on the table and unwrap it.

"Is Sven going to be okay?" Calypso asks sweetly from my side.

"I hope so." I pull the tiny pink baby out of the rag and realize there's about a fifty-fifty shot for this guy. "You already did good by giving him a good strong name."

A quick inspection shows no visible injuries and he's squirmy. All good signs. But his eyes are still sealed shut, he doesn't have any hair, and a tiny little umbilical cord is still attached to him. All bad signs about his chances.

"First things first, we need to get him a little bit of sugar water to help stabilize him." Tucking him safely into my sports bra, I head toward the kitchen and start grabbing all the ingredients I need.

"Um… did you just…?"

I look over my shoulder at Matthew who has the strangest look on his face.

"What?" Now I'm self-conscious. Do I have tooth-paste on my chin? A booger hanging out of my nose? I have some sort of stain on my jammie top, don't I?

"You just stuck a squirrel in your bra."

Oh yeah. I guess he's never seen me do that before. Hazards of working in wildlife rescue, I don't even re-alize what I'm doing until someone points it out.

Clearing my throat of my embarrassment, I turn back to the job at hand and spend a little more time than necessary making sure the water is at the right temperature for my mixture. "It's a sports bra. When they're this little, the best way to get them warm is skin to skin contact."

Matthew doesn't say anything so I take a chance and glance over at him. He's nodding and watching me closely as I pour water in a small bowl. "Makes sense. I guess I just never thought of doing it for an animal. Seems… strange."

I scoff. "You'll just have to trust me when I say a squirrel in my bra is hardly the strangest part of my life."

I gather the rest of my supplies and the three of us head back into the small dining area. Since it's just me, I don't need it for actual dining, so it ended up being a combination of Luke's bedroom and my blog room. Mostly Luke, though.

His oversized cage is set up on top of a large towel on the table for easy clean up. Extra rags and clean food bowls sit on top, next to branches of fresh leaves sticking out in various spots. Squirrels like to chew on bark and leaves so I have to change them out regularly. Of course, that also means never walking too close to the cage without paying attention. Impaling yourself on a branch is never fun.

I settle myself on the chair and pull Sven out of my bra. "Come here, baby. Let's see if we can get you to eat something."

"Can I watch?" Calypso moves closer, eyes focused on the wiggly thing in my hand. He's barely the length of my palm. Wrapping my fingers around his body to keep him warm and his head where I want it, I bring the syringe to his mouth and hope for the best.

"Baby squirrels don't eat very much," I explain as I encourage him to lick the drops of water. "But they have to stay hydrated so even if he doesn't want it, we have to make sure he finishes some."

"Why sugar water?" Matthew asks, leaning forward, just as intrigued in what I'm doing as his daughter. "Shouldn't he have milk or something?"

"He will." I get a little lick out of Sven. "With the

fall and the loss of heat, the sugar will give his system a little boost. Plus, he's used to mama's milk and soft nipples. The flavor will encourage him to try to get used to a different way of eating. There ya go, little one," I coo, and click my tongue at him like his mama would.

Sven doesn't need much encouragement. The second he gets a taste of the sugar, he goes for it. That's a really good sign.

"Look, Daddy, he's eating it!" Calypso's excited voice makes me smile. It's always fun watching these babies thrive. I just hope he continues this direction.

"He's doing a good job—" I'm cut off when a two-pound, adult male squirrel suddenly jumps on my shoulder.

"Oh god!" Matthew yells and takes a huge step back, pulling Calypso with him. "There's a squirrel on you!"

Rolling my eyes, I glance over at the menace sitting on me, flicking his tail territorially.

"Sure. Now you come back."

I ignore Luke, who is chittering away, clearly unhappy that there is another squirrel in his domain. Never mind that Sven's so small, he doesn't even know he's alive yet. In true Luke fashion, he needs to show Sven who's boss.

"So, this is Luke," I say with a head nod.

"You really do have a pet squirrel." Matthew's eyes

are wide and his back is against the wall like he's afraid to make any sudden movements. Calypso tries to step forward, but he holds her tight against him.

I glance down at my shoulder again. It's as if Luke has suddenly realized there's not just a new squirrel in the house, but new people too. "Pet is a relative term. He thinks he owns the place."

"You have a pet *squirrel*."

Calypso finally breaks free and moves closer. "Can I pet him?"

"No, honey! Squirrels can be mean." Matthew moves to grab her again, but Luke makes a sudden movement, and Matthew is right back up against the wall.

"That's only if you try to grab him. If you're super gentle and slow, Luke will probably even sit on your shoulder."

Calypso's eyes widen with delight, while Matthew's continue to widen in fear. How in the world he had enough bravery to pick up Sven, I'll never know.

"Here." I hand Calypso a pecan. "It's Luke's favorite. Feed it to him and he'll get used to you."

Slowly, she reaches out to Luke. The closer she gets, the more he recognizes what she has to offer. Finally, he sniffs the nut and snatches it from her hand, settling himself back onto my shoulder to eat.

"I did it!" she exclaims. "Did you see that, Daddy?"

"You have a pet squirrel?"

I roll my eyes again, only this time it's at Matthew. "He's not a pet. He's a rescue."

"What's the difference? He's an adult squirrel, and he's sitting on your shoulder. Oh god! He's sitting on my daughter's shoulder!"

Clearly tired of having to put effort into reaching for his food, Luke scurries down my arm and hops onto Calypso. She's giggling as Luke nuzzles into her hair like squirrels do when they're exploring and looking for food. I give her another pecan to feed him and he pops out from under the dark ringlets, looking like he has his own wig on. It makes me laugh, so of course I do what any good hostess would do while her guest is freaking out—I grab my phone and take a picture.

"Seriously, Matthew. Luke isn't your average everyday squirrel. He can't live in the wild so he never went feral." I turn my phone around to show them the picture. Calypso's giggles get more pronounced. Even Matthew looks like he's fighting back a laugh. Or at least a chortle. Maybe a sob. Regardless, the more he watches his child interact with the animal, the less hysterical he seems.

"But, why can't he live outside? In trees."

Luke seems to think that's his cue to greet our other guest, as he swivels on Calypso's shoulder, takes one look at Matthew, and jumps. Matthew makes a garbled, strangled sound as Luke lands on his shirt, then scurries to his favorite perch, his shoulder.

Not wanting to make any sudden movements so I

don't startle the girly-man, I slowly reach out, shifting Sven in my palm. "Here. Take this pecan, and just feed it to him."

I'll give Matthew one thing; he's trying really hard to not pee his pants. Or let out another high-pitched screech.

Taking the nut, he hands it to Luke, who immediately sits up and starts eating. As long as it's not peanuts, he's pretty easy to please.

Matthew lets out a quick breath and a sort of smile or grimace forms on his face. "He's eating, huh?"

Calypso nods. "He likes you, Daddy."

"Yeah. I have a squirrel on my shoulder." I try to not laugh, biting on my bottom lip as he stands stone still.

"You do. You're doing really good," I say, still using a gentle tone for Matthew's purposes, not Luke's. "If you reach up, you can probably pet his head too."

Watching Matthew try to overcome his fear of squirrels is like watching a cartoon. I know what's about to happen, but it seems like there's no way. Until suddenly, Matthew touches the top of Luke's head, Luke immediately falls over, and Matthew spends the next few seconds trying to catch him before he falls and hits the ground.

When he finally has Luke in his hands, Matthew keeps looking down at the squirrel and up at me, then down, then back up shock written all over his face.

"Ohmygod, I killed your squirrel!"

Thankfully, Sven is done eating so I pop him back in my bra and stand up, approaching an almost hysterical Matthew.

"I'm so sorry. I didn't know I was so strong," he babbles and I try really, really hard not to laugh at the fact that he immediately assumed his giant model muscles crushed Luke's brain.

"You didn't kill him." I take Luke from him and press him up to my neck, giving him a quick hug and stroke. "He's sleeping, see?" Holding him out, I point out the obvious rise and fall of Luke's furry chest.

Matthew blinks a couple times. "Wait. He just fell asleep?"

"He has the rodent version of narcolepsy. Or at least that's what we think. It's the only way the vet could describe what happens," I explain as I turn to put Luke away. "That's why he can't live in the wild."

Matthew comes a little closer and watches as I settle Luke in his cage. "Yeah, I can see how he'd be easy hawk food."

My jaw drops and I cover Luke's tiny ears. "Don't say things like that when he's sleeping. You'll give him nightmares."

"Seriously?"

"No."

"Daddy!" Calypso interrupts what is possibly the strangest conversation ever. "Carrie has your picture on her wall!"

Aaannnnddd she starts the most awkward conversation instead.

In what I've come to know as his typical Matthew fashion, he turns to me with a smirk, the infamous dimple on display. "She does, huh?"

"Wow. You seem awfully confident in your sex appeal after practically running screaming from a rodent four seconds ago."

He shrugs nonchalantly. "I feel emotions. I'm comfortable in my sexuality. But I do wanna know why you have a picture of me. Is it framed? Do you kiss it at night?"

Satisfied Luke is fine and he has enough food for when he wakes up, I close his cage. "Yes," I deadpan. "And Olaf didn't run away. I stole him so I could get close to you. I even planted Sven in your yard."

Matthew's face actually pales. Does he not understand sarcasm?

"Seriously, Matthew?"

"I mean… models have weird stalker things happen all the time."

I shake my head and turn away from him, wondering what the hell Calypso is even talking about. It doesn't take long to spot the picture on my corkboard.

"Oh yeah. I forgot I put this up here," I say as I pull the postcard down and hand it to Matthew. "Donna Moreno's new book comes out next week. I didn't want to forget to post my review."

Matthew's eyebrow quirks. "Suuure. That's why it's up there."

I see he's no longer worried about me peeking in his windows. Calypso, on the other hand, is more interested in my photo light box and the props inside.

"What does this do?" she asks, very obviously holding herself back from touching things without asking.

Without missing a beat, I start taking some of my favorite colorful swag out and setting up a small scene. "This is my light box. I put things in here when I want to take a picture. Let's see, we have a coffee mug and a glove. Let's see what we can do with this."

I snatch the postcard back out of Matthew's hand and stage the scene. Putting on the black gloves, I put one hand around the mug and lay the postcard next to it. Turning the whole set on, I take a quick pic with my phone and show Calypso who squeals with delight.

"See how it turned out?"

"It's so pretty!" she gushes. "Look Daddy! She made you look pretty!"

I smile victoriously at him, but he's too busy staring at my corkboard to notice. I'm not sure what's caught his eye. It's just a mishmash of reading schedules, author events, and swag I need to use in my pictures.

"You're a fan of Blind Fury?"

Oh yeah. I guess that old ticket is up there too.

"Love them. That's the only time I've ever seen them live." I gesture to the ticket I now know he's looking at.

Digging his hands in his pockets, Matthew suddenly looks nervous. Not He-Just-Killed-Luke nervous. More like game night nervous.

"You know they're coming to the Convention Center this weekend."

My jaw drops because no, I didn't know that. "Seriously? How did I miss that?"

"Obviously it's because my picture distracted you every time you looked at the corkboard."

I laugh because that was actually pretty funny.

"Sadly, I don't have any distracting pictures, so I knew they were coming," he continues, cocky, arrogant Matthew back in charge. "And guess who has two tickets?"

"Ugh." I drop my head back and look at the ceiling in disappointment. "I'm so jealous. I wish I could go, but I'm sure tickets are sold out."

Matthew squeezes his eyes tightly and I'm not sure if he's about to sneeze or pulling himself together. Either way, he blurts out the words I wasn't expecting. "You misunderstand. You want to go with me to see Blind Fury in concert?"

The debate in my brain takes all of half a second. Do I want to go see my favorite band with a hot guy who makes me laugh and brings me baby squirrels to put in my bra with very little judgement?

"Yes. Yes I do."

# Chapter 13

*Matthew*

I'm probably a little more excited than I should be to see Carrie tonight. It isn't a date but just knowing we're going out by ourselves makes it a little more significant than playing kids board games on my living room floor. Not that I didn't fully enjoy our night at my house or even the one at hers with that weird sleeping squirrel, it's just that tonight feels different. Even the way she didn't hesitate before accepting the invitation didn't surprise me too much.

Of course, calling my buddy Kevin and demanding he sell me his ticket was pricey. Not only monetarily but I'll also be helping him move into his new place next weekend. If I know Kev, I'll be doing most of the heavy lifting while he directs me where to go. It'll be worth it.

As I hit send on my final email of the week, a little face pops up on the other side of my desk. I pretend to be startled sending her into a fit of giggles.

"You scared me, Sprite."

"Daddy, you're so funny when you get scared. Your eyes go like this." I watch as she tries to make her eyes wide but only succeeds in scrunching her nose.

Shaking my head, I motion for her to come around the desk. Hopping up on my lap, she wraps her arms around my neck and squeezes. The scent of her strawberry shampoo mixed with sweat from playing fills my senses and I sigh. I know moments like this are going to lessen over the next few years so I appreciate them while I can.

"How was school?"

Leaning her head back, she groans. "It was okay. We had to work on our writing. I don't know why we have to do that. Everyone has a tablet these days, can't we just type out everything?"

"Writing is important. I do it every day. The time for computers will come. Let's close this place down and see what Grandma's doing."

I go through the steps to log off the system, noting there are still a couple hours until I have to pick up Carrie. Calypso skips out the door as I flip the light switch and follow her down the hall toward the main part of the house. My dad is sitting in his recliner, glasses low on his nose as he reads on his tablet and Mom is in the kitchen, unloading grocery bags.

"Hi honey. What time are you picking up your date?"

"Mom—"

"Just let me have this, Matthew. I have so few joys in my life."

"Oh for goodness sake. Look, we're friends and I had an extra ticket. Don't make more of this than it is."

Ignoring me, my mom cuts up an apple and scoops a little peanut butter on a plate before sliding it in front of Calypso as she settles on one of the stools at the counter. I snag one of the slices as my daughter tries, and fails, to smack my hand.

"Nobody likes a thief, Daddy."

"My apologies, baby. Be good for Grandma and I'll see you in the morning."

"Daddy!" she screeches, stopping me before I can kiss the top of her head. "Will you ask Carrie to send me a picture of Sven? I want to make sure he's okay."

"Honey, she sent one this morning. I showed you on the way to school."

She opens her mouth to argue, but I hold my hand up to stop her. "Fine. I will shoot her a text right now."

`Me: Sprite asked if she can see a picture of Sven.`

`C: Sure.`

Minutes tick by and I all but give up when my phone vibrates.

`C: Sorry, I had poop on my hand.`

`C: <photo attachment>`

Eww.

Me: Poop?!?!

C: Yeah, you know human—or in this
instance, squirrel—waste.

Me: Umm... gross.

I shiver at the thought and tap on the photo.

"Here you go. Sven in all his pink glory."

"Oh, he's getting bigger. Did you see, Grandma?
We saved him. Daddy thought he was a zombie."

Funny how her recollection of how it all went down
changes depending on who she's talking to. "And, I'm
outta here. Be good."

"Don't rush over on our account," Mom says with
faux sweetness. I know her game. "You know, if you're
up late, or need to do anything in the morning."

Groaning, I rub my hand down my face. "Boundaries, Mother."

I leave her to answer the rapid-fire questions about
what I would need to do on a Saturday morning from
an inquisitive six-year-old as I pat my dad on the
shoulder and head out of the house. Serves her right
for insinuating I'll be up late for any other reason than
the concert. As I turn the ignition and my phone connects to the Bluetooth, another alert of a text message
comes through.

C: Are you sure you wouldn't rather just meet there?

Me: Nope. I'll pick you up at 6:00.

C: If you're sure. I feel bad. At least let me pay for parking.

Me: See you at 6:00.

I can only imagine how frustrated my short response has her. I envision her pink lips clenched in a fine line, her eyes squinting as she tries to come up with a retort. Unfortunately for her, my phone is set to send a message that I'm driving. She'll just have to stew for a while. Maybe I'll even "forget" to turn off the auto response and see how annoyed she is when I pick her up.

"Are you going to check your phone all night?" I tease as Carrie picks up the device for the fourth time since we were sat at our table.

"I'm sorry. I don't mean to be rude. It's just that usually I'm the one who cares for the newborns. I'm worried."

"And struggling to give up control?"

Scoffing, she reaches for her whiskey and takes a small sip. I mimic her move with my own glass and watch as she pretends to be offended. The problem with that is she's not. And I'm right.

"Fine. I'm struggling a smidge. I know Jamie can handle it, but I'm worried. Can you imagine if something happens to him? How will we tell Calypso?"

Her concern for my daughter and her feelings triggers something in me. Delilah loves Calypso and does the best she can, but the reality is, the primary woman in my daughter's life is my mom. And while she loves her more than anything, to have another woman show complete concern for her… it's different.

"Well, we'll deal with that if it becomes an issue. How about tonight we just have fun? I mean, we're seeing Blind Fury. That means there's no room for distractions."

"You're right. I still can't believe you had an extra ticket. I'm so excited. How many times have you seen them in concert?"

Before I can respond, the server appears with our food. She places the plates in front of us—grilled salmon and a side of steamed vegetables for me and a club sandwich for Carrie—before placing a few extra napkins on the table and leaving us alone.

Our conversation is stalled for a few minutes, as we take our first bites of dinner. Once I've tasted everything, I take a drink of water and pick up our conversation where it ended.

"I've seen them in concert about six times. I never miss an opportunity, and once I even went after a signing in Vegas."

"Wow! You really are a fan. I think the only thing I've seen six times is *Legally Blonde*."

Stealing one of her fries from the plate, I stuff it in my mouth, a huge grin on my face as she growls at me. That move and her response breaks up whatever awkwardness we were filling with small talk as we go about finishing our meal. As much as I wanted to order fries of my own, they are a weakness of mine, and I have a shoot coming up soon. There's no room for extra water weight when it comes to spending ten hours in front of a camera with your shirt off. And sometimes your pants.

I manage to slip my credit card to the server while Carrie is in the restroom and am signing the receipt when she slides back into the booth. I ignore her mumbles under her breath while I place the card back in my wallet. Glancing up at her, I smirk at her stance. Sitting back with her arms across her chest, she's trying to look angry. And failing miserably.

Instead, she looks sexy as hell. Her long hair is curled tonight, the locks brushing the tops of her breasts. The fitted black long-sleeved top she's wearing has a cut out right at her cleavage, and I'm not ashamed to admit I've settled my gaze on that spot a few times tonight. Neither of those points compete with what her jeans do for her ass. Again, not ashamed to have lingered on that as she walked in the restaurant ahead of me.

"I said I wanted to buy dinner, Matthew."

"Too bad, so sad. Say thank you and let's go. You don't want to miss a minute of the show."

Rolling her eyes, she slips on her jacket and grabs her purse before moving out of the booth. I gently guide her through the restaurant, my hand on her lower back. When we get to the door, a couple is entering but the man stands outside holding it open as we step through and out onto the street. He smiles at me as his wife mumbles something like "young love" before stepping through the door. I don't bother to correct him.

It's a short walk to the concert so we fall in line with the masses and quietly make our way to the Convention Center, enjoying the evening. Until we arrive and Carrie groans at the long lines.

"Have no fear," I say as I grab her hand and tug her away from the crowd and to a door marked "VIP."

Pulling the tickets from my back pocket, I hand them to the woman standing at the door with a scanner. The sound of the beeps confirming our VIP status is music to my ears as we are ushered through the door.

"Umm… how much were these tickets?" Carrie asks, still letting me hold her hand as I walk us through the masses and toward the concession stand.

"Not too much. Okay, what are you drinking? The hard stuff is only served at the main bar and you can't take it out to the seats. So beer, one of those spiked teas, or wine?"

She looks from the concession stand to the sign with directions to the bar. As much as I'd love one more whiskey before I switch to water, I also don't want to miss any of the show. Beer it is.

Carrie, on the other hand, is still deciding. "Not a beer and wine fan?" I ask, squeezing her hand.

Looking down at our linked fingers, she lets out a gasp and snatches her hand back. I'll ignore how much that sucks. For now.

"I hate beer and no way I'm drinking fake spiked tea in a can. That's just wrong on so many levels. I guess wine it is. But be warned. It goes straight to my head. I cannot be held responsible for the extreme giggling that may occur."

"Giggling is never a bad thing."

"You say that now. I'm not exactly a quiet person."

"Eh, I think I can handle whatever you throw my way," I say before stepping up to the counter to order our drinks.

Then, I almost crash into the kids next to me when Carrie pushes me out of the way to pay. When I start to protest, she places her hand on my mouth to shut me up. On instinct, I stick my tongue out and lick her hand. It's the same move I do to Calypso when she tries to keep me quiet. I'm happy to report it has the same effect on Carrie as it does my sprite.

"You are disgusting," she groans, wiping her hand on my shirt.

"And you are making it hard for me to be a gentleman."

"It's a beer, Matthew. Relax. Now, take me to the seats so I can get my concert on."

Laughing, I shake my head and motion for her to follow me. Again, afraid I'll lose her in the crowd, I take her hand in mine. It's only because she's small and could easily be lost. I don't care if her little hand feels pretty damn good in my hand.

We make it to our seats just as the house lights dim. The crowd roars and Carrie stops in her tracks. Turning to look at her, the darkness doesn't stop me seeing her stand with her mouth open. I guess she's finally figured out just where our seats are.

Leaning down, I whisper in her ear. "Get ready to have your mind blown. Seeing them this close is the only way to go."

Without another word, I tug her along and down the aisle toward our floor seats. I wasn't kidding when I said up close is the only way to see Blind Fury. The three hundred bucks I owe Kevin for his ticket are worth it as the guys take the stage and Carrie's face breaks out into the biggest smile I've ever seen. With the first strum of the guitar and beat of the drums, she starts swaying her hips, taking a sip from her wine. I stand next to her, watching her in my peripheral as she sings along to every song. Her cup is empty and I take it from her, waving it to see if she wants another. Nodding, she smiles and turns her attention back to the band.

I make quick work of going back to the concession stand to get her another wine. While I'm there, I grab us both a bottle of water and myself a bag of candy. So much for my shoot in a few weeks. I'll just have to work extra hard tomorrow with my workout. As I return to our row, Carrie is now in full dance party mode. Her arms are over her head and her hips are moving in a circular motion. If I didn't know better, I'd think she was using an imaginary hoola hoop.

Standing next to her, I hand her the wine. Before she takes the cup from me, she wraps her arms around my neck and jumps up and down, pulling my neck with her.

"Thank you for this! I'm having so much fun!" Her voice is extra loud in my ear, but it's the warm breath skirting across my skin that I notice most of all.

I don't bother answering, nothing can be heard. Instead, I give Carrie her wine and unscrew the top of my water just as she shifts so she's standing in front of me. Her hips are swaying and her ass bumps into my crotch more than once. To save myself and any future children that I may father, I rest my hand on her hip and slow down her moves.

Bad decision. She's gone from her own dance party to a seductive slow bump and grind against me. I have a feeling giggles aren't the only thing wine does to her. From the way she's moving, I think a little hellcat lurks inside her and wine is its catnip.

Apparently I was wrong. I may not be able to handle everything she's throwing my way.

# Chapter 14

*Carrie*

The volume on the radio is low in Matthew's truck. Or maybe it's at normal volume and my eardrums haven't normalized yet after a three-hour show plus two encores.

It. Was. Amazing.

Matthew wasn't lying when he said up close and personal is the way to go when seeing Blind Fury in concert. I still question his truthfulness about what kind of a deal he got on those tickets, though. Not that I'm pushing it. I'm grateful he took me out on the town. It was one of the best night's I can remember in a very long time. Unfortunately, it's about to get super awkward.

Part of the reason I wanted to meet him close to the venue was to avoid the whole walking me to the door scenario. It's always uncomfortable when you don't know if there's going to be a good night kiss or just a hug. Am I supposed to invite him in for drinks? If I do, does that mean I'm offering him sex?

It's a whole anxiety filled process for me that I don't enjoy.

Right now I'm trying not to think about it. I want to enjoy these last moments of the world's best... date. Not a date. Just friends. Or is it a date?

"Tell me about your blog."

Matthew's surprising question breaks me from my nervous thoughts. I look over at him, the light from streetlamps making his face dodge in and out of shadows as we drive.

"Hmm?" I ask, not certain what he wants to know.

He smiles playfully at me and tries again. "Tell me about your blog. I know you review books, but how did you start? Why do you do it? Give me the skinny on Carrie Mibooks."

I roll my eyes at his use of my blogger name. It's less about anonymity and more about having an online persona, something I'm sure he's familiar with. I wouldn't know since I don't follow him on social media. Although maybe I should change that now that we're dating. Or concert buddies. And co-parenting a squirrel. Whatever. Man, I'm a lightweight. Three glasses of wine and I already overthink everything.

"Well, I guess it's pretty standard. We've been blogging for about five years and we've got a bit of a following."

"We?" he asks, keeping his left hand on the wheel, leaning his right arm on the center console. "Who's we?"

A wine giggle bursts out of me because that question is the funniest thing I've ever heard for no reason whatsoever.

"Have you even read my blog?"

Matthew bites back a shy smile, those damn dimples that sell thousands of books on full display. Busted. "No. But have you looked up my portfolio?"

"I don't have to. Your picture was on my corkboard, remember?"

He doesn't even try to hide his amusement this time. "Okay, okay. You win. As soon as I get home, I'll pull up your blog and read the whole thing, start to finish."

That's a lofty goal for a man who hasn't even read the book he's on the cover of. "That will take hours, if not days. Maybe just read some of the most recent stuff. I think Celeste posted something new today. I can't remember."

"Who is Celeste?"

"She's my blog partner. I review books and she does theater, musicals. Things like that."

"So it's not just a book blog? I'm confused."

I think about how to answer his question. Originally, we started out only reviewing books, but realized quickly that Celeste's passion was more in the performance arts than in the written word. It was just a tiny hobby back then. Not the explosion to include followers and advertising space like it is now. It doesn't make enough to pay the bills or anything, but my Australia travel fund is growing steadily. I don't tell Matthew all that, though.

"We've discovered that there are a couple different kinds of reader," I explain. "The first loves books more than anything. They will choose a book over television, movies, a party, even dating." Matthew's eyes widen, clearly shocked by someone voluntarily missing out on the opposite sex for the written word. "It's not uncommon for them to devour two to three hundred books a year."

"A year?" he exclaims. "I don't think I've read that many in my entire life!"

"Obviously you aren't our demographic. Now I know why you haven't looked at it yet," I joke and catch his eye. For whatever reason, in this moment we end up holding gazes. I don't know how it happened, but here we are.

This is exactly the kind of walking to the door moment I was afraid of.

Clearing my throat, I face forward quickly and continue babbling. "The other kind of reader is more about the story, whatever form that comes in. They love books, but they also love music, plays, and musical theater. They just love hearing a well-woven tale."

*Well-woven tale? Geez, Carrie. How much did you*

*drink tonight?*

"And which are you?"

"I am sort of in between," I admit. "I can do some theater, but if my nose isn't in a book, you're more likely to find me binge watching Netflix originals."

"I'm more of a Prime lover myself," Matthew states and I can't help but look over at him again. "That Jack Ryan is a pretty awesome guy."

I raise one eyebrow in question. "Got a bit of a man crush, do you?"

Matthew just laughs as he pulls into my driveway. "There are worse people to crush on." And then he turns serious when he throws it into park and looks over at me. "And way better people to crush on."

Umm… is that his way of saying he has a crush on me? Way to throw me right back into my awkward anxieties as soon as we get back to my place.

"Come on," he continues without realizing the turmoil I'm feeling, "let's get you inside."

Matthew hops out of the truck, but it takes me a few seconds to pull together my nerves before I grab the door handle. Of course, he's already there, opening the door for me, helping me down, holding my hand all the way to the front. Manners. Matthew has manners in spades. If I wasn't so damn nervous, I'd be excited about all the physical contact. It's nice being treated like a lady, not just the woman who smells like rodent.

"I had a really nice time, tonight," I remark, trying

hard to turn on some false bravado as we stroll up the front path.

"Really? With as many books as you've read, you use a cliché end of the date phrase like that?"

Just like that, the false bravado leaves so my sarcasm can rear its ugly head. "You're right. How about this?" I turn to face him, stopping on the front stoop. "I had fun, man." And I punch him on the shoulder. "Better?"

He chuckles lightly, dropping my hand to rub his shoulder. "Not even close." Grabbing me, he pulls me to him, and I know what's about to happen.

He's about to kiss me. Ohgod, he's about to kiss me. What do I do? I don't want to kiss him!

But maybe I do. Do I? I don't know anymore.

*Relax, Carrie. Just go with it…*

Quickly, I position myself for maximum kissage and we lean in, but at the last second I change my mind and turn the opposite direction so he kisses my ear. My ear!

Matthew immediately pulls me into a hug, his chuckles bouncing me against his body while my hands hang at my sides like noodles. No matter how I stand here or how amazing he smells, and dang he smells good, I can't hide my own humiliation. He was going for a kiss and I turned.

This. This is why I don't like the end of dates. I always end up doing something stupid that makes it awkward. Fortunately, my good friend Convention Center Pino Grigio is giving me a tiny bit of bravery to face this situation head on.

"I'm so sorry, Matthew. I really like you." I pull away from our embrace to finish this conversation. "But I'm not interested in a physical relationship."

He chuckles lightly again, but I can't tell if it's in embarrassment or for some other reason I'm missing.

"You know I wasn't trying to kiss you, right?"

And cue more humiliation. Apparently I read this entire situation wrong.

"Uh…" Think Carrie! Use your wine brain to turn this whole thing around! "Then it looks like we're on the same page. See ya."

I swivel to my door and quickly try to thrust my key in the lock, but Matthew grabs my arm first.

"What do you mean we're on the same page?"

"We're not getting physical. You. Me." My hand flies around willy-nilly between us in my effort to em-phasize who I'm speaking about. "You don't wanna sleep with me. I don't wanna sleep with you," I ramble, fumbling with my keys as I try to get out of dodge. Un-fortunately Wine Brain also comes with Wine Fingers and I can't get anything to work right.

"Who says I don't want to sleep with you?"

"You just said you didn't."

"No I didn't."

Frustrated at my lack of coordination, I huff. "It's

fine, Matthew. I'm celibate anyway."

I did not. Just. Say that.

Yep. Yep, I did. And everything comes to a screeching halt with that one little sentence. Closing my eyes tight, I pray that when I open them again, I'll have been dreaming.

No such luck. Instead, Matthew is tugging on my arm to turn me around.

"Wait. You're celibate?"

Oh good. Just the kind of conversation I wanted to have after a first date/concert/meeting, *whatever.*

"I'm not judging," he says, but no one actually means that when they say it. "I'm just curious... why?"

This is the conversation I don't like having with people because it's always awkward. One of two things usually happens—they assume I need to overcome some sort of trauma, or it's laughed off like it's a joke. But as I look up at Matthew, I realize he's not asking for entertainment purposes. This isn't about getting a good, personal story out of me. It's like he can see that there's something more there.

"I already told you I wasn't interested in a physical relationship," I say quietly, hoping that'll be the end of it.

"That's different than being celibate."

"So?"

"So I know you've dated before, which tells me there is a reason for your celibacy. And as your friend and the father of your baby squirrel…" I smirk, because yeah. That was kind of clever. "I feel like it's important."

I distance myself from him and cross my arms over my chest. Normally, I wouldn't be so likely to open myself up, but a couple things are running through my mind. One, he let me come over for dinner and I know he doesn't usually bring women around his daughter. Or at least, I assume. Regardless, I know it took a certain amount of trust to do it. Two, he told me about Calypso's mom which is a pretty personal story. And three, Pino Grigio.

Damn that Pino.

"I'm not a virgin so it's not about keeping myself pure or anything like that."

"So then what is it like?"

I peek up at him, his bright green eyes sincere and focused only on me, rapt attention on his face. I'm not getting out of this without spilling my guts so I might as well do it before I sober up too much.

"It's a well thought out, personal choice."

"I figured out that part already."

I bite my lip and look to the sky momentarily. The concept itself is simple, but sometimes I feel like it's hard to explain. I've come this far though. I might as well try.

"I just… I think relationships today are too sex focused. Especially in the beginning. I sort of expected it in college. That's when you are exploring who you are and what you want out of your life. You know what I'm talking about."

He nods because he does. Calypso is living proof of how a lot of us behave in our early twenties when we're on our own and have no responsibility except deciding whether or not to skip our eight o'clock class.

"I just started noticing that after the luster of the physical part sort of dimmed, most times there wasn't any relationship left. I don't want an accidental relationship that evolved from a healthy sex life. I want a healthy sex life that evolves from a solid relationship."

Matthew nods slowly and I can tell he's absorbing my words. "So you want a love story worthy of a romance novel."

I smile at his chiding. "I'm more realistic than that. But yeah. I want my next relationship to evolve from common interests and genuine care for each other. I feel like if sex is secondary to other stuff, it's a stronger bond. And a stronger bond makes for better sex anyway," I add on in a mumble to myself.

Matthew cocks his head and moves closer. "Excuse me? Did you just say you need a strong bond for good sex?"

I roll my eyes at him. "Not exactly. But come on. You have to admit sex is way better when there is an emotional connection, not just a physical one."

He shrugs, not quite agreeing with me but not disagreeing with me either. "I never really thought about it."

"Of course not. You're a guy. Sex is mind-blowing no matter what for you."

"Well, it's blowing something. That's for sure."

I burst out laughing. "Ohmygod, you did not just say that."

He smiles like telling me something funny is a victory on his part. "I did. But I also understand. You want a good, solid foundation before going there. I get it."

I smile shyly, trying to enjoy this moment because honestly, it could be the last. More than once a guy has expressed interest in me, only to suddenly lose that interest just as quickly when he finds out what my boundaries are. "I'm not looking for a hookup, Matthew. I want more than that. I'm worth more than that. And I think that's why you intimidated me at first. I'm not one of the women who will sleep with you at a signing because what happens there stays there."

His face suddenly changes into one of confusion. "Wait, what?"

"It's okay. I'm not judging. Well, maybe a little." I go for the joke but it falls flat. "I just can't be that person."

Matthew shakes his head, his eyebrows furrowed. "I… wait… one of what women who will sleep with me at a signing? I don't… what does that mean?"

A humorless laugh huffs out of me. "Matthew, the grapevine is pretty quick with romance readers. We love stories, even if it's gossip about a male model sleeping with readers."

His hands cover his mouth lightly and I'm feeling just as confused as he looks. Why does he look like I've just pulled the rug out from underneath him?

"Carrie, I don't know who you've been talking to, but I've never slept with a reader. And certainly not at a signing."

I huff in irritation. "You don't have to lie to me. I heard it from more than one source. It's okay. It's your business."

"No, you don't understand. I don't know where that rumor started, but it's a million percent not true."

"Wait… what?" Now it's my turn to be confused.

"I've had one one-night stand in my life and ended up with a kid. And every time I go to an event, there is an element of fangirl crazy. I purposely stay far away from that."

"But you hit on me the first time we met."

He opens his mouth to respond and then seems to change gears. "Uh, yeah. That was actually because I was trying to prove to Donna that I don't always get the girl."

"Hold on." I hold my hand up because this conversation has suddenly gone from being personal to completely convoluted. "You're saying you've never slept with a reader?"

"Never," he says as he slowly shakes his head.

"But I've heard it several times. Matthew Roberts, the cover model on Hazel Scott's books, sleeping with readers."

"Um, I've never been on a Hazel Scott book. I'd love to. She's got a huge reach, but she's never asked for me."

What the hell is happening here? "What? Yes you have."

Pulling my phone out of my clutch I swipe it open and pull open the internet. Typing rapidly, I read what I'm doing. "What cover model is on Hazel Scott's books. There." I turn the screen around to show him what I'm searching. "This should settle things."

When the results load, I gasp and throw my hand over my mouth. "Ohmygod it's *Nathan* Roberts." Eyes wide, I look up at him in shock. "It wasn't you."

It takes about two seconds for the shock to wear off and for Matthew to burst into laughter. "All this time you were avoiding me because you thought I was the man whore model?"

"You don't have to call him that," I say sheepishly. And a little hypocritically since I've been apparently judging Matthew all this time.

"No, it's what he's known as in our field. Everyone knows about him. Well, the model that has no problem spending time with the ladies, anyway. I just never asked who it was."

Matthew keeps laughing and I drop my chin down to my chest. "I am so embarrassed."

"Don't be," Matthew says. "It all makes sense now. No wonder you were so cranky with me."

I cross my arms, partially relieved. Partially irritated that he's finding so much enjoyment in my misplaced judgement. And partially pissed at myself for being such a scatterbrained mess that I can mix up the names Nathan and Matthew. Maybe my mother was onto something with her Ritalin talk.

"Don't be mad." Matthew moves toward me, putting his hands on my arms and rubbing the night chill away. "Anyone could have made a mistake. You were protecting yourself and your boundaries. Besides, you were right about one thing."

"What's that?"

"You *are* worth more than just a hookup. You're worth it all. Now go get that weird sleeping squirrel fed and go to bed. You need to sleep off some of that wine."

I laugh softly, grateful he isn't going in for a kiss again. I'm too embarrassed to even consider locking lips tonight. Having no more problems with the lock, I let myself in and I quietly wave goodbye before closing the door behind me, strangely sad that our night is over. I'm glad we've cleared the air, but there is a good possibility it's the first and last date-thing we'll have together.

Sometimes it sucks having different boundaries than most twenty-somethings that I know. Maybe it's because I'm a romantic at heart, but I want a man to prove beyond a shadow of a doubt that he's willing to sacrifice to make a relationship with me work. And sex? That's a big thing for most men. It's the ultimate sacrifice for some people.

"Hi, Lukey. Do you need some more nuts?" I ask quietly, peeking into his cage. He wakes up for just a few seconds to look at me, then turns to bury himself under the blankets again. "I guess not. Goodnight, then."

Without Sven here to feed, it doesn't take long to get ready for bed. Before I know it, the evening has been showered off of me, and I'm climbing under my own blankets, the night already becoming a distant memory.

Just as I shut off my lamp, my phone lights up. It's a text from Matthew.

M: I have a confession. I really was going in for a kiss. I was just trying to save face in front of you after you turned. Sleep well, Carrie.

His words make me smile and maybe a little relieved. If he's not embarrassed, then neither am I.

# Chapter 15

*Matthew*

The book industry has changed a lot in the last few years. When I first started this gig, I didn't have much to do in the way of marketing or staying visible on social media. Then the indie book community blew up, the number of authors grew rapidly as did the demand for models. When I met Donna Moreno everything changed. We not only hit it off professionally but became friends. As her friend, I want to support her in any way I can. Unfortunately for me, I told her that one day and that's why I have to do the one part of this job that makes me break into a cold sweat.

Live social media videos.

It's one thing to record myself working out and edit that down to a ten second clip. But this whole live thing is not only nerve-racking, it feels ridiculous. The cover I'm promoting today has me lying on my stomach, shirtless, looking at the camera. It's a simple pose on the surface but the amount of direction the photographer gives me about moving my chin, my elbow, the way my fingers hang. It's absurd. Yet, there I am, in my black and white glory with my triceps engaged and my hair standing on end. Bedhead and bedroom eyes.

This will do nothing to squelch the rumors Carrie informed me of. I can't help but chuckle at that thought. No wonder she was so adamant to stay far away from me before. Hell, I don't want anything to do with the man whore model either. It's just not the type of person I want to associate myself with. Add her celibacy to the assumption I was sleeping around, her distance and attitude makes sense.

My phone buzzes in my shorts pocket while I set up the tripod for my phone. It's the third text from Donna this morning with a reminder to go live. As if I could forget. She also sent an email, tagged me in a few posts, and I'm sure if I look outside there's a carrier pigeon sitting on my front step with a note strapped to his back.

D: I've been stalking your stories. There is NOTHING MATTHEW!

Me: R-E-L-A-X I'm setting up now. I had to drop off Sprite at school. I'll be on in about ten. My hair isn't quite "bedhead" per your request.

D: Well mess it up! The ladies love that. TEN MINUTES!

Laughing I slip my phone back in my pocket and

continue setting up. Yes, I have to actually set up for this video. It's like a really bad made-for-cable-television movie. First, I mess up my bed so it looks like I've been sleeping restlessly, or sexing it up. Then, I move to the bathroom to "mess up" my hair.

While I'm adding pomade to my do, my thoughts drift to Carrie and our conversation on her porch. I knew she was nervous on the drive so I tried to keep the conversation neutral, choosing to ask about her blog. A safe topic.

Never did I expect her to tense up as much as she did when I went in for a kiss. I don't know what I thought she'd do, but turning her head so I became acquainted with her ear instead of her lips wasn't it. It was like being an awkward teenager again, a girl turning her cheek to avoid my kiss so I did what any reasonable man would do. I hugged her. Awkwardly. Her limp body in my embrace was almost funny, but then she hit me straight in the gut.

*"I'm not looking for a hookup, Matthew. I want more than that. I'm worth more than that."*

She's right. She is worth more than a hookup. And, what's funny is she has no idea I've been thinking the same thing. Not only about how great she is but also being over hookups in general. I want more too. For me and for Calypso. Do I think Carrie is that person? The one I'm willing to risk bringing into our lives, taking a chance on our feelings? I don't know.

There's just something about Carrie. The way she was with Calypso, not only the first night they met but every time since. She's patient and doesn't mind answering the most mundane of questions. Her laugh is ridiculous but could easily destroy the worst of days. She's beautiful. Not only in her looks, but in her heart. I meant what I said. She is worth more.

But no sex? At all? That's not something I expected. I'm also not sure if it's a deal breaker. I'd like to say it isn't, but it also isn't a topic I've encountered before. If we were to get serious, would she change her mind? Would I have to make do with me, myself, and I? Or is that asking too much? I don't know the answer, and it has my thoughts tangled.

My phone vibrates again and I roll my eyes, not bothering to respond. Pushing aside my thoughts of Carrie, I walk back into my room and set my tablet up on the tripod. Settling under the covers, the sheet and comforter low on my hips, I check the screen to see if the waistband of my shorts is visible. Dammit, it is. I will not take my shorts off. That's just taking this video to a level I'm not completely comfortable with. Instead, I unbutton them and lower the waist a little before pulling the comforter up a little farther.

Twisting, I make sure my arm is positioned in a way that puts the intricate tattoo on my shoulder on display. Here goes nothing. I tap the live button and throw myself back on the pillows, left arm over my head, eyes relaxed as I smirk at the camera. The dimples I hated as a kid are in high demand these days. I feel like a complete weirdo lying like this. But there ya go, the number of viewers is rapidly increasing. Fifteen. Twenty-seven. Sixty-four.

"Hey everyone. Matthew Roberts here."

One hundred fourteen.

"How are y'all doing this morning? Is it morning where you are?"

I see the comments jumping quickly, hellos and wave emojis. The reaction emojis are flying across the screen. Two hundred four. Time to engage a little.

"Thanks, Lisa. I hope you have a great day too."

"Oh Michelle, I don't think I'll be at the Denver signing. How about Dallas in February?"

Three hundred seventeen.

I continue commenting for a few more minutes, throwing the occasional wink out when requested. I keep the responses neutral, not giving up too much of my personal life. I refuse to use my daughter in this aspect of my life and have become pretty well versed in deflecting topics back to books or the viewers themselves.

"Whiskey is my drink of choice, Candace. If I see you at the bar, we'll have to share a toast."

When the viewer tally hits three hundred seventy-two and seems to stall, I reach over to the nightstand and lift the book that is the reason for this video in the first place. Adjusting myself, I do a double take at the comment that floats across the screen.

*I would love to pay you a visit in your hotel room one night, Matthew. I'm sure we would be great togeth-*

*er. I like it rough. Just like Jayden in Before Tomorrow.*

My eyes widen. Not only does this woman want to come to my random hotel room, she wants to have sex. And thinks I'm a fictional character in a book because I am on its cover. Okay, maybe Carrie had a point about the rumor mill. I can see how if you weren't paying close attention to our names, you could assume I was taking people up on offers like this. Note to self: stay at a different hotel than the event. And book your room under an alias.

"Have you guys seen the cover for Donna Moreno's upcoming release? I was honored when she asked me to be part of the series."

Holding up the book, I watch as hearts fly across the screen.

"It's great, right? Make sure you've preordered your e-book copy before the release next month."

"Yes, Laura. I'm always willing to sign the paperbacks whenever I'm with Donna at an event. Hopefully we'll see you in Dallas. Okay everyone, I need to get going. Thanks for hanging out with me this morning. Congrats to my good friend, Donna Moreno, on her new cover. Bye, all."

I toss the book to the side and lift up to click the end video button when I see the final comment. *I'm told I have a great tongue.* And, I'm done. No more live videos. Harmless flirting is one thing but propositioning me with a great tongue is a little more than I want in my life these days.

Once I confirm the video is stopped and shared, I throw myself back on the pillows. This time, the position isn't about looking sinful and sexy for the viewers, it's more to contemplate what exactly I'm doing in my life. Not allowing myself to second guess anything, I tug my phone from my pocket and pull up my text messages.

Me: How's our baby boy?

C: He's getting stronger. Looks like he's going to make it. Better get ready to pay me all the child support.

Me: What is the going rate for a squirrel baby? Can I pay you in pecans?

C: I'll have to consult my attorney.

C: Read any good blogs lately?

Me: Yep. Turns out bloggers are really knowledgeable and witty.

C: Obviously.

C: Have a good day.

Me: You too.

With a smile on my face, I toss the covers from the bed and get myself ready for the day job. Gotta make that pecan money.

# Chapter 16

### *Carrie*

Stopping Matthew's video, I pull out my ear buds and try not to grimace at the comments. This is a time for relaxation, not to tense up. I'm getting my first pedicure in a month and although it's not my usual place, Jamie has been raving about it so I thought I'd give it a try. I'm a sucker for a good pedicure.

The video started out super sexy. No surprise there. He's sexy. Plus, it's part of his job as a cover model. Of course he's involved in the promotion of the books that he's featured on the cover. Social media is such a huge part of the release process and these days, it's pretty standard to do something interesting for a cover reveal. Knowing Matthew as well as I do now, I have a feeling he put in a whole lot of effort to make a well-staged event. Yet, I also wouldn't be surprised if he was wearing the bottom half of a snowsuit and two pairs of socks under the covers.

He looked every bit the sinful and sexy cover model with his shoulder covered in beautiful intricate colors and bedhead as he interacted with his fans. The icky part for me was in the couple of hours since he posted it, hundreds of comments have been left. Many of them are so gross and inappropriate, it's a wonder they haven't been reported. The offer of being the meat in a Matthew Roberts-Spencer Garrison sex sandwich was particularly cringeworthy. After our date… thing, the whole situation kind of reiterates my point about why I want a solid relationship before jumping in the sack, and I kind of hate that.

Don't get me wrong, people can date or have sex however they want. I don't care. I just don't understand when the act of sex become so much more important than the getting to know each other part.

It's… frustrating. Physical intimacy is important to me. Am I the only single person in the world who thinks that? Surely not. Frustrating or not, I have to remind myself my perfect match will understand why it's something I have to do for me and be glad to go without sex.

Okay "glad" may be reaching. Maybe just willing. Resigned? Humoring me? Whatever. We'll be on the same page. That's the most important part.

Dropping my phone on the small table next to me, I grab Donna's upcoming release and prepare to read while my technician grabs one of my feet from the water. I'm so far behind on this read and I have a meeting with Celeste next week to go over timelines for the blog. She's going to freak out if I don't have my review written. I've never missed a deadline but at least a few times a year I cut it close and stress out. It's become part of our process.

I get behind.

She freaks out.

I catch up and get everything done right on schedule.

She relaxes and has fifteen reviews ready to post at a moment's notice because she's so far ahead.

It's called balance.

I try to get into this new story, which is amazing by the way, but the technician is being kind of rough with the cuticle scissors. I grunt a little when she tugs, hoping she'll get the hint, but she doesn't even notice. I couldn't be so lucky.

Shaking my head, I stick my nose back in my book, trying to lose myself in the story of billionaire tycoon Roberto Amore and his temporary secretary, Lola. Yes, it's an overused trope, but Donna Moreno's books are a guilty pleasure for me, no matter what. I'm kind of hoping a surprise baby shows up by the end. If we're going to go for cliché, I want them all! Nothing keeps my attention more than a super-rich boss trying to decide how to break it to his family that he knocked up his secretary!

I can't seem to concentrate on the story as much as normal, though, when the callus shaver comes out and the woman at my feet goes at it like I've been living barefoot in a forest all my life. It's distracting and, frankly, I'm a little afraid.

Seriously, this is who Jamie recommended? Am I at the right place?

Grabbing my phone, I shoot off a text to make sure I didn't end up at the wrong salon.

Me: You recommended that place at 8ᵗʰ and Parker, right?

J: Yeah! Ooh La La Nails. They're the best. I was there earlier.

Me: Well the lady I got is NOT happy about doing my pedicure. I think she's taking out some pent-up anger on my feet.

J: eek! Does she have flowers on her dress? Kind of older?

Me: YES!!!

J: Haha! I've never seen her before today, but she did mine the same way when she started with me. Then she cut me and was super nice after that.

Me: Probably because she was worried.

J: No doubt.

None of this conversation is reassuring, but it does confirm why I should have gone with my first instinct when she told me about this place. Jamie isn't known for having the highest standards, but I took her word for it. Lesson learned. Next time, ask if blood was drawn.

Joke's on flower dress lady. Little does she know that I snuck Sven into her place of business in my bra, when the sign clearly says "No Pets." I couldn't just leave him in the car and I won't have time to go get him from home before going to work. I had to prioritize. Painted toenails and reading time won out.

Although, I'm still having a hard time reading because the nail clippers are out and—

"Ouch!" I exclaim and just as Jamie predicted, the tech finally seems to notice my feet, instead of everything else around her.

"Oh! Sorry," she says and begins rubbing my foot gently. "Sorry. It's tiny. I'll be careful."

*"Thanks," I say but I'm thinking, You should have started off being careful.*

For the second time, I grab my phone.

Me: SHE JUST CUT ME!

J: So it should be all good now.

Me: Except she just pulled out peppermint oil and is about to rub it all over my legs, including in the cut!

Jamie doesn't respond, probably too busy laughing her ass off. Which is actually okay. My favorite part of a pedicure is the leg massage. This is the time when I truly let go. I lean back, close my eyes, and just enjoy having my muscles rubbed. I always give a larger tip if they focus on the bottoms of my feet. The shelter is almost all cement to make it easier to clean, but it's rough on my tootsies.

My thoughts drift as the relaxation hits and for some reason Australia pops into my mind and all the things I want to do there. Matthew's right. I think I want to spend more of my time outside the city. While I wouldn't mind a day or two to explore the city limits, I'm so curious about the terrain and the wildlife. I want to see a kangaroo and hold a koala.

Hmm. I wonder if Matthew did that. I should ask him—oh. Well. I might as well ask him now since the world's worst nail technician just got up and walked away. Where the hell is she going? Seriously, is this woman on drugs? She may be only in her sixties, give or take a few years, but something tells me her capacities aren't all there. At least it gives me time to text. We can do that right? Text? He asked me about Sven this morning, so it's not weird between us. I think.

Well now I'm angry with myself for ruining my favorite part of a pedi, which is just the feeling I need to get over myself and text already.

> Me: Did you hold a koala in Australia?

Matthew answers quickly, maybe quicker than normal. I wonder if he's getting a shitty pedicure too and is welcoming the distraction.

> M: You can't hold koalas. It's some sort of policy.

What? Well that's disappointing.

Me: Are you sure? I work in wild-life rescue. Surely they'd make an exception for me. Maybe they have a koala with narcolepsy. I'm an expert in that.

M: I'm sure they do since koalas sleep like twenty hours a day.

Me: Sounds like my ideal day. Speaking of sleeping, I saw your live video. It was… interesting.

M: Let's not discuss that, shall we? Some of those comments made me want to run out and eat a dozen do-nuts. Maybe shave my head.

Me: What's wrong? You don't want to be part of a Spencer Garrison-Matthew Roberts sandwich?

M: I don't even know who that is, so no. Wait. Does he look like Jack Ryan? Then maybe I'd consider.

I snort a laugh as my nail lady sits back down.

"What's so funny?"

Now she wants to talk to me? When the pedicure is almost over? *"She's working super hard for that tip, huh?"* I think sarcastically. But I politely say, "Just work stuff," and point to my phone. Maybe that'll get me out of here faster. At this point, fighting the traffic in the Popeye's lunch line sounds more relaxing.

Ooh. Chicken sandwich. That sounds good for lunch.

```
Me: I'll have to see if Jack Ryan
is available. We could both get so
lucky.
```

```
M: Suuuure. Celibate for me, but
get ole Jacky boy involved and sud-
denly it's on.
```

```
Me: Everyone has a price, buddy.
That's mine. TTYL.
```

Tossing my phone aside, I grab my book again. If I can get through just one chapter, I'll be happy at this point. But no such luck. Once again, my phone chimes with a message.

"I quit." Dumping the book back on the table, I grab my phone. No sense in pretending I'll get anything accomplished at this point. Right now, I'm more worried about leaving here with all my toes.

```
J: How's it going? Did the pepper-
mint burn?
```

```
Me: Not much. She's painting my
nails now. Hopefully between the
lines. I'm not expecting much be-
cause she only massaged ONE LEG!
```

```
J: Seriously?!
```

```
Me: In her defense, she did a kick
ass job on that one leg. I'm only
side eyeing her because of it in-
stead of full on glaring.
```

```
J: I think we need to find a new
place.
```

Understatement of the year.

And maybe I need to find some friends with better and higher standards.

# Chapter 17

*Matthew*

I love my child. I think she is the most beautiful, smart, and hilarious human on earth. She's also stubborn, frustrating, and has a very loud, off-key singing voice. The day started off great and somewhere around three this afternoon turned into chaos. By the time I picked Calypso up from my parents' house, she was talking a mile a minute and making a dozen plans for our day. Unfortunately, I forgot to turn the hose off before I left to get her and the normally nice and well-maintained backyard became a mudhole with Olaf as its ruler.

Two hours of clean-up and a dog bath that quickly turned into my little sidekick needing a long bath of her own, I'm finally able to sit down for five minutes. If only it were quiet. Instead, my own little wannabe pop star is performing her own concert and her efforts are wailing, I mean serenading me, down the hall.

"Daddy! Daddy! Are you here? Can you hear me?

Daddy!"

Groaning, I push myself off the couch and pad my way down the hall. Peering into the bathroom, I smile at the scene before me. With her hair covered in bubbles like a little bubble hat, a bubble beard, and bubbles popping all around her, she's sitting with her head tilted back, mouth open to shout. It may be slightly evil but I can't help myself.

"You rang?"

Her screech is louder than normal thanks to the bathroom acoustics. She jumps, eyes wide with water splashing out of the bathtub.

"Daddy! You scared me!"

Laughing, I sit down on the toilet seat, a huge smile on my face. "Sorry, Sprite. I couldn't help myself. Now tell me why you're shouting after me."

"I was thinking I haven't seen my baby Sven in like four hundred years. He must be so sad and miss me. Can we call Miss Carrie?"

"It's been two days since you saw a picture so much less than four hundred years. And Miss Carrie is probably busy."

"No. She's probably sad we haven't checked on her and Sven. We should be better friends, Daddy. Grandma would be so dispontated."

I knew when I told my mom to mind her own business and stop asking me if I had a girlfriend now that I'd taken Carrie out that somehow she'd find a way to still bring it up. I'm just surprised it took her partner in crime this long to mention it.

"I think you mean disappointed. And your grandma needs to get a hobby."

"Oh, Daddy," she says with her hand reaching out to pat my leg. "Grandma's favorite thing to do is make me snacks. It makes her happy."

Chuckling, I bend down on my knees and help my little Miss Know It All finish her bath and wrap her up like a snuggle bug in a fluffy towel. As I carry her over my shoulder, setting off a string of giggles, my phone rings with a text notification in the other room.

"Get dressed, Sprite. How do you feel about ordering pizza for dinner?"

"Okay but no green stuff on mine," she says over her shoulder as she begins digging in her drawers for something to wear.

Walking out of her room, I make my way to the kitchen to dial up my favorite pizza place. I don't indulge in pizza often, but I'm feeling like today is a perfect cheat day. I'll also order a salad for good measure. Before I can pull up my contacts, the phone buzzes in my hand, reminding me of the unread text.

C: I see the appeal of your man crush.

Smiling, I quickly tap out a reply.

Me: Welcome to the Jack Ryan crush club.

C: I assume you're the reigning president of said club so tell me, is there some sort of initiation?

Without allowing myself a second to think about it, I respond.

Me: Yep. You have to stick our son into your shirt, drive over here, and share a pizza with me. Or Sprite if you don't like green things on yours.

I wait while the three dots bounce and then stop and start again. And stop.

Me: Stop typing and deleting. Just say "Okay, Matthew. See you in a bit."

C: I'm only putting Sven in my shirt because he misses his big sister. And we're out of pecans. Time to pay up, squirrel daddy.

Laughing at her sass, I quickly call in our order for pizzas and salad. As I finish the call, Calypso skips into the room dressed in a pair of bright pink leggings with stars on them and a *Brave* T-shirt I could have sworn I put in the donate bag. A year ago. But it isn't the ill-fitting shirt that catches most of my attention, it's the way her brush is stuck in her hair. This is not going to go well.

"What did you do?"

"I was doing my hair and it kinda got stuck."

"Honey, that looks like more than stuck. Go grab the detangler and big comb. I'll get your stool and meet you in the living room."

Her little lip pops out, and I see the first signs of tears. She hates when we have to work out knots. Her poor little head is too tender for the amount of work I have to do. Thankfully, we only have to do this a few times a year.

"I know you hate this, but we have to get started before it dries. I have a surprise for you too. Now hop to it."

At the prospect of a surprise, she adds a little pep to her step as she sets off to get supplies. Meanwhile, I check on Olaf, who is exhausted from his day of mud-slinging, before making my way to the couch and flip on the kids movies we have cued up on our favorites.

I've managed to work out the knots of half her head when the doorbell rings. I stand, lifting my leg over her like I'm some sort of male Rockette as my daughter sits fixated on the movie playing. Other than a few wails as I tugged on her hair, Calypso hasn't moved. She's almost like a robot without batteries.

Opening the door, I'm greeted with a smirk and a furry head peeking out of a V-neck T-shirt. Suddenly I find myself doing something I never fathomed was possible. I am jealous of a glorified rodent.

Is this what my life has come to? Just a few months ago, Carrie was giving me attitude and almost refusing to let me buy her a drink at an industry event. Now, she stands at my front door, a grocery bag in her hand and dressed very similar to my daughter. Except instead of a Disney character on her shirt, Carrie's reads "I like books, you not so much."

It's then that I am really grateful Olaf ran away and brought her into our lives. I want to continue to get to know Carrie and build on the friendship we've started. The concert was a great insight of what could be, and it's something I want to explore.

"As much as I love standing here watching you think, this ice cream is going to melt and Sven is probably going to poop on my chest."

Shaking away my thoughts, I step back and motion for her to enter as I snatch the shopping bag from her hand. With one hand holding on to the critter in her shirt, she shrugs off her sweatshirt and grabs it before it falls to the ground.

"I haven't told Sprite you were coming. She may scream. Loudly. And, if I know my kid, and I do, there will likely be a victory dance."

"For me or this guy?" she asks, pulling Sven from her shirt and holding him up to her face like she's going to kiss him.

"Honestly? I have no idea. Come on in."

We make our way to where Calypso sits, still not moving from the position I left her in. Carrie looks to me and I shrug before clearing my throat. Nope. No movement. I try it again. And if it's possible, I think she's more frozen.

"Well, Carrie. I guess you'll just have to take Sven home. Looks like Sprite is sleeping sitting up."

At the sound of my voice, the little monster turns to face us, half her head a tangled mess and the other her usual springy curls. As expected, she jumps up and does a really intricate end zone style dance.

"Oh, Miss Carrie! You brought him! Does he miss me? I told Daddy he probably does. Did you know that we went to that big store with all the things that Daddy says makes him buy things nobody needs and got a big bag of nuts? We did! It's this big." With her arms wide, Calypso tries to demonstrate how big she thinks the bag of pecans is that I grabbed the other day from the big box store.

"Well, I think Sven will be very happy with his big bag of nuts. Umm, what is happening here?" Carrie asks, motioning to Calypso's hair.

"Tangles. It happens every so often. We were just working them out when you got here. Come on, Sprite. Have a seat and we'll finish up."

No sooner are the words out of my mouth than the doorbell rings again. Looking from Calypso to Carrie and then the direction of the door, I wonder what I should do. Falling into our world seamlessly like the last time she was here, Carrie walks around the couch and sits in the spot I vacated.

"Alrighty little one. I'll work on this squirrel's nest on your head if you'll hold Sven. Be gentle; he's still very tiny."

"Car—"

"You better grab those pizzas before they get cold. We've got this. What are we watching?"

I stand there for a few beats, watching as Carrie starts combing Sprite's hair as she catches her up on whatever movie she's watching. I knew I was starting to crush on my little blogger friend, but I had no idea how much until now. Seeing her with my daughter, making her giggle and not squirm at all as she works on her hair, opens up a piece of me I wasn't sure existed anymore.

# Chapter 18

## *Carrie*

Booting up my computer, I pull out my blog calendar and notes from last month's meeting with Celeste. We have a lot to discuss, including a potential new advertiser. Unfortunately, I'm having a hard time keeping my mind on work. Memories of last night at Matthew's house continue to run through my mind.

It is in the top two most fun nights I've had in months, and we didn't even do anything exciting. We ate pizza—well, Calypso and I ate pizza. Matthew had salad because he has a shoot coming up and we wouldn't want his muscles to look bloated or whatever models worry about. Me? Not a model, and I love a good stuffed crust.

While eating the gooey goodness, the three of us watched a show where a couple of teenagers ended up in a 50s style beach movie. There was a lot of singing and dancing and I was oddly entertained by it. Fortunately for me, Calypso fell asleep on her dad this time, so I was able to watch the ending to see how the main characters made it back through the time warp.

The more I spend time with the Roberts, the more I like it. And that scares me.

I can feel myself getting too attached to this little family. I think about them all the time and wonder what they're up to. It's confusing because I don't know if Matthew feels the same, considering my well-established boundaries. A man has needs, ya know, and I don't plan on being the one to fill them. So where does that leave us?

*Whatever, Carrie, I think to myself as I open my video messenger app. You've got bigger things to worry about than whether or not Matthew like likes you.*

It's like I'm in sixth grade all over again. I guess it doesn't matter how old you get, wondering if the guy you're crushing on feels the same never changes.

Time to act like an adult. I have business to discuss.

Clicking the accept button when it rings, Celeste's boobs come into view.

"Ah!" I scream and sit back, throwing my hand over my eyes. "Why are you trying to poke my eyes out online?"

She backs up, sitting on her chair so I can see her, not just a massive amount of cleavage. She may be tiny, but she's got huge knockers. They're always getting in her way. "Sorry. I dropped my pen right after I called you and of course it rolled halfway across the table."

"Well, it was a lovely hello," I say sarcastically, tucking one foot underneath me and settling in for what could be a long conversation. We don't do this often because when we do, we get chatty. Up to three hours chatty.

Celeste shrugs, her curly blonde mop immediately springing back in place when her shoulder drops. "I got a new bra. It better make me look good for the price I paid." Picking up her notepad, she doesn't lollygag around, instead getting right down to business. "Okay. First things first, I don't have three hours today. Tickets for the next Prince of Darkness con go on sale in thirty-eight minutes so I have to be finished with this and have my mouse hovering over the purchase button by then."

"Isn't it still ten months away?"

"Nine," she corrects. "After that obnoxious flu that knocked me out this year, I can't risk losing out on tickets. I will get Hunter Stone to sign my playbill! I *will*!"

"Calm down there, psycho. We won't let you lose your chance." Mostly because I know how devastated she was earlier this year. She had been looking forward to the event for so long.

Celeste nods once and I know from experience that means the topic has been discussed appropriately and we're ready to move on. "Next item, I confirmed that new advertiser we talked about."

"Nice. Who is it again?"

She clicks around on her computer while she talks, probably multitasking. It used to bother me that she wasn't keeping 100 percent of her attention on our conversations, but I learned quickly that she is one of the only people I've ever met that can truly keep all of her attention on the task at hand, while juggling three other things. It's a useful skill. And a weird one.

Me? I can't keep track of my own socks, let alone all the schedules she has. Just another of the many reasons we complement each other.

Hot mess, meet list maker.

"It's called Tiger Talent. They're a talent agency specializing in acting classes, modeling classes, things like that," she explains. "They want to do a bi-weekly run for three months."

"Ooh!" I say with a smile. "That's a nice little payout."

More clicking of her keys. "It's not bad. And hopefully it'll open up opportunities with other agencies or maybe some touring theater groups." A dreamy look crosses her face. "Could you imagine if the touring company for *Kinky Boots* advertised on our blog? I would die."

"With as much traffic as the site has had the last few weeks, it's not an unreasonable goal."

Celeste shakes her head like I'm being ridiculous. "Don't get my hopes up. By the way, their marketing team already has the graphics they want used, I'll just need you to copy edit for any errors."

"On it, boss." And I am, jotting it down on my own to-do list which may or may not get lost at some point.

"How's it going on your end?" she asks, moving us right along. No surprise there. She lives for lists and organization, but currently, she lives for her chance to meet Hunter Stone. I glance at the time and know her pulse is probably beginning to race at the prospect of securing a ticket to see him.

"Good. Visibility for new releases is climbing and click through is adjusting accordingly. I've secured one of those new ad contracts we talked about too. That publisher I made contact with last month wants to get some visibility on their new release."

"Ooh, good one. We could potentially secure long-term ads out of them." Celeste continues to type away, no doubt taking notes on this meeting. Maybe I should do that too. Nah. I'll get a detailed e-mail later, I'm sure.

"I know. And another lead came in yesterday. I got an email from the organizers of an author event. I'm pretty excited about that one, obviously."

Celeste's eyebrows rise in interest. "Oh, I like that. A win-win for them and us. With your reviews and our reach, it may help with their ticket sales."

I nod in agreement. "That's exactly what I was thinking. It's only a one-month ad to see how it does, but if the numbers look good, I can reach out to a few more event coordinators as well."

Celeste blows out a breath, and I can tell she's suddenly feeling frustrated.

"What's up? Why are you making that face?"

The clacking of her keyboard stops and she looks me dead in the eye. "What face?"

I wave my hand around, gesturing to her face. "The one that says you're frustrated. Usually you reserve it for me when I'm close to missing my deadline."

That intimidating eyebrow quirks again. "Are you?"

"Am I what?" I know my shifty eyes are giving me away, but I'll never admit defeat.

"Are you behind?"

"Not by much."

She groans and drops her head on her arms. See? It's our balance.

"Seriously, Celeste," I plead. "I'm not that far behind. I just keep getting distracted from this book, so it's taking me a little time."

Her head pops up, blonde curls bouncing in her face. "It's Donna Moreno. How bad could it be?"

I scoff. "Excuse you. Do not put words in my mouth. I didn't say it's bad. I said I've been distracted."

"By what?" she asks, eyes darting to the corner of the screen where I know the time and date sit.

"You mean besides a baby squirrel that has to eat every five hours and the world's worst pedicure?"

She cocks her head, and I know she's sizing me

up. It makes me nervous, to be honest. Like she can see right through me. Can she see how Matthew has invaded my thoughts, making it impossible to read? Can she tell I've been spending more time looking at him on the cover of Donna's new book than reading the words inside of it?

"I call bullshit on the squirrel because you're always doing that," she finally says, "And while I'm not doubting the terrible pedicure, I think something else is going on."

I sit back in my chair, crossing my arms defensively.

"However," she continues, "I have just twenty-four minutes until tickets go on sale so I'll ignore it for now. Instead, I'll use it as a segue to our next topic. I know we've tossed around the idea of bringing on a third blogger." I roll my eyes at this continuing topic of conversation. "But I think we should revisit. We're starting to get stagnant, and I don't want that. So what do you think for real?"

The same thing I thought last time we talked. It would be nice to have another person contributing to the workload, but the financial part of it kind of sucks.

"We're finally to a place where we're making a little money. I just hate the idea of it being a three-way split." Resting my arms on the table, I lean in. "I know that's not very business minded, but I don't know if the workload justifies that expense yet."

"I've been thinking about that part." I can tell by

the gleam in Celeste's eye and the tap of her pen that she's found a solution she thinks I'll like. "What about my roommate, Anna?"

Not the heavy-hitting solution I was expecting, but I can run with it.

"What about her?"

"Well, you cover books and television adaptations. I cover performance arts and some movies. If we're going to expand, we need to think about covering everything audio related. Music, podcasts, maybe even audiobooks."

She has a good point. Readers and theater lovers listen to music too. If we're trying to bring in new followers, it's not a bad way to go. Still, it won't be an easy transition.

"I like what you're thinking, but why Anna?"

"Because she's busting her tail trying to make a name for herself in the music industry. Who better than a semi-professional musician to critique the latest in music trends?"

Another good point. But I may as well throw Debbie Downer into the mix.

"And how are we supposed to pay her while we wait for advertising to follow?"

"We don't."

I furrow my brow at the excited look on her face. I feel like I'm missing something. "So make her work for free? In my experience, that doesn't usually go over well."

"You have no experience," Celeste spouts off. "Besides, as we're building, we can do a trade for ad space. We can ease her in slowly since we need time to build the pages on the website anyway. And when her next single releases, we give her a free ad to help her generate some sales."

Nodding, I have to admit the idea has merit. "Talk to her about it. If she's on board, that would be great. If not, I don't know." I run my hands down my face, feeling as exhausted as I probably look. These overnight feedings are still killing me. "But you're right. If we become stale we'll start losing followers. We need to stay fresh, and this could be a good way to accomplish that."

Celeste taps a few keys, no doubt a note to revisit the topic later pending Anna's answer.

"What else is on that list of yours? You have less than twenty minutes."

She doesn't even look up from her notes to respond. "I have a timer set." Of course she does. "The last item we need to discuss is why you keep twirling that pink plastic ring on your thumb and if it has anything to do with why you're distracted lately."

Quickly I look down and realize, she's right. The ring Calypso gave me last night for being the "bestest squirrel brother mommy in the history of the world" has been sitting in a pride spot next to my computer since I got home last night. Because who could resist beautiful plastic jewelry with a pitch like that? I just didn't realize I'd picked it up.

"Umm…" I stutter, trying not to give myself away. "I got it from a little friend. That's all. You know… animals and… all that."

"Mm hmm." She doesn't sound convinced. "I don't believe you. Your face is as red as your shirt."

I gape at her. "It is not! I can see myself in the little box and… oh shit. Good lord, I look like a tomato."

"Like I said." Sitting back, she crosses her arms, only this isn't a defensive move. She looks more like a petite little bouncer wanna be. "Spill."

Sighing dramatically, I cave. Mostly because she's not going to let up. Also because I have to get it off my chest. But primarily because she's not going to let up. Whatever. She's relentless as she… sits. Staring. And waiting. It's disconcerting.

"Fine. I got it from a friend's six-year-old daughter, okay?"

"Keep going."

I throw my hands up. "What do you mean by that?"

"You're leaving out details. Keep going."

I huff and puff and try to throw her off the trail, but to no avail. "How can you be so sure I'm holding back?"

"Because I'm a stage manager," Celeste retorts. "For actual actors. And this performance"—she pauses and points her finger in my direction, mimicking my move from her boob-filled greeting—"is the worst I've seen in a long time."

Well shit.

I try to stare her down, but we both know she has a while until her alarm is going to go off and there's no way I can hold on that long. When it comes to the battle of stubborn, she wins every time.

"Fine!" I throw my hands in the air again and ignore her victorious smile. "It's a *male* friend."

"So you're dating someone."

"No," I scoff. "Maybe. Not really. I don't know."

Celeste squinches her eyes and scratches her head, making her mop even bigger, which I refuse to point out so she can fix it because she's irritating me. "Is this about that sex thing again?"

Cue another scoff from me. "It's not a sex thing. I've made a conscious decision to not just hand out that part of myself to any Tom, Dick, or Harry that comes along."

"Is his name any of those?"

"His name is Matthew," I say slowly, unsure of where she's going and not trusting it.

"Problem solved. Sleep with him already."

I love Celeste. I do. But she doesn't understand my decision. It's something we'll never see eye-to-eye on since she's all about "free love".

"That's not helpful," I deadpan.

"I know, I know." But does she? Does she really? "It usually makes it easier to figure out if you've been friend-zoned or not if you're having sex."

"Really. Because I seem to remember how muddy the waters were in your last relationship for that very reason."

Celeste points her finger at the screen dramatically. Theater nerds, ugh. "That was an isolated case by a jerk who wanted to sleep his way to the top of the theater world."

"I know. And I'm not trying to turn it around on you. It's just not as cut and dry as I would like it to be. We've hung out a couple times. I like his kid. She's funny. And yes, he knows there will be no physical intimacy."

"So you friend-zoned him."

I open my mouth to argue with her but stop. Because holy shit. Did I friend-zone him without meaning to? Quickly, I rewind the conversation we had that night.

I turned.

He kissed my ear.

I told him we weren't having sex.

I became acquainted with myself, in the biblical sense, with the picture of him next to my pillow. *Not that he will ever know that part.*

I texted him about Australia the next day…

Groaning, I drop my head to the table with a loud

thump. "Oh shit. Did I friend-zone him?"

"No idea. I don't even know who this guy is."

And I will never tell her. Because bad things happen when I toss things like names and scenarios out into the universe. It's like Murphy's Law. The minute I say how I feel out loud something thwarts it all.

"Wait just a gosh darn minute!"

Uh oh. Celest doesn't exclaim much. She organizes, argues, and processes. She might even be combative. But exclaim isn't usually her thing. Unless she's putting puzzle pieces together. Puzzle pieces called Murphy's Law.

Lifting my head just enough to look at her, I see her focusing on something over my shoulder. "What?"

"Why do you have that picture still on your corkboard?"

My eyebrows shoot up and I turn to look, probably turning the color of my shirt again. Realizing what it is, I turn back around and lie through my teeth. "So I don't forget what's coming up."

The most annoying imitation of a buzzer comes out of Celeste's mouth. If she never makes that noise again, it will be too soon. "Try again. You never leave things on your corkboard once you start reading, which you already have. You use the post cards as a bookmark."

"So I forgot? So what?" I shift in my seat uncomfortably. She's onto me. The question is how long can I deflect before her timer goes off?

"Liar!" she shouts, banging her hand on the table, which makes the computer vibrate. These theater types are so dramatic. "You have a picture of Matthew Roberts on your corkboard. Matthew Roberts has a daughter."

"How do you know that?" I demand.

"Everyone knows that," she says without stopping her rant. "You said you're dating a Matthew that you don't know if you friend-zoned because you told him you weren't sleeping with him, but you're tied up in knots because cover models always have women chasing after them so what if he only thinks you friend-zoned him when really you want him to woo you, but you don't know if he can because he has a six-year-old daughter who you also love because she gave you that fancy piece of jewelry you're messing with again."

Immediately, I toss the ring away, wondering how in the hell she said all that without pausing or taking a breath.

"Also," she continues, finger in the air momentarily as she pauses for dramatic effect, "ohmygod you're dating Matthew Roberts!"

And this is why I didn't want to tell her. Listening to her squeal and clap for joy was not on my list of things to do today. Neither was explaining the situation to her, but clearly I'm not getting out of it now. Why hasn't that timer gone off yet?!

"Okay," she says, pushing her hair out of her face. "I'm calm. I'm calm. Now tell me everything."

Reluctantly, I do. Well, not everything. I don't tell her about the kiss. Or about Delilah. Or even much about Calypso. Some things should stay between two people, especially when one of your friends is trying to write a kick-ass screenplay. No one needs to make my life into a best-selling anything.

Truthfully, it feels good to get it off my chest. To let someone I have a reasonable amount of trust in know my insecurities and help me process my feelings out loud. To just hear my fears.

"So, I don't know where we stand," I say when I catch her all the way up. "It doesn't feel weird or anything. It just doesn't have that hint of promise anymore."

"Did it ever?"

I shrug because, maybe? Like right before he tried to kiss me there was a small moment that could have been that hint. Or maybe I imagined it. It's possible he was only looking for a fling when I offered him my ear and not my lips.

"Listen, I am the last person to talk to about relationships because mine never work out." I huff a laugh because Celeste isn't wrong. Any advice she gives I usually take with a grain of salt for that reason. "But maybe you need to tell him you're sorry you accidentally friend-zoned him. That puts the ball back in his court, and it'll get clearer."

"That is—" I begin but am cut off by the obnoxious sound of her timer, the one she keeps because it's apparently the only noise that will actually wake her up.

Celeste's hands begin flying around her keyboard and mouse as she prepares for what she would argue is the fight of her life.

"Listen, I want to chat more, but if I don't get on this—"

"I know, I know," I say dismissively. "Go get your tickets."

She smiles and blows out a deep breath, probably in preparation for all the physical exertion her fingers are about to endure. "Thanks. Love ya. Oh and Carrie?"

"Hmm?"

"There's a squirrel sticking out of your shirt."

The screen goes blank just as I look down. Sure enough, Sven has maneuvered his way to the collar of my shirt. Even more exciting, though, he's looking around.

Gasping, I reach down and pull him all the way free, tsking my tongue at him in my best mama squirrel imitation. "Look at you, big boy. One of your eyes is finally open. Hi there. There's lots to see in this big wide world."

He keeps blinking and looking around, likely in a bit of shock from all the light and colors.

"Your daddy is going to be so happy to see this."

And then I pause and think about what I just said.

I have potentially friend-zoned the father of my

baby squirrel.

My life has hit a new level of ridiculousness.

# Chapter 19

*Matthew*

In the weeks since I donned that awful teal monstrosity some call an Elsa dress, my daily routine has changed a little. Now, if Olaf uses his "there's a critter on the ground" bark, I do a perimeter search of the yard. Okay, I do that anyway because while he told me about Sven, our dog isn't exactly a reliable source for other potential orphaned animals.

The second addition to my day is talking to my new best friend. My relationship with Carrie has evolved from virtual strangers with mutual friends to her easily becoming one of my favorite people. Sure, she likes to give me a hard time and ask me random questions about Australia and international travel in general, but she also calls me on my crap and reminds me to stop and enjoy life.

Her zest for knowledge reminds me of a younger me. The guy I was before dropping to the ground for twenty quick pushups to get my muscles ready for a photo shoot so I can spoil my daughter and prepare for her future. Yes, twenty pushups. It's enough to engage my muscles but not really break a sweat.

This morning after I dropped Sprite off at school I had an overwhelming desire to drive to the shelter. Without a valid excuse, I didn't do it. Sure, I could have picked up some donuts or maybe her favorite chai tea on the way. Friends buy friends breakfast, right? It's a sign you are a good friend and care about the person. Maybe if I use the word "friend" enough, I'll start seeing her more that way than what my heart—and body—actually do.

I used to think I had walls up, that I was afraid of putting myself out there and seriously dating. Hesitating to bring someone into our lives. Now, I see that I simply hadn't met someone I wanted to incorporate into our little family. A person I could not only trust with my daughter and the aspects of my life, both modeling and single dad, but who respected Delilah and her place in our lives. Becoming friends with Carrie has been seamless, but the undeniable attraction I have, we have, has me wishing for more with her. She fits. She respects who we are, how our family isn't necessarily traditional but it works.

Full disclosure, her declaration of celibacy did cause a little pause. It wasn't something I've encountered before, but it is also something I respect. And, truthfully, understand. Her desire to have a solid relationship first made me rethink my own boundaries, and it's something that pops in my head often. Daily. Sometimes hourly.

Physical intimacy is important, but it isn't a deal breaker. Trust, honesty, and a willingness to put in the work matters more. I know that, now that I have a daughter. One day, Calypso will be dating and the idea of her not being respected enough to build a foundation before giving up the most precious part of her makes me sick. And leads to some random online searches for how to keep your daughter from dating until she's thirty. Apparently, other than a one-way ticket to Mars it's unlikely I will be successful.

"Okay, Matthew, I think the electrician will only be another twenty minutes or so. You still doing okay?"

I turn my attention to Shane, the photographer. I've been here for hours, and we have managed two pictures. The power in this building keeps going out and we haven't been successfully able to accomplish much more than me doing a set of pushups and climbing into the bed before the lights flicker and the room goes dark. Normally, we'd reschedule but since the holidays are approaching, it's today or never. If we cancel, I don't get paid and the author doesn't get her custom photos. Since this is a very popular author, and she's recently announced a movie deal, neither of us wants that. The potential for exposure is too great.

"I'm good. I think I'll step out and take a quick walk, get my energy levels back up. I'll make sure I'm back in twenty." He nods and returns to the group of people standing around in a circle, phones in their hands as they frantically tap away.

The weather has dipped a little in temperature, so I grab my sweatshirt and tug it over my head before slipping my wallet into my pocket. Retreating toward the door and out of the studio, I tap my social media and begin liking and responding to tags and mentions. The elevator ride to the first floor is quick and I'm out onto the street in minutes. Looking left to right, I spot the telltale green awning on the corner and turn in that direction for a much needed caffeine fix.

My phone rings as I step off the curb.

"Hey, Mom," I say in greeting.

"Hi honey. How's it going?"

"They're saying twenty minutes."

Her sigh tells me she's worried about me finishing this shoot in time. I don't dare tell her I have the same fear. As a surprise, I bought tickets to Christmas on Ice for Calypso. The look in her eyes when I told her last week was more than I could have expected. To say she was elated would be a tremendous understatement. Of course, she's been planning her outfit for days. Last night I had to break it to her that the dress she wore as flower girl in my cousin's wedding was a little too much for this type of event.

Instead, my mom took her shopping today for something special and new to wear. About an hour ago, I received a text message with her sitting in a big teddy bear chair getting a children's pedicure. My little girl is getting the full princess treatment and I know she's looking forward to our father-daughter date night. So am I. Only, a part of me is worried I won't make it.

"You know your father or I would happily take her but we have this retirement dinner to attend."

"I know. It was a complete rookie move on my part for telling her in advance. I should know better."

"Maybe you can exchange the tickets for another night?"

"This is the last performance on this leg of the tour for our region. I think it heads west before shutting down for the year."

I approach the door to the crowded coffee shop and step aside to finish my call as people scurry in and out, all dressed more for winter than I am. I suppose when the average temperature is closer to eighty-five than the seventy it currently is, numbers are irrelevant. We're freezing.

"What about… never mind."

"No, I'm open to suggestions. I don't want to disappoint Sprite, but the potential future income from this shoot could allow me to take us on that Disney cruise I've been eyeing and still add a chunk to the college fund. I also don't want to cancel the gig."

"I was just wondering if maybe your friend Carrie would take her. Calypso adores her and from the little you've told me, the feeling is shared."

My mind starts spinning at what she's suggesting. Not because it's crazy or without merit, but because it seems natural. Simple and within reason. I have zero hesitation when it comes to Carrie doing something with Calypso on their own. I have no doubt my daughter would much rather hang out with another female instead of me, something she doesn't get nearly enough of.

"That's a great idea, Mom. Let me hang up and call her. Hopefully she doesn't have to work tonight and doesn't have an aversion to people dressed as popular animated characters while they ice skate."

Laughing, Mom says goodbye and I open the door and head inside for a little pick-me-up. Placing my order, I step aside and peruse the display of cups and other retail items. It's only minutes before my name is called and I step up to retrieve my drink. Doctoring it up with some cream and sugar, I take a sip to check the sweetness level. Satisfied, I check the time and confirm I have about five minutes before I need to be back on set.

My phone vibrates in my hand as I exit the store and a quick glance sends an immediate smile to my face. It just so happens to be the one person that elicits that reaction from me and the person I was just going to call. Instead of responding to her text about tipping in Australia, I hit the call button.

"Hello?" Her voice is confused and… a little out of breath.

"Why are you out of breath?"

"I was moving things around for a shoot. I have

to get some new graphics done for upcoming releases. Wait. Why are you calling? You're supposed to be doing a photo shoot for some unknown author who you won't tell me about. Stupid NDA."

Chuckling, I step off the curb and jog across the street. The sign said "Don't Walk" but I feel like living on the wild side.

"It's been a shit day and we've accomplished nothing. I stepped out for a coffee while they try to get things ready."

"Oh no! Don't you have that thing with Calypso tonight?"

"That's actually why I'm calling. But first, tipping is almost non-existent in Australia. That's something we'll talk about when the time comes. Add it to the list."

Carrie lets out a long breath before there's a pause on the line. I wait for her to speak, but when she doesn't, I look down at the screen to make sure the call didn't drop.

"Are you there?" I ask as I approach the building where the shoot is taking place.

"Oh yeah. I was doing as instructed and adding it to the list."

Of course she has an actual list. This girl is so determined to go to Australia it's not even funny. I hope she can make that dream a reality one day.

"So, what are you doing tonight?"

"The usual. Solving crimes, saving the world. Why?"

"How do you feel about ice skating?"

She lets out a squawk of excitement and it triggers an emotion in me I haven't felt in a long time. No, ever. Making Carrie happy and giving her a reason to make that sound of joy is something that hits me deep to my core and is a feeling I want over and over again.

# Chapter 20

*Carrie*

Reason number one why people have kids is because of moments like the night when Calypso fell asleep on me. Practically angelic when they're deep in slumber, it's enough to make anyone's ovaries explode.

Reason number two? Special performances geared toward children. Not like school plays or band performances. Heaven knows people don't have children to attend those. No, I'm talking about big budget productions with light shows and professional entertainers.

I have been dying to see Christmas on Ice because it looks like so much fun. The costumes and music alone would be entertaining but on ice? That's taking things to an epic level. How creepy would it be if a twenty-something, childless woman shows up in a princess dress and sits all alone?

Hella creepy.

So when Matthew asked me if I could take Calypso last minute, I may or may not have blown his ear drums out with my squeal. He doesn't need ears to flex his man muscles anyway. He'll be fine.

My only hesitation was meeting his mother under such odd circumstances. That's a big deal, isn't it? Meeting his mother? I was probably overthinking the whole thing, which was completely unnecessary anyway. It isn't like we're a couple. Heck, we're not even dating. Matthew is my friend. A friend I'm unbelievably attracted to and who I talk to everyday.

Since Mr. and Mrs. Roberts were in a rush to get to a retirement party, they practically threw the tickets at me through their car window when they arrived at my house. Meanwhile, Calypso jumped from the moving vehicle with the *Mission Impossible* music playing in the background, her skirt flying in the wind.

Okay, maybe it wasn't that dramatic. But there certainly wasn't time to chitchat before we all said our goodbyes. It's a good thing, too, because after a forty-five-minute drive across town, Calypso and I got a primo parking spot at the Convention Center. That's a great thing since there's a fifty-fifty chance I may have to carry her to the car at the end of the night.

"Ooh!" Calypso exclaims, hopping up and down excitedly making her ringlets bounce too. "They have princess wands! And they light up!"

The child in me is excitedly waving around her credit card, ready to purchase two. But the adult in me needs to be practical.

"Do we really need those?" Need, want. It's all relative at a place like this. "We already bought matching tiaras, T-shirts for us and your dad, and we're getting those refillable Olaf water bottles when we get snacks. Is a princess wand necessary?"

"Yes!" she yells without hesitation. "What if it's dark while they skate? How can we see what we're eating?"

"Good point."

And the child in me wins out. To be honest, adult me isn't sad about it at all. The holidays are upon us. It's supposed to be the most wonderful time of the year and if spending boatloads of money on unnecessary crap that makes us smile is the way to do it, so be it.

The line moves quickly and before I know it, we're now the proud owners of twenty-dollar light-up plastic wands, our refillable Olaf bottles, and an ornament for Calypso's tree because of course we need a yearly reminder of this momentous occasion.

Oh and a drawstring bag to carry it all in. It'll be twelve dollars well spent when Calypso decides she's done carrying all her purchases.

Making our way to our seats, I'm impressed to see Matthew didn't skimp. We aren't front row, or anything, but being seated in the first row of the second section so the only thing in front of us is the railing isn't too shabby either. Especially since there is a lot to see.

The ice rink itself isn't that big, which makes me

do a double take. How in the world are the performers going to be able to jump and spin in that small of an area? No matter. They're professionals after all, so I'm sure they'll be fine. Besides, whatever they do will be exciting. The floor to almost ceiling blue sparkly curtains are teasing us with what's to come by hiding whatever is backstage from the audience. I'm glad because while she's only six years old, Calypso would surely spot every out-of-costume performer and be outraged at the shenanigans. There are rock and forest decorations strategically placed around the stage and next to the floor seats, so I know there's going to be a large amount of audience interaction. Not that I ever questioned that. This is a national touring company after all.

It's crazy to think it wasn't long ago that Matthew and I were standing on the ice, well it wasn't ice then, watching Blind Fury perform. Flashes of the night in my mind send a wave of warmth across my skin. Not that I'm complaining. There is ice nearby, it's a bit cool in here without my lady flashes of heat.

"Are you excited?" I ask once Calypso is settled into her seat.

She responds by happily nodding, eyes wide as she stuffs cotton candy in her mouth, legs in motion as they dangle.

"Good. I'm kind of glad your daddy got stuck at work. It's always fun to have a girls' night."

"And you look way prettier in a dress than Daddy did."

I laugh and whip my phone out, ready to capture the moment for all time and send it to Matthew so he relaxes. As grateful as he was that I stepped in, I know he's also concerned she'll be disappointed he couldn't make it. The first three text messages said just that.

Based on her squeal when the lights begin to dim, I think she has other things on her mind.

Quickly, we get head to head, making sure our tiaras are on full display. One pic is all I get before Calypso's attention is on the moving spotlights and I'm no longer her concern. The distraction gives me a chance to text the picture to Matthew without her asking to scroll through the pictures on my phone like she did in the car. I don't know why she expects me to keep a daily picture log of Sven's childhood.

And I don't know how she found that exact folder either.

M: I see you both have been crowned princesses for the night.

Me: Night? Try permanently, buddy. We have matching wands and T-shirts to prove it.

M: Please say you aren't spoiling her. I try to limit how much crap she comes home with at these things.

Me: Princesses can't be spoiled. Only indulged. Because we deserve it. Now be quiet. I'm pretty sure my prince charming just skated by.

Matthew responds with an angry face emoji which makes me laugh and then think. What does that mean? Is he mad I've admittedly spent a little too much money on character merchandise that likely won't work by next week? Does he think I'm actually hunting for a date with his daughter next to me? Is he jealous?

I still have a hard time reading him. That's probably my own darn fault. Celeste was right. I need to acknowledge the potential friend-zone label, and maybe apologize, so the ball is back in his court. But I'll do that later. Right now, I have a shrieking six-year-old who is squeezing my forearm so hard in excitement, I'm pretty sure I'm going to end up with a bruise.

"Look, Carrie! It's the princesses!"

Sure enough, one by one they float across the ice. Our favorite queen of all time is first in the line, her blue dress billowing out behind her as she sings about letting go of all her turmoil and being who she is. It's impressive, to say the least. I could barely walk in the same costume without tripping over my feet. I have no idea how she doesn't run the blade over her outfit.

For the next two hours plus, Calypso is transfixed into a magical world of rock people and kingdoms and the kind of sisterly love we all should be so lucky to experience. It's engaging and exciting.

For a six-year-old.

Me? It lost its luster at about the forty-five-minute mark. I almost fist bump the two-year-old next to me when he starts shouting, "Mama! Go home!" I'm feeling the same way, kiddo. But then the most random thing happens—a storm blows in.

No, not on the ice, although that happens too. I'm hearing thunder over the magical booms of the show and only one kind of thunderstorm is powerful enough to do that.

A quick check of the weather on my phone confirms what I suspect—a super cell formed right over top of us. It'll probably come in, dump a whole lot of rain, and leave just as quickly. But the thunder amplifying the intensity of the story line? That's what fascinates me.

For a short time. And then I want to run for my life again.

Let's face it, two hours is just too long for something like this. Not for the kids, necessarily, but for the parents. I think maybe Matthew should take her next year. The dress doesn't drag on the ground when he wears it and the braid holds better in wig hair.

"Did you have fun, Calypso?" We swing our clasped hands back and forth, me hauling the loaded drawstring sack on my back as we move with the crowd toward our car. I was right about that super cell. There are huge puddles everywhere.

"Why do you call me that?" she asks, without any form of irritation, just inquisition. "Everyone else calls me Sprite."

"I guess I never thought about it. Do you want me to call you Sprite?"

"Yes, please." Even at this late hour, she still remembers her manners, which is more than I can say for some of the other kids around us. Of course, I've had to tug her to the side so she doesn't jump into the puddles. You can't win them all.

"Well then, Sprite it is. You didn't answer my question. Did you have fun?"

"Yes! It was all so pretty. The princesses! The reindeer! Did you see when the nose fell off the snowman?" She continues to babble excitedly about every part of the show that caught her attention, which is basically all of it. I don't mind. Benefit number three of having kids is experiencing everything through their eyes.

Don't get me wrong, I enjoyed parts of being here tonight, but it wouldn't have been nearly as much fun if it weren't for her energy and joy. It's almost like getting in touch with my inner child.

Popping the lock on my car, I help her climb in, still babbling, and make sure her booster seat is nice and secure. Taking my time between closing her car door and opening my own, I take a second to breathe in the smell of rain on the pavement. It's one of my favorite scents. Probably because it reminds me that all the yuck on the pavement can be washed away—just like all the yuck in our lives.

I shake my head at myself. I have no idea where that philosophical thought came from. Maybe all the lights and noise damaged my brain.

I wait for the car next to us to pull out before climbing into the driver's seat and immediately yelp.

"What the hell?"

"Can't say that," Calypso chides. "Grammy says h-e-double hockey sticks is a bad word."

"Yeah, well so is what I'm about to say because my car is flooded!"

Sort of. A quick look around shows there is water all over the seat of my car and the floor around me, but nowhere else. Looking up, the drip is clearly coming from my sunroof and landing on my face. And it's cold.

"Son of a bitch. That super cell jacked up my car!"

"Can't say that either!"

I put my hand up to calm Ms. Sassypants down. "Okay, okay. I just need to figure out what to do."

Fortunately, I have extra towels in my trunk in case of wildlife emergencies. Or sunroof explosions.

Quickly, I clean up the mess, even though my pants already soaked up most of the water. I was hoping the dress did the trick but I couldn't be so lucky. That thing is already almost dry and I took it off approximately thirty-seven seconds ago.

"Carrrriiiiiiieeee…" Calypso begins to whine. "I'm tired. Can we go home?"

Suddenly that sugar high she was on doesn't seem like such a good idea.

"Yeah, hang on, sweetie. I'm almost ready." Grabbing my car key, I put it in the ignition and say a quick prayer to the gods of ice that whatever exploded in my front seat, didn't make its way to my engine. "Please turn on. Please turn on."

I turn the ignition, the normal rumble indicating the car has come to life. "Eureka!" I yell and toss my hands in the air. As soon as I do, I push the ceiling the wrong way and drops of rain fall on my face again.

Note to self... touch nothing.

Backing out of the parking space takes no time at all, but getting out of the lot itself? That takes a while. I was prepared to wait in line, but I wasn't prepared for my car to start doing weird shit.

Like all the lights on the dashboard coming to life at once and start beeping weird. I immediately throw my hands up in the air, like I'm touching something to make it go haywire. It all stops almost immediately so now I'm questioning what kind of magical hell this is.

No time to dwell on that. Instead, the windshield wipers start wiping at rapid speed even though I didn't turn them on. I should know better than to grumble about it because Calypso starts screaming about the ghost in the wipers.

Hasn't she crashed from the sugar yet?

All in all, it takes over an hour of weird shit and sweet talk to get my car to Matthew's house. But she makes it... and promptly dies in the driveway.

Dropping my head to the steering wheel, I groan. Now what am I supposed to do?

"We made it!" Calypso yells and quickly scrambles out of her seat and out the car door, forgetting all her new things behind her. She must be the only kid on the planet that complains about being tired while in a moving vehicle and doesn't fall asleep.

Taking my time, I gather everything up and drag myself to the front door where Matthew is waiting. This night has officially exhausted me. Or maybe I'm having my own sugar crash.

"She looks happy." Matthew has a huge smile on his face before it drops. "What's wrong? Why have you been crying?"

"Crying?" Confused, I wipe my face and find more drops. "Oh those aren't tears. It's been raining freezing rain in my car the whole way home."

Now it's his turn to look confused. "*In* your car?"

"Oh yeah. A super cell decided to form above the parking lot and apparently my sunroof has a leak."

His eyes widen. "Oh no."

"Oh yes. And now my car is dead in your driveway, so I need to wait for my ride share to show up. Is that okay?"

"Why do you need a ride share?"

"Um… to get home?"

"Do you need to get home to the squirrels?"

I shrug not knowing what that has to do with anything. "Jamie has them tonight."

"So spend the night here."

I blink once. Blink twice. Blink a third time. He's inviting me to spend the night? Doesn't he remember he's been accidentally friend-zoned.

Grinning at me, he chuckles lightly. "In the guest room, Carrie." *Oh that makes more sense.* "You're exhausted, your car is dead, and the news just reported another storm is on the way. You might as well stay here."

"And we can have a slumber party!" Calypso shouts, scaring the crap out of me. Where did she come from? I don't have a chance to ask her when she grabs the drawstring bag out of my hand and skips away. Her high is definitely lasting longer than mine.

Still, who can say no to an offer like that?

# Chapter 21

## Matthew

Whoever said "the early bird gets the worm" was obviously a bird and not a person. Sure, I'm the one that set my alarm for this ridiculous hour. What was I thinking?

It was made all the worse because I invited Carrie to spend the night which meant little sleep for me. But come on. She'd spent hours sitting in an uncomfortable seat with my sugar-amped daughter because I couldn't, and from the looks of the haul Sprite was lugging around in that bag last night, she also spoiled her rotten with presents. All this brought the news reports I've seen about the dangers of ride shares to the forefront of my mind, and I wouldn't have been a good friend letting her climb into one so late.

All valid reasons for inviting her to use the guest room. Of course, none of them are the truth. Standing on the stoop, mascara running down her face, her cute little nose the color of a ripened cherry, my heart dropped to my stomach. The idea of her in pain or upset was like a kick to the gut. I'm just going to skirt right past those feelings and stick with the fact that I like her, she's my friend, and the idea of having our morning conversation in person makes me happy.

Yet, knowing she was only down the hall wearing my T-shirt while she slept made falling asleep difficult. I counted sheep. Recited the alphabet. In Latin. I even tried reading one of Donna's books, assuming it would put me to sleep. It didn't. If anything, it jump-started my libido while I cast the lead characters as Carrie and myself. A cold shower, more staring at the ceiling, and I finally fell asleep four hours before my alarm jarred me awake.

With my basketball shorts on and my teeth brushed, I make my way down the hall, peeking in on Sprite before heading to the kitchen. Quickly, I write a note to Carrie before flipping the brew button on the coffee maker so it's ready for me when I'm done with my workout. With my minimal sleep, I need to wake up my muscles and my brain before facing the day. Or more accurately, my daughter's retelling of her Friday night adventures.

"Hey buddy, it's early for you," I whisper to Olaf as I lean down to scratch the top of his head. He nuzzles into my hand before turning in a circle and lying back down onto his bed.

Stepping out into the garage, I press the button on the wall to roll up the large door, letting the cool air roll through the space while I do some quick stretches. The birds are chirping and the squirrels are clicking. I can't believe I know that squirrels click. Or cluck. Whatever it is, they are doing it, and I laugh to myself. The storm cooled off the night but I can already feel how humid the day is going to be. Slipping in my ear buds, I step outside and punch the code into the garage door before I take off for my morning run.

The upside to being up and out this early is the lack of movement in the neighborhood. Most houses are quiet, only a few curtains open. Normally I wouldn't take off for a run with Calypso at home, but knowing Carrie is there made it a no-brainer. And because the universe is clearly trying to tell me something, just thinking of her, the song playing comes to an end.

The slow beat of my favorite song by Blind Fury begins and unable to stop myself, a huge grin appears on my face. It's the same song Carrie was dancing her ass off to at the concert. Not just dancing but grinding against me while she sang at the top of her lungs. Turns out, it's her favorite song too.

As one song turns to another, my speed picks up. I follow my usual route and by the time I get back to the house, my muscles are warmed up and my mind is clearer. I know what I need to do. It's time to break my self-imposed rules and take Carrie out on a real date. One where there's no question about what we're doing or its definition.

"Eight." Hold, two, three.

"Nine." Hold, two—

"Oh, uh, oh, wow."

Dropping from the pull-up bar my feet hit the ground with a thud and I turn to look at Carrie. She's standing in the doorway from the house, her hair messier than it was when she closed the bedroom door last night and my T-shirt hitting her almost to her knees, while holding a cup that says, "My daughter is awesome." Visions of the scenes from Donna's book flash in my mind and I fold my body forward and touch my toes. A necessity as those thoughts send all the blood from my head to below my waistband.

"Morning," I say as I release a long breath.

"Good morning." The raspiness of her voice does nothing to help my situation, so I take a deeper breath before exhaling. I send a little prayer that I have this under control and slowly rise to face my house guest.

"Sleep good?" Taking a sip of water from my bottle, I take a chance and glance her way.

Nodding, she lifts the cup to her mouth and takes a sip. We stare at each other a few minutes, neither of us speaking a word when a lawn mower powers up across the street, breaking the silence.

"I did, thank you. I called for a tow truck. They said it would be about an hour."

"Oh."

I don't know why I'm disappointed in that news.

Of course she needs a tow truck. It isn't like she can move in here with us. That's insane. I obviously need food. Protein. Vegetables. Something to nourish my mind because with that random thought, my blood sugar must be low.

"What time did you get up? It looks like you've been out here a while." Her eyes scan the floor where my various weights are sitting.

After my run, I did a circuit of weight work. While I keep a relatively clean house, my workout space leaves something to be desired. My mom hates it. Thankfully, she hasn't had to deal with my poor gym housekeeping since I moved out of her house three years ago.

"About an hour. I went for a run first. I only have a few more sets and I'm done. Is Sprite up yet?"

"Nope. I think she's sleeping off the sugar high. I probably should have cut her off at the cotton candy. It's no excuse, but I am only used to caring for squirrel babies, not actual human children."

Laughing, I chalk my hands again before I say, "Well, I think kids and sugar are like squirrels and pecans. I've seen Luke annihilate a pecan and have no doubt Sprite did the same with her treats. How about when I'm done here, I whip us up some breakfast?"

"Sounds goo—"

She stops mid-sentence as I jump to the pull-up bar. My hands gripping the metal before I suck air into my lungs and power my body up, chin over the bar. I can feel Carrie staring at me, her eyes like lasers on my skin. Then I hear it. Why now? Dammit, how am I going to explain this?

Giggles, whispers, and then, "Who's that?"

While I try to come up with a story, I increase the speed on my movements, cranking out two more pull-ups before dropping to the ground. Hands on my hips, I breathe in and out, trying to regulate my heartrate. Turning my head slowly, I linger a little on Carrie, her eyes wide as she peers around the doorway to look at the owner of the question.

"Oh. My. Gosh," she whisper yells, amusement written all over her face.

"What?"

"You have a neighborhood fan club!"

"I do not." I do. But it's not my favorite part of the day so I will never admit it.

She laughs quietly, probably trying not to scare off the lurkers. "You so do. I'll prove it. Do some more chin-ups?"

"What? No." My words say I'm defying her request, but my body moving back into position says I want to see what she thinks is about to happen.

"Seriously. Just do like"—she waves her hand at me—"five. Just five. But do them slowly. And flex hard."

Shaking my head at whatever this is, I comply and slowly pull myself up, straining with the movement of lifting my entire body several feet in the air.

Behind me, Carrie quietly gives a play-by-play of the women I'm now ignoring. "And here comes another one. Oh! She stumbled on a crack in the sidewalk. Get ready for the water bottle to drop in three... two... one..."

The sound of a water bottle hitting the pavement makes me huff out a laugh, which makes me drop to the ground in time to see its owner chasing after it. The other two women smile and wave before rushing behind their friend. When I turn back to Carrie, her eyes are wide in amusement.

"What?"

"I told you. You have the neighborhood cougars all a fluster. You know it too, don't you?"

I furrow my brow a bit as I admit the truth. "I may have put it together before now."

"That's what I thought." She looks out the garage door, trying to see if our little fan club is still within hearing distance. "I bet you perform for them too."

Perform? Like dance? What is she talking about? I know the expression on my face is one of confusion while hers remains unchanged.

"I have no idea what you're talking about. What's in that mug? Did you find my whiskey?" I tease.

She bats my hand away as I grab for her drink. "Seriously? No, there's no whiskey in here. But if you touch my caffeine, you will witness my wrath." She steps down from the doorway and into my personal space. She smells like Sprite's strawberry shampoo thanks to the shower she took last night. We've stood this close before, but something is different today. Not just that she's standing before me, a scowl on her face, wearing my shirt.

"Okay, babe, you're going to have to tell me what has you looking at me like you're ready to poke my eye out."

She props her hand on her hip, careful not to spill with her other hand, and purses her lips. I've seen this look. It's the same one women have given Kevin when he uses one of his awful pickup lines. Crap.

"You just gave those women a show with your… your… tattoos and muscles all sweaty and… and… ugh. Then you *charmed* them with that damn smile of yours. It's the same one you have on the cover of Unbound. I know because ninety percent of the online reviews are about that smile and not Donna's amazing words. Not that your smile isn't worth the recognition, but that story is so beautifully written—"

"I did not give them a show, Carrie," I interrupt with a laugh. "Hell, I didn't even know they were there." She responds with a "pffft" sound and I don't have a choice but to cave. "Okay fine. So I have a fan club." Carrie's face quickly changes to one of victory. I better explain myself quick. "I try not to think about it very often, because it's weird. I mean, not like stalker weird. School bake sales are a little awkward, but they never cross a line. It's part of the job," I ramble. "I'm just working out…"

"With the door wide open."

"It gets hot in here."

"Shirtless."

"Sometimes I have to give them what they want."

I say it playfully, but from the look on her face I immediately know I've said the wrong thing.

Her shoulders drop, all the sass and gusto she had a few minutes ago evaporating before my eyes. "And that right there is why I don't give men what they want."

Is that what she thinks I want? To be like any other Joe Schmo walking the streets? Meet a girl and get her into bed? That's so far from what I want it's not even funny.

Turning, she steps back up into the doorway to the kitchen and then pauses. Is she waiting for me to respond? I need to respond. Shit.

"Carrie, wait."

With her back ramrod straight, she doesn't move, giving me a chance to say something.

"I'm sorry. I didn't mean that the way it sounded. I was just playing around with you. But beyond a wave here and there, I don't engage with them when they walk by."

Her back may be to me, but I see her relaxing. The tension in her back loosens before she spins to face me. Gone is the scowl and disappointment. Thank goodness.

"You don't owe me an explanation."

"That's just it," I begin. Taking a tentative step toward her, like she's a skittish animal, my voice is low as I continue, "I do owe you an explanation. Because you laid all your cards on the table a couple weeks ago, now it's my turn. I think we should go out again."

"I'm sorry I accidentally friend-zoned you."

She says it so fast, I'm not sure she even heard me ask her out. But I'll take it. At least it starts an honest conversation between us. "You didn't friend-zone me."

"I didn't?"

"Nope. Did you feel friend-zoned?" I ask before taking another step toward her.

When I'm in her space, I watch as her eyes slip from my face down my torso. It's a slow perusal, one I don't mind. When I'm close enough to touch her, I lift my hand to hers. She's still gripping the coffee cup in her other hand, and I'm actually a little concerned she's going to snap the handle right off with how white her knuckles are.

"I mean, kind of. No. Okay, I don't know. What do I know Matthew? Until a few weeks ago, I thought you were a mindless model who spent his free time flexing in the mirror while he kissed his biceps and regularly slept with readers."

Barking out a laugh, I squeeze her hand.

"We'll get back to that presumption later. Just so we're clear, I don't feel friend-zoned, and I didn't friend-zone you. Maybe a little surprised by your admission, but not enough for me to mark you off some invisible list of dating material." She whacks me playfully on the chest. "And, before you ripped me a new asshole, I did ask you out again. What do you say?"

Chewing on her lower lip she shifts on her feet and then makes my entire day by nodding. Lifting her chin with my finger, I give her a slow smile, one that is strictly for her. I want to kiss her. The need is overwhelming. When her tongue slips between her lips, I take that as an invitation when a loud scream of excitement startles us both.

"Carrie! You're still here! Yay! Where's your crown? Let's go find it!"

Laughing quietly, I drop my hand and wink at Carrie before Sprite shouts for her again and she scurries away. Like a squirrel.

# Chapter 22

## Carrie

*It's kind of chilly out, so I need to wear jeans. I could go with the distressed skinny ones that make my ass look like I do squats daily. Looking at them, I'm not quite sure I want to risk it. They're getting kind of old and the purposely torn look is starting to tear not so purposely.*

*Oh! I could wear my new dark skinny jeans. Except they have an elastic waist. If my shirt rode up that could be embarrassing with a muffin top...*

"Would you hurry up already?" Jamie yells from my bedroom, interrupting my internal dialogue as I slide the hangers back and forth trying to decide what to wear on my date tonight.

It's not like I have a plethora of options. If we were going to a hospital or a costume party, I'd have lots of scrubs to choose from since that's my normal work attire. But unless Matthew is the world's worst date planner, I probably need to wear something a little nicer.

"This would be a whole lot easier if I knew where we were going," I shout back through my closet door, holding up both pairs of pants to inspect, still running through the pros and cons of each.

"So text him and ask."

Giving up on making the decision myself, I carry them both out to show Jamie the options. "I would, but that feels so... I don't know... friend-zone."

"Here we go again," she mumbles and then points to the darker pair. "Those."

Tossing them on the bed, I put my hands on my scantily clad hips. Fresh from the shower, I didn't want to sweat through my clothes by putting them on before my hair is properly dry. Besides, I'm fully clothed in my under attire. Nothing Jamie hasn't seen before.

"Listen here, Linda," I start. Which makes Jamie roll her eyes and turn her attention back to Luke, who keeps attacking her hand and running away when she runs her fingers on the bed. "I am trying to put my best foot forward."

"By spending hours trying to decide between two pair of jeans? Sounds like you're neurotic, not getting prepared."

I drop the tough guy act and plop down on the bed. Luke immediately attacks the towel on my head.

"I just don't get it, James. He's just so... so... everything. And I'm just so… me."

"You say that like it's a bad thing."

Reaching up to pet my squirrel, he dodges my reach then thinks better of it when I scratch behind his ears. Yep. Everyone has a price. Even wild animals.

"It just doesn't make any sense. He could have anyone he wants, but he asked me on a date?" Jamie groans but I ignore her. "He knows I'm not giving up the goods, so what's his angle?"

"Do you hear yourself?" Jamie chides and I turn to look at her. "There is no angle. He likes you. And I, for one, am getting sick of listening to you overanalyze."

Just then, Luke pounces on my hand, his eyes go blank, and he falls over asleep.

"See?" Jamie says. "Even Luke is tired of hearing you second guess everything."

I scoff. "He has a disability."

"Or he's sick of listening to you say the same things over and over again." She smacks me on my bare leg, making me yelp. "He likes you, Carrie. There's nothing weird or nefarious about it. Or at least there's not at this point. If you continue with your crazy, he might change his mind. Obviously sex isn't a deal breaker for him. Being certifiable might be, though."

I sigh because she's right. It's been so long since I've gone on a second date, I don't know what to expect, and that scares me. If this even is a second date. The concert was just a friends thing, wasn't it?

Hell, I don't know at this point. The only thing I do know is I've always heard that date number three is *the* date. If you go out that many times, it's sort of an unspoken rule that sex is on the table. Which is why I usually don't get past date number one. It doesn't seem right for me to know with absolute certainty that no one is getting any orgasms for a long while and not let whoever I'm dating in on that. Once my motor gets running, it's hard for me to stop, so I try not to even put the key in the ignition. If it's something that is going to cause problems, it's better to know in advance so they can cut things off. And they always cut things off. Or ghost me. Usually ghost, but we all know why.

With Matthew, though, it seems like he's okay with my self-imposed celibacy. No one has ever been okay with it before. That's why I'm so stumped.

"Enough thinking," Jamie announces and starts pushing me off the bed. "You don't have time to sit around. He'll be here in forty-five minutes. Do I need to feed Sven?"

Standing up, I look at the time. "Yeah. He could eat. Did you see his eyes are open?"

Jamie smiles widely. "I love this age. They're so cute when they're still all wobbly and fall over when they try to sit up on their back legs."

"I know. This is when they start growing so fast, though. I'm glad he doesn't need to eat every two hours anymore, but it's sad thinking he'll be out on his own in just a few weeks." I push my bottom lip out in an overexaggerated pouty face.

"Not to worry. You'll always have your buddy, Luke." We both look over at him sleeping soundly on top of the wet towel that remained put when I stood up. "Do I need to put him back in his cage while I get Sven?"

"Nah. He's usually out for a solid hour when he has an attack."

Jamie shakes her head and grumbles, "Weirdest thing I've ever seen," as she walks out of the room and to the kitchen, leaving me to my clothing dilemma.

Deciding on the dark skinny jeans was cake compared to finding a top. Because of the elastic waist, I didn't want it to be too tight. But most of my flowy tops are thinner material and it's December. I'm naturally cold and need a sweater even when it's fifty degrees out. No judgement. I may have grown up in New Jersey, but I've turned into a Texas girl. I'm not built for chilly weather.

Unfortunately, I don't have a flowy sweater so I went with one of the aforementioned tops and a cute black leather jacket over it. It's stylish, comfy, and keeps the elastic bulge from becoming too apparent.

The only thing left to figure out is shoes. Sadly, I don't have time to drive Jamie nuts by trying on twelve different pair, as the doorbell just rang.

I race to the front, so Matthew isn't stuck waiting outside, but somehow Jamie gets there first and is already letting him in. How the hell did she do that?

"Hey Matthew," I say and his face lights up with a huge smile. I've got to admit, it's nice knowing I put that look there and any residual nerves fade away. "This is my friend Jamie. Jamie, this is Matthew."

They reach over to shake hands and without missing a beat Matthew says, "Oh yeah. I think you were twerking behind me when I saw you at the shelter."

Jamie can't hide her embarrassment as her face turns bright red.

"You saw that?" I ask through a laugh.

"No one has ever caught me before." She seems stumped, and clearly rethinking every time she's pulled that number on a customer.

Matthew winks at her, making her blush even more, which I find hilarious. "Well, the glass was pretty reflective that day."

Jamie looks over at me, wide-eyed and I know what she's thinking.

"You better stop making fun of the boss behind his back."

She just nods, mouth still clamped shut. Seriously. I've never seen her so taken aback. It's pretty amazing, actually.

Grabbing Sven from the towel pressed up against her very blotchy chest, I turn back to Matthew. "Before we go, I thought you might like to say hello to your son."

Matthew's eyes light up like a kid on Christmas morning as he takes the baby squirrel out of my hands and begins talking to him. "Hey buddy. Look how big you are. And all that fur. You get your hairiness from your daddy, don't you? Huh?"

I glance over at Jamie who's looking at me with the same amused expression on her face.

"You seem to have gotten over your fear pretty easily," I jest.

"It's hard to be afraid of something so tiny and cute," he says to Sven, not me. "You're not a big, bad rodent like Luke are you? Huh? No. You're still small and harmless."

"And you guys were making fun of me for being the weird one?" Jamie whispers in my ear making me snicker. She's not wrong. To an outsider, watching Matthew coo at a squirrel and call him his son could seem awfully strange.

"Wait." Matthew suddenly looks up and begins looking around. "Luke isn't out, is he?"

Oh boy. This could be fun. For me and Jamie, not Matthew.

"He is actually."

Just as I suspected, Matthew's eyes get huge and he starts inching backward toward the wall. I know Jamie is highly amused by this turn of events but tormenting the poor man before he takes me for steak and lobster is probably not the best of ideas.

"Relax, Matthew. He had an episode. He's asleep on my bed." He visibly relaxes and I gently take Sven back and hand him over to his babysitter. "Which means we need to leave before he wakes up, and since I don't know where we're going, you get to choose my shoes." I pick up the two pair off the floor where I dropped them and show him. "I've got cute booties if we're going somewhere sit down. Or if we're going to be walking a lot and it's more casual, Chucks." I see-saw my arms so each pair goes up and down.

"I never told you where we're going?"

"Nope. I've had one hell of a time figuring out what to wear because of it."

"You can say that again," Jamie grumbles and I shoot her a dirty look. No reason for him to know I'm off my rocker. Yet. That's more like a fifth date admission.

"I don't know a lot about women's footwear unless you mean shoes that light up when you walk or Velcro." I nod in understanding because I can see that. Throw in some princesses and I'm sure that's most of what Calypso owns in the shoe department. "But I thought we'd go to Dave and Buster's and try our hand at air hockey."

I like this idea. "Chucks it is," I announce and hop on one foot while trying to put the other shoe on. "But I'm warning you, buddy. I'm the queen of air hockey."

He laughs and offers his arm to help steady me while I finish putting on my shoes. "Those are fightin' words. And you need to know, I'm still the reigning Roberts champion from our last family reunion."

Grabbing my purse and throwing it over my shoulder, I wave goodbye to Jamie who already promised to lock up when she leaves. "You don't scare me. I've seen your competition. It's easy to beat at least one of them when she can barely see over the top of the table."

He throws his head back and laughs. "Is that so?"

"Totally so."

"Well then," he says as he pulls the door closed behind him, "let's do this."

# Chapter 23

## *Matthew*

I consider myself an excellent air hockey player. I wasn't kidding when I told Carrie that I'm the reigning champion in my family. That's saying a lot because I have younger cousins who assume they'll take me down at each family gathering. Cocky punks think playing drunken beer pong means they can do anything.

Taking in a deep breath, I grip the plastic paddle in my hand and lean down, eyeing the goal on the opposite end of the table. The cool air skirts across my skin as I exhale. Her giggle is distracting, but I won't let it get me this time. She may be up three games to my zero, but this one is mine.

"I have faith in you. This one is going to make it."

Growling, I shoot my gaze to my opponent. The huge smile on her face won't get me this time. She giggles again and I wait. Wait for her eyes to close as those sweet giggles turn into a full belly laugh.

Three.

Two.

Shoot!

"And he scores! Victory is mine!"

Eyes wide, her laughter stops on a dime as she tosses her paddle onto the table. Hands on her hips she attempts to look offended by my win but that doesn't last long when she starts shaking her hips in a weird looking victory dance.

"You did it! I mean, I'm still the winner but good for you!"

Stepping around the table I approach her and lean against the table, arms crossed over my chest. With a quirked brow, I wait for her to finish her celebration dance.

"Thanks for the dance."

"Anytime. So, what's next? Skee-ball? Old school Pac-Man?"

"Food. I'm starving."

Her face falls and I can't help but laugh. Taking her little hand in mine, I tug her behind me. "Come on, if you're nice I'll let you eat more wings than me."

"Oh, I do love a good chicken wing. How do you feel about dipping sauces?"

I weave us through the crowd toward the restaurant, her hand still in my possession. A group of women cross the path in front of us and I come to a quick stop to avoid running into them. Carrie stumbles into me, releasing my hand, which would suck but it doesn't because both of her hands land on my back.

One of the women in the group stops, eyes wide as she looks at me. I know what's coming as soon as her gaze floats across my body. This is my punishment for those college years when I was a ridiculous flirt and did the same thing to co-eds. Closing my eyes I take a deep breath and exhale, about to offer up the smile the neighborhood ladies appreciate when that ridiculous laugh from Carrie overshadows even the sounds of the video games.

The straggling woman is pulled away by her friends as I spin on my heel to look at my date. She's bent over laughing. And snorting.

"You about done?"

"She… they… you… ohmygod, I can't breathe and I may pee my pants."

Not responding, I slip my hands in the front pockets of my jeans while I wait. It's only seconds but she stands, wiping the tears from her face and smiles up at me.

"It doesn't matter where you go, does it? The cougars are everywhere."

"Oh stop," I grumble, grabbing her hand again and leading her away. With her behind me, I take the opportunity to smile and laugh with her. Not that I'll let her see, but damn, that was pretty funny.

By the time we reach the hostess stand, her hysterics have subsided and the grip of her hand is a little tighter. As we follow the kid to the table, Carrie breaks the silence and says, "You didn't answer me."

"About what?" I ask as I slide into my side of the booth. I watch as Carrie does the same and slips off her jacket, setting it to the side.

"Dipping sauces with wings. Where do you stand?"

"Is this a trick question?"

Shaking her head, Carrie doesn't respond when the server approaches our table. After reciting her script, she takes our drink order and steps away. Carrie rests her elbows on the table and with her chin in her hands, a smirk on her face.

"It's not a trick question, Matthew. Some people are fans of blue cheese dressing while others stick to a basic ranch. I did have a friend once who actually liked honey mustard. I thought it was gross but to each his, or her, own. The question is, what's your poison?"

Pretending to think long and hard, I rub my chin with my thumb and forefinger and look her in the eyes. She quirks a brow, and I don't think she's ever been cuter. Prettier. More beautiful. Hell, she's just her and that's perfect. The server returns with our drinks and takes in the two of us in a stare off. Wisely, she sets my beer and her Jack and Coke down but before she can run away, Carrie and I order our food without breaking eye contact.

Carrie's eyes widen just a bit, my order obviously taking her by surprise. She may be waiting for me to explain my dipping choices, but what she doesn't know is why I'm still quiet. Her blog actually inspired this date. She wrote an entire post about how dates are depicted in books. One of her complaints was the realness of how the hero plans a date with the heroine. I think her words were something like "How come none of these guys just take the girl out for a basket of wings and a beer? Not everyone wants to eat oysters and sip champagne."

"Why choose one when you can have both?"

She picks up her glass and takes a drink. This isn't a sip or a tasting of the cocktail.. It's then that she recognizes the question and immediately starts coughing as she chokes.

"What did you just say? Did you—"

"Read your blog? I told you I did."

"I wrote that like two years ago."

Winking, I lift my beer to my lips and take a sip. Like a normal person not like my date who was channeling her inner frat boy, guzzling her drink.

"But seriously, I always get a side of both. Sometimes you just have to indulge."

"You ordered a salad," she deadpans. Then we both break out into laughter.

It isn't long before the server returns with our food. A basket of wings, a salad, and extra dressing for dipping later, we settle into our seats. Neither of us speak at first, just sitting in comfortable silence. Carrie and I talk multiple times a day so we don't have to fill the space with small talk. In fact, this doesn't even feel like a first date. Or is it a second? Does the concert count? I didn't officially declare it a date but still, it was to me.

"Did you give your mom that discount code for the book sleeve?"

"I did. She may have bought herself a few things too. I had no idea blogging had such perks."

She smiles and nods. "Yeah, it's kind of cool when we are able to offer discount codes to our readers. I think Sprite will really like the sleeve and book."

"You called her Sprite." My smile grows. I've never heard her refer to my daughter by her nickname.

"It was her idea. Is that not okay?"

"No, it's great. I'm just surprised. Other than family she doesn't allow anyone to call her by her nickname."

With a small smile, she dips her chin and takes a small drink from her glass. The silence that is normally comfortable is a little awkward. The server catches my eye and starts his way toward us.

"Everything tasting okay? May I grab you another round?"

"We're good, thanks."

He nods and leaves us alone.

"Hey," I say, reaching across the table tapping the

top to catch Carrie's attention. "I should have said it when we were at your house. Before you pulled me away from our child by threatening me with Luke. You look beautiful."

A light pink tints her cheeks as she whispers, "Thank you. I'm still not going to sleep with you."

Sucking in too much air, I start choking in response. What the hell? The server's chuckle catches my attention and I quickly turn my head toward him. Lips pursed as he tries to suck down a full belly laugh, he clears the empty plates and slowly pulls the check holder from his apron, placing it on the table. He must assume this date is about to go up in flames.

"Okay…"

"Just in case you thought the compliments, wings, and inferior game play were the way to get me in the sack."

"Inferior? Come on now, I kicked your butt at the basketball game," I respond while placing my credit card in the holder.

"Yeah well, I scored two hundred tickets on only one round of Whack a Mole. Inferior."

Shrugging her shoulder, she looks off to the left, her eyes focused on the television. I follow her gaze and know for a fact she is not interested in bobsledding. Is that even a regular sport outside of the Olympics? Huh. Interesting. We're both looking at the men running and jumping in the sled when the server returns with my credit card.

"How many tickets do you have on that card?" I ask, pulling her attention back to me as I scribble my name on the slip.

"At least a million."

"So math isn't your thing, I take it."

"Oh hush Mr. Financial Advisor. Not all of us get the warm and fuzzies from numbers. Is there somewhere we can check my balance?"

Nodding, I stand from the booth and watch as she slides out doing the same. I motion for her to go ahead of me and step behind her, my hand on her lower back as we exit the restaurant. Looking around, I spy the Winners Circle display in the corner and open my mouth to say something to Carrie when she breaks out into that weird victory dance again.

"Oh yeah, that's all for me. Do you see how it is named after me?"

"Uh, what?"

"Winner's Circle. That's me. I'm the winner here. Come on, Matthew, I have prizes to claim." I let her take me by the hand this time and drag me across the building to claim her bounty.

Twenty minutes. It took her twenty minutes to choose her prize. Then put it back. And then claim it again. Two thousand tickets. I didn't even think that was possible. Mostly because I had two hundred forty-six.

While Carrie walked out with a book safe and a crap ton of candy, I am the proud owner of two bouncing balls and a licorice rope. Clearly I am the winner in this scenario.

Now, as our date is coming to an end, nerves I haven't felt since I was nineteen take over. My hands are sweaty, and I'm pretty sure it'll be a two antacids kind of night. Sitting to my right, Carrie is blowing bubbles, courtesy of one of the mega gumballs she snagged while singing along to the music.

"I don't remember these losing their flavor so quickly. It's actually pretty disgusting."

"There are napkins in the console here if you need to get rid of it."

Faster than I can blink, she whips open the console and spits the gum into the paper. The extra spitting may be a little much, but who am I to judge? When she eyes the water bottle in the cup holder, I chuckle.

"Go ahead," I say, nodding to the water.

"Bless you. Seriously that gum was offensive. I'm throwing out all the other balls before you take this bag home."

"I don't know why you think giving my daughter all that candy is a good idea. You saw what that cotton candy did to her."

Turning in her driveway, I put the truck in park and kill the engine before turning toward her. Smiling, she scrunches her nose and then snorts out a laugh.

"Ah yes, but the beauty of this candy is you'll deal

with the fallout and not me. Besides, Ring Pops and candy necklaces are something every little girl should experience. It's a rite of passage."

"If you say so. But if she's bouncing off the walls and driving me crazy, she's coming for a sleepover."

Not waiting for a response, I slip out of the cab and round the truck, grabbing the handle just as the door opens and she hops down to the ground. Carrie walks ahead, her book safe clutched to her chest and steps up on the porch. I still don't know what that thing is for. I'm not sure she does either, but it is some sort of an accessory for her library so of course she had to have it.

"Here, gimme that thing." Taking the safe from her, I watch as she searches through her bag and retrieves her key and opens the door.

Tossing the keys into her purse, she takes the safe from me and sets it on the floor along with her purse before turning back to face me. With her bottom lip tugged between her teeth, her eyes wander all around, anywhere and everywhere but on me.

"So, the no sex thing."

She gasps. Well that caught her attention.

"What about it?"

"Does that include kissing? Is kissing off the table?" I ask while she blinks rapidly. Okay then. When she shakes her head, I take a step forward and take her hand gently. "Do you think it would be okay if I kissed you?"

More blinking and a very slow nod, I lean in and brush my lips across hers. It isn't a passionate kiss. There's no tongue or moaning, just a slight brushing of my mouth on hers before stepping back. Her eyes open ever so slowly, a grin taking over her face.

"Thanks for letting me take you out again. Sleep well, and I'll call you tomorrow."

Stepping down from the porch, I peer over my shoulder to see her standing there, her finger on her lips. That simple gesture makes me feel like a million bucks, but the grumbling in my stomach reminds me that even the million dollar man needs an antacid.

# Chapter 24

*Carrie*

It has been a long week. Partially because I really want Friday to get here so Matthew and I can go out again while Calypso is doing her grandparents' night. That kiss we shared was as chaste as they come, but the emotion behind it was so much more.

See this is why I have to make sure I'm on the same page as any potential dates. Once my motor is running, I'm a goner, and Matthew definitely knows how to rev my engine with his lips.

The other reason I can't wait for the weekend is because the holidays are upon us, and that means lots of well-meaning parents planning to give their children pets for Christmas. Since the rescue is between baby seasons in the wildlife realm, guess who gets suckered into working the front and smiling through the application process? No, not Jamie. Me. Every day, I have to sit at the desk, a smile on my face and nod my head as each parent tells me how excited their child will be for their first pet. What I don't do is tell them how many of those same pets will end up back with us by spring break because they didn't realize how much of a commitment an animal would be. It happens every year.

Although each parent has the best of intentions, the process never gets easier. I hate that by March the kennels will once again be at capacity with little furballs that didn't make the family cut.

What makes me happy, though, is the text I get from Matthew saying he and Calypso are on their way over to my house. Apparently, Sprite has a present for Sven, and she can't wait to give it to him.

I keep wondering what kind of gift she could possibly have for a squirrel. If it's a Barbie bike, she's going to be disappointed when he eats it.

A knock at the door puts a little spring in my step as I bust a move to let my guests in. I could use some little girl time to boost my spirits again.

"Hey. Come in." I throw the door wide open so they can get in faster than the cold air. It's not cold by Minnesota standards or anything, but this cold snap is nothing to dismiss either. Shutting it behind them, my immediate attention goes to Calypso, who is already jumping up and down excitedly.

"I brought Sven a Christmas present. Can I give it to him? Please?"

Her wide eyes are impossible to resist, so of course I say yes. Besides, curiosity is killing me.

"Why don't we take your coat off first, Sprite," Matthew says with a smile, his gaze moving to mine where we have an awkward moment. You know the one I'm talking about. That first time you see one another after the first kiss when everyone sort of knows how the other person feels but isn't totally sure and you look at each other and blush, maybe look away again, until everyone is comfortable again.

Yeah. That awkward moment.

It doesn't last long though, because Calypso's excitement about the mystery present is contagious. Dropping her coat on the floor for Matthew to deal with, she races to the dining room where his cage is, the present still in her hands.

"Oh, Carrie! He's awake!" She continues to bounce up and down because apparently she never runs out of energy. Or maybe because she never runs out of the candy I gave her. Who knows?

Coming up behind her, I open the cage door to get him out. "You have to be very quiet around him, Sprite," I instruct and she immediately stops bouncing. "We don't want to scare him. Squirrels can be really skittish."

I take that moment to look up and see Matthew peeking around the corner.

"Apparently grown men can be skittish too," I joke, but Matthew doesn't seem to notice, his face keeping the same scared expression that he had last time he was here. "Relax, Matthew. He's locked up in his cage."

True to form, Luke takes this moment to pounce against the cage and buzz, flipping his tail to show everyone who's boss.

Seeing that he's in no immediate danger, the six-foot-tall, full grown baby blows out a breath and quickens his steps into the room. "Cool. I mean, it's fine if he's out. It's your house and all. I just... yeah. It's cool."

My smirk suppresses the grin threatening to overtake my face. I don't think watching someone who looks like him react to my sweet Lukey like he does will ever get old. While he's side-eyeing the cage to make sure Luke can't get out, his daughter has no fear whatsoever.

Calypso sets the present on the table while I shift Sven in my hands, holding him tightly so he doesn't try to crawl away. She begins to gently pet his head, clearly enthralled by her furry brother.

"I brought you a present, Sven. Do you want to open it?" Picking up the small package, she holds it up to me, a confused look on her face. "How's he gonna open it?"

"That's a good question," I say, pretending there are a whole lot of options. "What if you hold him and I open it for him?"

Calypso's eyes widen, and she nods vigorously with excitement.

"You have to stay calm though," I gently remind her as I hand him over and get him situated on her chest.

He's hanging on like he's attached to a tree, which is no small feat for a little guy like Sven.

Taking the small package out of her tiny hand, I carefully pull the wrapping paper apart. It's clear that Calypso wrapped it herself, which makes it all the more special. Vaguely, I hear the click of Matthew's phone as he takes pictures of this moment. He must have some serious zoom on that camera to get anything worthwhile with how far away he is from the cages.

Gently, I pull a soft blue square of fabric from inside the package.

"I made it myself," Calypso announces quietly, her hands petting Sven and holding him in place.

"Well, you cut up a blanket without my permission, anyway," Matthew clarifies with a chuckle.

"Right. I made it." She rolls her eyes at Matthew's obvious inability to understand what it means to sew. "He's all by himself in the cage so he needs something to snuggle with."

I don't bother telling her that squirrel nests are made of pine needles, sticks and rocks so he probably doesn't care that much, because her thought process is way too precious.

Placing the fabric over Sven's tiny body, Calypso moves her hand and wouldn't you know it? He proves me wrong when he immediately snuggles down into it and falls asleep. I swear, none of the animals in my house want to do what comes naturally. Bunch of prima donnas.

Calypso gently sways back and forth like a mama holding her baby and looks around the room. "Where's your Christmas tree? And your stocking? Christmas is tomorrow."

Matthew, seemingly over his fear now that his daughter has taken one for their team, comes up behind her and puts his hands on her shoulders. "Christmas is next week, honey. And she probably can't have one because Luke might get lost in it."

I snicker. "Oh I'd find him once he fell out of it. I actually don't have one because I'm Jewish."

Matthew's eyebrows furrow. "Really? I didn't know that."

Holding my hand up to stop him, I clarify. "I didn't say I was religious but it is how I grew up. So, no Christmas tree for me but see? I have my menorah on the mantel with all those pretty candles."

Looking over at my fireplace, her big eyes are full of questions. "So you light them all like on your birthday? And blow them out?"

I smile at her innocent question. The more I get to know Calypso, the more I realize kids have this amazing way of relating to the world around them. I've also learned not to let certain opportunities pass you by. Explaining one of my most favorite traditions to her counts.

"It's a sort of celebration, but not like for your birthday."

"Then like for what?"

Looking up at Matthew, I silently ask his permission to answer her question. Just because I think it's a cool story, doesn't mean some parents aren't sensitive to any kind of religious information their child hears. Last thing I need is for Matthew to storm out of here because he thinks I overstepped a boundary of some sort. We've had enough boundary discussions lately.

He gives me a quick nod, though, so I know it's okay to continue. "A long time ago there were a bunch of people. They had a really tough time and were really poor." I know I'm simplifying the story of the Jews being freed from Egypt, but she's six. Her attention span isn't really that long so I need to hit the highlights and quick before some twinkly lights distract her. "These people had to use oil to light candles so they could see in the temple, but they didn't have enough to last very long. Except, one little thing of oil lasted a whole eight days. So we light the candles to celebrate the miracle of light."

Calypso stares at the menorah for a few seconds then turns to me, a sweet look on her face. "That's it?"

"Sprite!" Matthew says, but I hold my hand up to stop him.

"There's a lot more to the story but I think that part is pretty amazing, don't you?"

"Yes, but…" Her eyes begin filling with tears. "Santa doesn't come to your house?"

I see where this is headed and as I have no desire for her to have a meltdown, I squelch her disappointment quick. "Oh honey. Don't feel bad for me. You may have Santa, but that menorah also means I have eight days of presents."

Her face immediately changes. "Eight days? Like Christmas every morning?"

I bobble my head because no, not like that at all. I don't want to disappoint her either, though. Why must children be so inquisitive?

"Not like Christmas exactly. But when I was your age, every night I would receive a new present to open. They started out small on the first day but by the last it would be something super awesome."

Calypso whips her head around to look at her dad. "How come I don't get eight days of presents?"

He chuckles lightly. "We're not Jewish, honey."

"Hrmph." She stomps her little foot, a scowl on her face and mumbles something that sounds suspiciously like "Stupid Santa." Thank goodness Santa doesn't monitor this house or that could have been a naughty list making statement right there.

Matthew ignores her, focusing on me instead. "Will you spend any of the holiday with your family?"

"Nah." I cross my arms and lean against the table, still watching Calypso enjoy holding Sven. "Now that I'm an adult, they go on an extended cruise every year. Besides, it's not easy to take off the time from work anyway. I just hang out with Luke, and we watch movies."

"You should come to our house for Christmas Eve dinner."

He says it so nonchalantly, it almost doesn't register. "What?"

"I said, you should come to our house for Christmas Eve."

I immediately begin shaking my head. "No, no, no. I can't intrude on your family time."

"What intrusion?" he asks with a shrug of his shoulder. "It's really informal. My parents come over, mostly to keep my mom distracted so she doesn't whine about how my brother left the nest and never comes to see his family on Christmas anymore."

"He doesn't?"

"He's in the military and stationed overseas. She's also dramatic and possibly hitting the eggnog a little too much."

Makes sense.

"It also means my dad doesn't have to be up and over to our house before the sun rises on Christmas morning. Plus we always have way more food than we need. So come on. It'll be fun."

I stand there, thinking through my options. Stay home by myself and watch Hallmark? Hang out at Matthew's and eat holiday food.

Sounds like a no-brainer to me.

"I'll be there."

# Chapter 25

*Matthew*

One of my favorite smells in the world is my mom's prime rib. Each Christmas Eve morning she blows into my house with her sacks of supplies and starts her cook prep. Slicing, dicing, and... whatever else it is she does. I have no idea but I know the Christmas music starts early, the coffee is brewed, and my kitchen looks like an episode of one of those cooking competition shows.

While Mom is here singing along to both traditional and modern holiday tunes, Dad stays home claiming that is the only gift he needs each year. Silence. Well, and the promise of hot buttered rum and pie.

Since Calypso takes her role as sous chef seriously, I'm able to take the day and get things done around the house I tend to put off. Okay, so I clean the bathrooms and do laundry. In my defense it's the crummy cleaning and laundry we all avoid. The tile grout and bedding. The people that follow my social media would die if they knew romance book cover model, Matthew Roberts spends his holidays washing princess bedding and scrubbing showers. Or maybe they'd like it. My mom says anytime my dad mops the floors she loves him a little more. Something about her love language.

*Keeping myself busy today was also strategic. It kept me from having to answer the dozens of questions my mom had about Carrie. Tell me about this job of hers. Is it only squirrels? How does she feel about your modeling? Where are you taking her for New Year's? You know your dad proposed to me on New Year's Eve, right?*

That last one has bounced around in my head all day and although that step is very far off, now I feel pressure to convince Carrie to spend the evening with me. Obviously, I want to spend the night ringing in the new year with her. I also know she's unbelievably leery when it comes to relationships.

"Daddy! Daddy! Where are you?"

Pulling a towel from the linen closet, I wait for my shouting child to find me. From the level of screeching, I have a strong suspicion she has been hitting the sugar. When her little body slams into my legs, I let out an "oomph" and brace myself so I don't smack my head on the door.

"Whoa there, Sprite. What are you—?" The rest of my question evaporates as I take in her appearance: flour covered cheeks, a tiara, candy necklace, and a little apron that says "Today I'm Making a Mess." There were never truer words than what is printed on that bright pink fabric.

"And you need a shower."

"How about a bubble bath?" Her little face lights up at the possibilities.

"We don't have time for that. We have a guest coming for dinner. Did Grandma leave?"

Nodding her head, she skips into her bedroom. I follow her into the room and watch as she gently takes off her tiara and candy necklace, placing them on her nightstand. It's these simple moments that I cherish. One day she'll be a teenager, full of hormones and probably some anger toward her overbearing father. These are also the moments I am sad that Delilah misses. She should see her daughter reveling in the wonder of a plastic piece of jewelry that she treats as if it's actually adorned with real rubies and sapphires.

"Okay, little one. We need to get a move on. There won't be time to do your hair so grab your shower cap and let's get you cleaned up."

Showers are a lot faster than baths any day, but since we don't have to wash and condition her hair, my little mermaid is in and out in no time. Since we tend to be a pretty casual family, holidays or not, she tugs on her new Christmas leggings and red sweater. I'm helping her adjust her tiara when my parents announce their arrival.

"Oh, Papa is here!"

"Hey, I'm here too," mom teases from the doorway.

"Yeah but you were already here. Papa probably had the sads because he didn't see me all day. Papa! I'm here! Where are you?"

Laughing, I stand from the bed and my mom shakes her head. "That child is too much. You need to find yourself a wife and give her a sibling."

And here we go.

"I managed that one without a wife."

Rolling her eyes, she pushes up the sleeve of her decorative sweater and glances at her watch. "That may be and while it wasn't the life choice we would have made for you at the time, she's a gift and we love her. Now, if Carrie will be here at six, you better get your ass in gear. It's a quarter till."

Shit. I move toward the door but come up short before mowing my mom over. She only giggles before stepping aside and letting me pass. Rushing to my room, I begin stripping off my clothes, tossing them aimlessly across the room before starting the shower. Making quick work of it, I take the speediest shower of my life. Toweling off, I get myself dressed and begin focusing on my hair when the doorbell rings. Of course she's on time.

I finish up and make my way to the living room where I'm greeted with Carrie kneeled down, eye level with my little girl. She's wearing a white sweater with her hair down in long loose waves. But it isn't the way her hair looks or the how the sweater hugs her body that has my attention. It's the way she's looking at my daughter, her eyes sparkling and her smile wide. I have no idea what Sprite is saying to her, it could be the grandest story or the silliest joke. I'll never know, and it doesn't matter, because from the look on Carrie's face, it's fantastic.

"Wow, that was the fastest shower I think you've ever taken. It's like you didn't want to miss anything. Or anyone."

"Mom," I warn.

"Oh hush. She's lovely. And, look at our girl. She simply adores her." I don't respond and then she pats my arm. "And I don't think she's the only one."

Rolling my eyes, I step away from my mom and move toward my girls. "Hey, you made it."

Smiling up at me, she rises as my mom leads Sprite away. She may drive me nuts with her meddling but right now I'm grateful.

"Looks like it. I hope it's okay, I brought Sven with me. Jamie is with her family, and I wasn't sure how late I'd be. Plus, he wanted to thank Olaf for saving him."

Glancing around, I don't see a cage anywhere and open my mouth to ask when she says, "I put him in the laundry room. Your mom distracted Sprite while your dad helped me. We'll take him out later and make sure she has time with him."

"Good idea. Can I get you something to drink? Eggnog? Wine?"

"Oh, umm… your dad mentioned hot buttered rum?"

Nodding I motion for her to follow me to the kitchen. I move around asking about her day as I pour us both a cup of the rum drink. That's when I notice the dish on the counter.

"I brought potato latkes. I hope that's okay."

"You didn't have to bring anything, you're our guest."

"It's no big deal. I also brought the gelt and my dreidel. Maybe I could teach Sprite a little more about my traditions? I don't want to overstep or any—"

"She'd like that. Thank you, Carrie."

With a huge smile on her face, she takes her cup and settles in on the couch where my dad and Sprite are sitting. The loud shriek from Sprite and boisterous laugh from my dad as Carrie pulls her items from a bag make it impossible not to smile.

"Papa, do you want to play?" Sprite asks my dad who immediately scoots himself closer to where they are sitting. He's never been able to say no to his granddaughter.

Carrie looks over her shoulder. "You wanna play with us?"

I hold my hand up. "Nope. I'm on backup cooking duty in case Mom needs help. I'm just going to sit and watch."

She nods once and turns back to the game, explaining the purpose of each piece and the rules.

"What I'm giving you right now is called gelt." Carrie passes out what look like gold coins in front of my dad and Sprite. "Each of us get ten to start."

"They're chocolate!" The thought of having candy in her hands before dinner makes Calypso a little too excited.

"They're made of chocolate, but right now we're going to pretend they're money," Carrie patiently instructs.

"Can I eat them?"

"It depends if you win the game or not."

Calypso doesn't appear to like that answer but complies anyway.

"Everyone puts one of their gelts in the middle. This is called the pot." All three of them toss one where Carrie indicates, although Calypso holds tightly to her nine remaining pieces. "You're going to spin the dreidel like this. Whatever side it lands on will tell you what to do."

Calypso looks closely at the wooden game piece. "I don't know what that says."

"That's because it's a Hebrew symbol that means 'nothing happens.' So all the gelt stays in the pot. Here." Carrie pulls out a laminated paper from her bag and places it on the table. "This shows all the symbols and their meaning. It will help us to not get confused. Are you ready to try, Sprite?"

She nods excitedly and picks up the dreidel, balancing it carefully on the table. Then she spins it as hard as she can and it goes flying across the room, nailing the wall.

"Um… maybe try a little less speed," Carrie suggests as Sprite bounds across the room to try again.

It takes them a while to get in the groove, but once they do, the competition gears up and all three are enjoying themselves. The pot is quickly filled then emptied and just when it seems one person is going to lose, suddenly they're back in the running. The hardest part is getting Sprite to stop jumping up and down long enough to spin.

Everyone is laughing and having a good time until Carrie finally notices what I knew was happening all along.

Gaping at my dad, she exclaims, "Hey you're cheating!"

As always, he immediately denies any wrongdoing. "I am not."

"You are too! You just added a gelt to Sprite's pile."

Calypso gasps and looks down, delighted at this turn of events. "Thanks, Papa!"

"No way!" Carrie continues to get riled up and this competitive side of her is making me laugh. "You can't do that."

Dad shrugs like he's naïve to the whole thing. "I was just helping out my grandbaby. We're a team."

"There's no teams in dreidel. Matthew, help me out here."

She turns around, palms up like she's waiting for me to say something. Which I finally do.

"Welcome to the Roberts family Christmas Eve dinner. This is why we stopped playing Monopoly."

And Calypso giggles as she takes a bite out of one of her gelts.

Dinner was delicious, the drinks were flowing, and Sprite was more excited to have Sven and Carrie celebrating with us than most of her gifts. Darryl was able to video chat with us, and my mom cried the entire time. He flirted with Carrie, she blushed, and I wanted to pummel him. I've never been the jealous type, but tonight while my brother charmed her into blushing and giggling, I wanted to stake my claim. Tell him to back off because she was mine. Then she told him he was sweet but not her type and I relaxed. With a huge smile on my face.

"I think Christmas was a success," Carrie says with a yawn, Sven nestled into her chest with his little blanket covering him.

"This is nothing. We still have our presents tomorrow."

"Wow. I know Sprite was jealous of my eight days of presents but I'm a little envious of her haul."

"Spoiled. You can say it. She's spoiled, and we're

doing a disservice to her."

When the topic of our conversation moseys into the room with a new stuffed squirrel in her arms, we turn our attention to her. Sheepishly, Calypso stands at the end of the couch, her bottom lip out in contemplation. With a raised brow, I wordlessly remind her of her promise.

"Carrie?"

"Yeah, honey?"

"I'm sorry Papa and I played creatively at your special game."

Okay well, it's not exactly the apology we discussed but it'll have to do. I'm exhausted and Santa still needs to eat his cookies and leave his gifts.

"Thank you for saying that. You know," Carrie says, sitting up to give her full attention to Calypso. "My holiday is only just beginning. Maybe you and I can try again tomorrow. If we're lucky your daddy may even play with us."

Relief washes over my baby as she smiles and nods her head in agreement. "Alrighty. I think it's time for little girls to go to bed. Santa won't come if you're awake."

"Okay, Daddy. Umm, Carrie, would you tuck me in?"

Her question doesn't shock me in the least but seems to have taken Carrie by surprise. She turns her head to look at me for guidance. With a slight nod and a loss of my brain cells, I hold my hands out to take Sven from her. She gasps and I shake my head.

"Give me the fur baby. Sprite, no stories. Straight to bed, okay?"

"Kay. Come on, Carrie!"

Dragging her down the hall, Calypso is rambling about her bedtime routine and prayers while I stand and take Sven to his cage. Once he's settled, I turn off the light and start moving toward the living room when a noise draws my attention to the hallway toward Sprite's bedroom. That's when I see something hanging from the entryway. Of course she did.

I stand on my toes and tug once then twice to pull it down.

"Whatcha got there?"

"Shit, Carrie. You scared me," I whisper yell.

"Sorry."

"Mistletoe," I reply, holding it up for her to see.

Her tongue slips between her lips and dart from the weed in my hand to my mouth and back again. Is she thinking of the last time we kissed?

"Carrie?"

"Hmm?" Weed. Lips. Weed. She's going to give herself a headache moving her eyes back and forth that fast.

"I'm a traditional guy. Mistletoe is a tradition."

Smirking, she focuses her eyes on me.

"May I kiss you?"

"Matthew, you don't have to ask me every time you want—"

I take that as a yes and slip my hand around her waist, pulling her body flush to mine. Surprising me, she doesn't hesitate and slides her arms around my waist, her hands gliding up my back as her chin lifts. Lowering my mouth, I capture her lips. Needing to touch her, I drop the mistletoe and grip the nape of her neck, my fingers tangling in her hair. The movement alone draws a sound that will stay with me forever. A mewl, not quite a moan or a whimper, passes from her mouth to mine.

Deepening the kiss, I pull her closer and then I feel her hands shift. Moving from my back to my front and for the slightest moment the thought of where her hands will go next sends a jolt of electricity straight through me. Then her hands grip my shirt and she slows the kiss before stopping it completely.

"I—"

"Stay."

"Matthew, I can't. I like you. Too much, I think. But nothing has changed. I still won't sleep with you."

"I would never ask you to go against your values. I like you too. Probably too much. Stay in the guest room. Have Christmas morning with us. I just want to spend time with you. Sven is fine and asleep. You know what they say, sleep when they sleep."

Surprising the hell out of me, she slides her hands

around me and lifts to her toes, placing a quick kiss to my lips.

"Goodnight, Matthew. I'll see you in the morning. Don't forget Santa's cookies."

Before I can respond, she spins on her heel and walks down the hall and into the guest room.

# Chapter 26

*Carrie*

Stretching my arms over my head, I find myself wondering what kind of mattress Matthew has for this guest room. It's still the most comfortable bed I've ever slept in, and also why it wasn't hard to convince me to stay over again. Like sleeping on a cloud, it has the perfect amount of firmness but still feels like I'm floating. Add the right number of pillows and fluffy blankets that keep me neither too hot nor too cold and it's pure heaven.

I could stay here all day. I also may be overthinking my sleeping arrangements right now.

No time to lie around though. As much as this bed is holding me hostage, Sven needs to be fed. Plus, while I may feel like lounging some more, my bladder is obviously hard at work.

Climbing out of bed, I tug on my pants and slip on

my bra. Nobody needs to see me running around without it. Instead of putting on my sweater, I opt to leave on the T-shirt I snagged from the folded laundry that was on the bed. Maybe I need to start keeping a change of clothes in my car. Slowly, I open the door, not wanting to wake anyone who may still be sleeping. Poking my head into the hall, I listen for movement but hear nothing. I quickly pad my way to the hall bathroom to do my business. Normally I wouldn't choose bubble-gum flavored princess toothpaste but desperate times don't leave me another option. I look like I just woke up, but there's no reason for my breath to smell like it. You never know when more mistletoe may suddenly appear.

*Too bad there isn't a quick fix for these eyebrows,* I think as I inspect my face in the mirror. Why didn't I deal with them yesterday?

I shake my head at my own laziness. Nothing I can do about it now. I've got a squirrel to feed before Little Miss Holiday Cheer wakes up. If last night was any indication of how things go around here on Christmas, I'd better be prepared for a small tornado to rip through the living room.

Quickly, I pass through the house, spying a plate of cookies and a glass of milk on the coffee table. A few bites are missing. I wonder if the guilty party was Matthew or Kris Kringle. With how much Matthew thinks about his food intake, it's more realistic to think Santa really was here.

Snickering to myself at my own joke, I round the

corner into the laundry room and stop dead in my tracks at the vision in my line of sight.

Matthew is sporting some sexy as hell bedhead, a white T-shirt, and the Christmas pajama bottoms Calypso gave him last night. Not a lot of men can rock sparkly snowflakes, but he makes it look sexier than it should.

What really has my breath hitching is watching him interact with Sven. He's holding Sven on his chest, rocking back and forth like he's a human baby, and feeding him milk from a small bottle. I'm fully aware that he's feeding a squirrel, but it's giving me visions of what he must have looked like as a new father—rocking his baby girl as he feeds and coos at her.

He must hear me approach because he looks up and flashes me a huge grin.

Aaaand I'm pretty sure one of my ovaries just exploded over the whole scene in front of me.

"What are you doing up so early?" he asks quietly.

"I needed to feed Sven, but I guess you beat me to it."

Looking down at our rodent son, he shrugs. "I was up anyway, so I thought you could sleep in. You can go back to bed if you want."

"Nah." I lean against the door jamb and rest my head. I may be up, but I'm not fully awake yet. "Once I wake up, I can't go back to sleep."

"That sucks. So no afternoon napping for you?"

"Nope. It's a curse." I push off the wall and take a couple of steps toward them. "Anyway, I should probably get this little guy and get out of here before Sprite wakes up."

Matthew looks up at me quickly, confusion and maybe a little hurt in his eyes. "Why? It's Christmas morning."

"I know." I try to stroke Sven's little head, but he starts sniffing my fingers wondering if I have any food for him. It makes it impossible to make contact with anything more than his nose. "I don't want us to get in the way."

"Carrie." He says my name in his dad voice, and I feel my last remaining ovary begin to rumble at the authority of his deep timbre. "You won't be in the way. In fact, if you aren't here, I'll have to explain to my daughter where you went and why, and likely there will be a hysterical breakdown. If you care about me at all, you won't put me through that."

My lips quirk in amusement at his dramatics.

"Plus," he continues, "we have leftover prime rib, and I was going to make a scramble."

And that cements my answer. For an animal rescue professional, I'm surprisingly supportive of the carnivore lifestyle.

"Now you're speaking my language," I joke, giving up on petting Sven, who has climbed from Matthew to me and is currently sniffing around in my hair. "Although I could probably go for some coffee first, if that's okay."

"One coffee, coming right up. Go make yourself comfortable on the couch." He quickly pecks me on the lips, which I enjoy a little too much, and I begin to wonder how my heart is going to take it when Matthew realizes I'm just a normal girl and not anything special. I know it's just been a matter of weeks since we've started spending time together and really had a chance to get to know each other, but he's become one of my favorite people in the world. He's so different than anyone I've ever known, and I find myself wanting to be near him, even if it's just sitting on the couch watching a movie.

Funny how things change when you get to know someone for more than their first impression. Just don't tell Donna Moreno. She'd have a field day, knowing I have to eat crow about her cover model. And then she'd probably turn it into a book or something ridiculous like that. Can you imagine reading about a hot model falling for a normal girl that spends her free time with animals that call trees their home? I can't.

Placing Sven back in his cage, he wobbles his way to the small box he now uses as a nest. That's the last we'll see of him for the next few hours, which gives me a chance to appreciate the cup of coffee Matthew promised before the festivities begin. I settle into the corner of the couch and enjoy the beautiful tree that is surrounded with more presents.

"Carrie!" a little voice squeals, startling me.

Calypso stands in front of me chattering excitedly

about Santa eating the cookies and how full her stocking is. She's not wrong. That sucker is oversized to begin with, but now it's overstuffed too.

"I'm sorry we didn't get you a stocking." Matthew hands me my steaming cup of joe and sits beside me. "I should have planned better."

"It's not like we knew I was going to spend the night." I take a sip, moaning at the goodness that is Folgers in my cup. Matthew's eyes widen slightly and I make a mental note that he likes that noise. Good to know. Not that I'll be using the information for anything, but knowledge is power and all that jazz. "Besides, I've never had a Christmas morning before, so I'm excited to see what this is all about."

His jaw drops open. "Never?"

"Did you forget the part about me being Jewish?" I tease and take another sip. Seriously, whoever invented coffee should have a statue somewhere. Huh. I wonder if there is actually a statue like that. I'll have to look.

"I didn't forget." He runs his fingers through his already messy hair and somehow he ends up looking sexier than he already did. It's so unfair. If I ran my fingers through my hair like that, I'd look like I stuck my finger in an outlet. "I guess it just seems foreign to me."

"I mean, I'm not a complete novice. I know what it's like, but I haven't experienced it. Besides, I have a feeling a certain someone is going to make the present process fun to watch."

"Can we open now, Daddy? Can we?" Calypso is practically yelling as she jumps up and down, too wired with excitement to wait any longer. I need to make sure she doesn't sample my coffee. The last thing this little one needs is caffeine.

Matthew turns to me and in his most sarcastic tone says, "Fun is relative." Then he pushes off the couch and heads toward the mantel. "Okay, Sprite. You can have your stocking. Wow." He pulls it down and pretends to have a hard time carrying it. "Looks like you've been a really good girl this year."

Calypso giggles and instructs her dad where to put her stocking. It barely hits the floor before she digs in, and basically recreates the scene from last night—wrapping paper flying everywhere, squeals of delight when each treasure is revealed, the soft sound of Christmas carols playing in the background as Matthew syncs his phone to the surround sound. Christmas morning is exactly like I've seen in all the movies. Except there's no snow. I'm a bit wimpy with cooler temps so I don't mind the loss.

The couch depresses next to me as Matthew sits down, and I can't help my contented sigh.

"This is just perfect," I breath and relax back into the cushions more.

"I'm glad you're having a good time." I feel him turn to look at me, but I'm having too much fun watching Calypso. It's another one of those moments where seeing this experience through her eyes makes it so much... *more*. "I hope this makes it a little better."

I look down just as Matthew puts a medium sized box on my lap. Based on the wrapping job, I'm sure Calypso had something to do with it.

Now I understand all her delighted shrieks. I'm having a hard time keeping my voice under control right now because I have a present! "Is this for me?"

He gives me a wicked grin and bites his bottom lip before answering. "There's more where that came from."

My jaw drops open. "Are you serious? Matthew, I didn't bring you anything."

"Sure you did. Sprite loves that stuffed squirrel. She named it Kristoff, by the way."

"No, I mean I didn't get *you* anything." Now I feel terrible, and it's making me anxious. It's one thing to bring a child a gift, but I didn't know we were at the point where we were exchanging gifts ourselves. I wouldn't know what to give him anyway. A tie for work? A low-carb recipe book? Some bronze tanner to slather on his incredible abs before a cover shoot?

"I can see your brain working overtime," he says quietly, and I shoot him an aggravated glare at his ability to read my mind. "Stop overthinking. This was impulse shopping, all the way around. Give me your cup."

"Fine," I say, caving to his request and handing him my beloved coffee. This is my first Christmas present. Why shouldn't I enjoy it? "Hey, Sprite!" I call out.

"Yeah?" She doesn't even look up from her new

toys.

"Did you get this for me?" She finally looks up to see me holding the box. When it registers what I have, her eyes widen, and she tosses the new doll she opened aside and comes racing over.

"Open it! Open it!"

I can't help but laugh at the fact that she's just as excited for me to open a gift as she was to open her own. There must be something really special in here.

Starting slowly because I want the moment to last, I begin peeling off the paper. That's short lived though, when Calypso's fingers get in the middle of it, ripping it open faster than I can keep up.

It's worth it. Inside the box is a wooden plaque with a painted picture of a squirrel. Only it's not just any squirrel. He's wearing glasses and holding a book. And because he's red I know without a doubt this sweet girl just gave me a picture of my Lukey.

"Sprite," I say, my voice full of emotion. "I love this so much."

Still bouncing, she replies, "You're the best squirrel mommy, and all mommies need pictures of their babies, so I got you a picture of Luke. Did you know that's Luke?"

I nod and blink the wetness out of my eyes because who cries over a Christmas present? I don't want to be ridiculous. "I did know. It looks just like him."

Well, not really. He doesn't actually have glasses,

but I still recognized him immediately.

"Daddy helped me pick it out." And she bounces away with that one final statement.

Holding my new prized possession to my chest, I turn to Matthew. "Thank you so much. I love it."

He nudges my knee with his own. "Yeah, we knew you would. But you have one more so put that down."

I do as he says while he bends down in front of the couch and reaches underneath it. I'm seriously confused as to what he could be doing, but I don't wait long. As he rises, he hands me a cylindrical shaped gift. It's about four feet long and must have been a bitch to wrap.

"What is this?"

He collapses back on the couch now that he's done with squats for the day. "Just open it."

This time I don't bother enjoying the moment. Because of how long it is I have to stand up to rip and shred like a good little girl who cannot contain her excitement. When I realize what's inside, I can't hide my surprise either.

"You got me a didgeridoo?" I screech, completely understanding why Calypso jumps up and down so much during the holidays. "This is amazing!"

"Since you're planning your bucket list trip, I figured you could get started early, learning how to play it."

Running my hand down the smooth eucalyptus

wood, I'm amazed by the intricate painting design on it. The didgeridoo has been used for centuries when indigenous Australians created the wind instrument. The sound is like nothing I've ever heard, deep and rich. I've watched videos of some of the most wonderful musicians creating music with it. I've always been fascinated by it and can't believe I'm holding one in my hands. It's the most beautiful thing I've ever seen. And likely the most expensive.

"I can't believe you got me this," I practically whisper, overcome with emotion for the second time in as many minutes. At this moment, I feel almost a "click" in place. Like everything about this, about Matthew, about our situation makes sense. *We* make sense. We understand each other and respect each other. We may even love each other. I mean, really. Nothing says love like an aboriginal wind instrument, right?

Matthew, who is completely oblivious to the existential moment I'm having, is almost as excited as I am. "The guy I got it from explained to me how to make it work."

Confused, I furrow my brow. "Don't you just blow in it?"

"I think there's more to it."

Shrugging, I decide to forgo any instructions he has and just go for it. Placing my lips inside the opening, I take a deep breath and blow.

Aaaand nothing happens.

"Like I said," Matthew says, clearly happy he was

right. "There's more to it."

"Okay, smart ass. What am I doing wrong?"

He chuckles lightly, and I can tell he's enjoying this way too much already. "It's like a vibration noise that goes through it. So you have to blow like this." He presses his lips together and blows, like he's making bubbles in a pool. That doesn't look too hard.

Pressing my lips together, I place them inside the hole again and try my best to blow bubbles.

*Pppppprrrrrrrrrrrbbbbbbbbbbbbb.*

"That sounds like a moose dying," Calypso says and Matthew bursts out laughing.

"I'm doing my best!" I argue and try it again.

*Ppppppprrrrrrrbbbbbbbbbb.*

"What am I doing wrong?" I ask. "Did you give me false instructions?"

"Nope," Matthew says as he reaches across to the coffee table and picks up his phone. "Try again. Only this time, I'm not missing the opportunity to catch it on video."

"You jerk." My words say I'm annoyed, but my eyes say I'm not that upset. "Don't you dare post that on your social media."

He snickers. "No guarantees."

I glare at him which just makes him laugh more. I'm regretting the bubblegum toothpaste. It would serve him right for me to have morning breath.

Closing my eyes, I focus on what my lips need to do, then get in position, and blow.

Once again, it starts out like a dying moose and then suddenly the timbre changes. My eyes widen but I don't dare stop blowing because I'm doing it! I'm playing the didgeridoo!

"You did it! You did it!" Calypso claps and yells as she bounces more.

Raising my hand in victory, I look over at Matthew, still blowing. He's smiling and laughing and hasn't stopped recording yet, the asshole.

Eventually, I run out of air and the noise stops.

"I can't believe I did it!" I gasp, trying to get my bearings while setting my precious new hobby on the floor beside the couch.

"It was pretty impressive."

Without thinking, I leap over the table, straddling him on the couch. "Thank you, thank you, thank you!" I say over and over as I press kisses all over his face, hoping he understands the gravity of my appreciation.

He chuckles and hugs me, not as tight as I would like but I don't think much about it. Until he says, "Um, Carrie? Calypso."

My body stiffens. Oh shit. I forgot there was a kid in the room. Slowly, I turn my head to see if she noticed me attacking her father.

Calypso is no longer jumping. She's standing still. Staring. Like those creepy twins in that haunted hotel movie.

I'm in so much trouble.

As suddenly as I jumped on Matthew, Calypso's face changes to a huge grin and she yells "Family hug!" running and jumping on us just like I did to her dad.

Matthew and I both laugh and begin tickling her, and he blows raspberries on her tummy.

Crisis averted.

And I have a new favorite holiday. Or at least I will. As soon as I crush Matthew at playing dreidel.

# Chapter 27

*Matthew*

When we were kids, my dad always grumbled about the holidays. I never understood how he couldn't love every single minute of the season. The cooler weather, decorating the tree, playing games, and watching holiday movies were something I looked forward to each year. Of course, like most kids I looked forward to Christmas morning. Santa never let us down, always hitting at least one of the big items on our list. He never left anything on the cookie plate other than a few crumbs.

Then I became a father. Sure, the first few years were easy because babies and toddlers are more interested in the boxes and wrapping paper than the gifts. Something changed about two years ago when Calypso realized the joy that is the Christmas List. Not only does she get very specific with her list, she also has a habit of choosing things that either require me to follow instructions for building or have so many damn plastic ties keeping it in the box I spend hours after she opens presents fighting to unpackage them.

Of course, she's passed out on the floor surrounded by paper and ribbon while holding her stuffed Kristoff. Carrie and I did manage to pull her away from the mess long enough to eat a little breakfast and call my parents. Then, she was right back at the mess which gave me time to sneak Carrie into my room and allow her a chance to properly thank me for her gifts with a kiss. Or three.

She surprised the hell out of me when she climbed on top of me and started placing random kisses all over my face after opening her present. I loved having her that close and uninhibited. Her smile was huge and her lips warm as the distance she's kept between us slowly vanished. Something changed with us this morning. I could feel the difference last night under the mistletoe but when I saw her this morning with messy hair and a line on her cheek from the pillow, I was more convinced.

Seeing her in my T-shirt again hit me straight in the gut. And by gut I mean heart. I realized as I held Sven in my hands and she teased me from the doorway that nothing has ever felt more real or right. Having her here with my family, spending the holiday with us and making new memories is something I want again. Not just for holidays but for simple moments. It's fast and we've only just started dating but I also know I'm too old to try and follow some weird society rule for how much time should pass before you know the person is right for you. For your child. Your family.

"Mother fuc—" Biting my bottom lip, I cut off my outburst before tossing the offending toy onto the cushion next to me. Why is everything on children's toys hard plastic? Seriously, I think I have more cuts and scrapes from these things than I would sticking my hands in a drawer of knives.

Glancing around the room, I regret not taking Carrie up on her offer to help clean up before she left. There is so much paper. Note to self for next year— gift bags. With a groan, I begrudgingly push myself up from the couch and grab a trash bag from the kitchen. The process is quick and I manage to have the room back to normal before making my way to the kitchen to tackle the chaos I left it in after breakfast.

With a final wipe of the counter, I toss the sponge in the sink and turn the light off. I should finish with those toys, but I also really want a shower and out of these snowflake pajamas. I'm a huge fan of lazy days in loungewear but thick sparkly pants are not the same thing.

Before I can make my way out of the kitchen, my phone chimes with a text message.

C: <photo attachment>

Opening the attachment I bark out a laugh of Luke on a shelf next to wooden Luke with his head cocked to the side.

Me: Someone looks confused. Or con-

```
templating squirrelicide.

C: Squirrelicide?

Me: Yeah, homicide by squirrel.

C: OMG! You are ridiculous. And
may be right. He has been staring
at his cartoon self for about 4
solid minutes.

C: Thanks again for including me
in your holiday. I had a good time.

Me: You're welcome. I think you
should come back over. We'll eat
popcorn and watch movies. Give you
the full Roberts holiday experi-
ence.
```

The three dots bounce around as she types and deletes her response. I know she wants to be here with us doing absolutely nothing, but something is still holding her back.

```
C: What makes you think I'm not
already living that awesome life?
I'm on my second movie and moved on
from popcorn to ice cream. You're
behind, pal.

Me: Ah, I see how it is. I've al-
ready been replaced by Ben AND Jer-
ry. You've broken my heart, babe.

C: Oh are we onto pet names, Schnoo-
kums?

Me: You bet your sweet ass. I'm go-
```

```
ing to hop in the shower. I'll call
you later.
```

With a huge smile on my face and some actual pep in my step, I make my way down the hall and to the bathroom. Now I need a good pet name for Carrie. It has to be epic and entirely ridiculous.

"Daddy, you are the most beautiful princess."

"Honey, I'm a grown man. I would be a queen."

Sighing, my pint-sized beautician snaps a barrette into place on top of my head. It's her third attempt to fasten the plastic clip, and I have no doubt there are just as many bruises on my scalp. She scowls at my proclamation before stepping back to assess her handi-work.

"Maybe you should just stay a boy."

I don't bother agreeing as she abandons me and starts talking to her assistant, Kristoff. Slowly, I un-tangle the accessory from my hair and drop it into the box to my right. Kicking my feet up on the table, I grab the remote control and flip through the channels, stop-ping on the news when the doorbell rings.

"Who is that? Maybe Santa forgot to leave one of my presents?"

Chuckling I shake my head. "I don't think that's the case."

Rising from the couch, I make my way to the front

door and hope it isn't carolers. I'm all about the holiday spirit but standing on my porch while strangers belt out holiday tunes is awkward. I never know what to do and I feel more like a dance club bouncer than a single dad playing dress up with his daughter.

Opening the door, I suddenly wish it was three groups of carolers than the surprise greeting me.

"Surprise!"

"Delilah. What are you doing here?"

"Is that anyway to greet someone on Christmas?"

Dumbfounded, I stand there for a few beats, my eyes blinking as I take in the woman who I spent one night with and received a lifetime of blessings. Her blonde hair is loose and carefree like her spirit. A long floral dress pools around her feet and I wonder briefly if she's even wearing shoes. That would be just like her to walk the streets of Texas barefoot so she could be one with the earth.

Shaking off my assessment of her, I step to the side and welcome her into the house. She moves through the doorway and whispers what sounds like a prayer under her breath as she sets a large bag onto the floor.

"You didn't answer my question, Delilah."

"I wanted to see Calypso. It is Christmas after all."

"We talked about this the last time you dropped in unannounced."

"Please don't be angry with me. I know I should have called but there wasn't time. My heart needed to be here with her today and I just couldn't stay away. Plus I only have two days off from my Dance Across Texas tour and didn't have any time to spare."

I don't bother asking about the tour. With her, there's no telling what kind of activity it really is. I'm sure it's dancing—that is her profession. But I never know if she's dancing backup for someone, dancing in a festival, or is riding in an old VW van circa Woodstock with people who still long for the days of making love not war.

No, I don't ask because I'm irritated. This is just like her, using her heart and soul as a basis for dropping in without discussing it with me first. Like I can tell her not to follow the parental need to be with Calypso. There's no way that's possible because it's how I feel everyday with our daughter.

Sighing, I force myself to put up a good front because there's no use arguing. It's only two days. "I'm not angry. Just surprised. Be prepared, I think her shrieking has increased ten decibels in the last month."

As we enter the living room, I clear my throat to get Sprite's attention. She doesn't react, completely enthralled with making her stuffed squirrel the next princess. Barrettes and all.

"Sprite, you have a visitor."

Turning her head our direction, her mouth falls wide open with shock all over her face.

"Mommy! You came!"

Jumping up, she runs to Delilah, those shrieks and

giggles louder and happier than I've heard in a long time. Wrapped in each other's arms they sway back and forth, talking a mile a minute. Suddenly feeling like a third wheel, I move to the kitchen and grab a beer from the refrigerator. I manage two pulls from the bottle before I'm interrupted.

"Daddy! Daddy! Look at my new wings."

I turn my head and smile at my little fairy. Strapped to her back is a pair of purple sparkly wings that she's trying to look at herself but only managing to spin in a circle. It's a little like Olaf when he chases his tail.

"Those are beautiful. You look like a real-life fairy."

"I know!" And she's so humble. "Will you take a picture for Carrie?"

Nodding, I grab my phone and snap a quick picture. Knowing that Sprite is thinking of Carrie makes me happy and a little sad at the same time. She shouldn't be thinking of another woman when her mom, the one she doesn't see but a couple times a year at most, is here with her. Before I can send the text, Delilah joins us. Squatting down to Sprite's height, she adjusts the straps before standing.

"I should be going. Would it be okay if I came by again tomorrow? Maybe take Calypso for a few hours?"

"You should sleep over! We could have a slumber party!"

With two pairs of identical eyes focused on me I

don't even hesitate before I answer. It's not a battle I'm going to win anyway, and it's not like she doesn't normally stay here when she pops in. "I'll just change the sheets in the guest room." Or as I prefer to think of it—Carrie's room.

"Actually, I prefer sleeping on the floor."

"Close to the earth?" I ask.

"Nah, my back has been bothering me and it's the only way I've managed a decent night's sleep."

Smiling, I go to the closet and grab some blankets and pillows and place them in Calypso's room while the two fairies giggle in the other room.

# Chapter 28

*Carrie*

I have found myself humming Christmas carols all morning long. Strange, for a woman who never once grew up so much as humming a holiday tune. Not strange for the girl who just spent her first Christmas with the boy she likes.

Yes, I know that sounds very middle school, but that's kind of how I feel. Giddy, anxious, butterflies in my stomach, resisting the urge to call him every minute of every day so I can giggle over the phone.

At least I didn't have to hold myself back from driving back over last night, knowing I had no way to get there. Who knew there was a silver lining to losing the rental car keys?

I figured they would show up by now, but no. I'm officially going to be late for work if they don't end up in my hand in approximately four seconds. Plus, I'm sure the rental car company will charge me an arm and a leg for a replacement.

"Luke? Did you steal my keys, sweet boy?"

My red-haired companion ignores me, too busy buzzing and flapping his tail at Sven, who is wobbling around his cage, completely oblivious to the challenge being thrown down outside his cage. This whole dance is as bad as watching the rodent version of West Side Story. The original version. Not the remake. Although, arguably dance-fighting is how I do it too, so I have no room to judge.

Flinging some clean rags that I haven't yet taken off the table, I cuss under my breath and realize I don't have a choice but to call in to work and let them know I'm going to be late. Dialing the number, I prop the phone on my shoulder and get on my hands and knees to crawl on the floor. Maybe this vantage point will work better.

"Thank you for calling Critter Keepers and Wildlife Rescue, where we rescue your critters. This is Jamie. How can I help you?"

"Hey. It's me."

"You could have interrupted me before I spilled out that whole obnoxious spiel."

Well. Someone's already in a cranky mood.

"Already getting calls about the beloved Christmas morning pets, huh?"

"Three of them. Why don't people invest in stuffed

animals instead of assuming a puppy won't pee on their carpet?" she whines. "I feel like it's a given they're going to destroy things. Does no one buy pet odor remover before bringing a new pet home?"

Leaning down, I look under the couch. "Ah ha!" I shout.

"Uh… did I just remind you to put pet odor remover on your list or something?"

Pushing myself off the floor, I take a quick deep breath. I really need to start exercising. "No. Sorry. I found my car keys. That's why I'm calling. Can you tell the boss man I'm going to be late?"

"On one condition." I roll my eyes because there is no telling what it will be. "Bring me coffee. Preferably the Irish kind."

I snort a laugh and quickly guide Luke back in his cage so I can gather my stuff. "I know you hate getting stuck on front desk duty, but I think drinking on the job might be frowned upon. However, candy cane mint hot chocolate is a good alternative."

"Perfect. I can pretend it's Goldshläger." The gagging sound I make is loud enough for her to hear. "Hey now! I love those gold flakes."

"Sometimes I wonder how you never became a sorority girl."

"They wouldn't take me. I'm too much of a wild woman."

Ohmygod, she's ridiculous. "Okay, Annie Oakley—"

"Who?"

"I'll be there soon. Don't cuss out any new pet owners before I get there."

"No guarantees," she says, and as we hang up I have no doubt she's going to bite her tongue all day long.

It's not that working the day after Christmas is hard. There's almost no foot traffic, most people exhausted from their celebrations or back to work after a few days off. There are just a lot of calls from people wanting advice on how to handle their new pet and where to get supplies. I get it. It's like learning how to take care of a brand-new baby. If that baby does its bathroom business wherever it sees fit and chews on anything in its path. In a word, it's overwhelming. But Jamie isn't the most patient person in the world when it comes to mammals of the human variety, and it's ten times worse when she's directing people to pet stores for things like toys, food, and dog beds. Lucky me, I get to hear her bitch about it all day. At least I get to go in late today.

Tossing my bag on the passenger seat, I crank the engine of my car. I still have two stops to make before getting to the shelter so fingers crossed the day after shopping traffic is light.

I haven't even made it to the stop sign when my phone rings. Glancing at the Bluetooth screen, I'm surprised to see Celeste calling.

Pressing the button to connect, I don't bother with a real greeting. We're cool like that. "What in the world are you doing calling me on December twenty-sixth? Aren't you with your family?"

"That's exactly why I'm hiding in my room making business phone calls." I have no doubt she used air quotes in that sentence.

"Is your mother already pressuring you to give up on your dream and move home?"

It's a long running conversation in Celeste's family—how working in the theater doesn't pay the bills. It's a constant source of irritation for her, but oddly she sounds more chipper than she should for someone avoiding her mother.

"Oh honey, that started the second I dropped my suitcase in the front hall. I just ignore her and ask about her latest beading project. That usually distracts her enough to move on."

I'm not at all surprised. Celeste and her mother have the weirdest relationship. They're best friends and worst enemies all at the same time. It's a dynamic I don't understand, so I gave up trying a long time ago. If it works for them, what's it to me?

"Anyway," she continues, "Anna said yes!"

It takes me a second to remember what she's talking about. Finally it hits me.

"Oh, Anna! Your roommate. Sorry that took me a second. I'm running late so my brain is racing," I explain since it's true. My thoughts have been spinning all morning. Of course, most of them are because of Matthew, but I'm not ready to share that little detail yet. We'll just let her think I'm frazzled because of the hot mess I am on the regular. "So she's trading reviews for ad space?"

"Yep. But she doesn't want to be known by her musician name on the blog."

"Understandable." Not that either of us use our real name either. Stalkers come in all industries. It's better to be safe than sorry.

"She's working on a couple of things already. It appears our website was impressive enough to the powers that be at a big music studio, that they went ahead and added her to their advance review list." Celeste giggles with delight and I don't blame her. It's hard to get publishers to give advance copies of books. I can't imagine how much harder it would be for Anna since we don't have a page on our site for music yet. She either knows someone important or our site really is that good.

I'm going with the latter, because it makes me feel like the hard work is worth it.

"That's really awesome. Plus, it gives us a little more breathing room on our own reviews." Which just means I have more time to hang out with my new boyfriend, or whatever I should call him.

Shit. What should I call him? Are we exclusive? Are we just dating? Is this a friends with very limited benefits situation? I guess we need to have some sort of conversation, which I actually dread. It makes me nervous to address things like this. All my insecurities like to come out to play. Stupid overactive brain.

Celeste and I chat a few minutes more about random business issues and how much eggnog she drank to get through yesterday. I don't have much time though, I still have a coffee run to make, and I'm a hundred yards from my first stop.

"Hey," I interrupt as she continues her rant on the flight delay that's already holding her hostage in her mother's house for six hours longer than she would like. "I sympathize with your plight, but I'm almost to my first stop, so I need to let you go."

"You aren't just going to use the drive-thru for coffee?"

Furrowing my brow, I dread fessing up, but I also feel a bit put on the spot. "I'm dropping a book off to Calypso."

"Calypso?" It takes her a second and I can practically hear when the light bulb goes off over her head. "Matthew's daughter? Ohmygod, are you lying to me and playing hooky to hang out with him?"

"Stop shouting. I'm in my car and the neighborhood can hear you."

"This is just so exciting," she continues at a volume I still find to be too high. "Your first fake illness to avoid work."

"First, I am not playing hooky. And even if I was, why are you so surprised? Really, it's not a big deal.

Yesterday I told Calypso about—"

Her screech makes my ears ring and although it makes no sense, I blink my eyes rapidly like that will help my ability to hear again. "You spent Christmas with them! It was your first Christmas and with Matthew Roberts!"

"I swear, if you make that awful noise one more time I will never speak to you again. Anna and I will vote you off the island, or blog, whatever. You know I don't celebrate Christmas. It was just a regular day for me and meant almost nothing," I argue half-heartedly because we both know I'm lying.

"So what kind of book are you dropping off? Is it some bedtime stories for you to read to her? Now I need to know all the things."

I sigh dramatically, but this is the part I don't actually mind telling her because it's kind of funny. "It's a book about Hanukkah decorations for kids. Calypso has decided that since Christmas is over and Santa is gone, she's converting to Judaism."

Celeste bursts out laughing. "She wants eight days of presents, doesn't she?"

I laugh along with her because she's right. "She has this whole intricate plan about how she'll convert back to Christianity again right before Christmas and then celebrate Hanukkah after every year. For six years old, I have to admit she's figured out a solid way to work the holiday system. Besides," I continue, "it's kind of fun to teach her some of my traditions. I've been lax the last few years, being so far from home. It's bad enough my mother is digging deep to hit me with some major guilt about not attending temple regularly. It was nice to talk about the holiday and made me miss the traditions I spent my childhood celebrating."

"And Matthew kicked your ass at dreidel," she deadpans, because she knows me so well.

"It was beginner's luck!" I burst in mock outrage. "I've got five more days to prove I'm still the reigning champion."

"Oh yeah. You've got it bad," she says under her breath. "But I'm warning you now, don't tell that child about your bat mitzvah."

"Oh hell no," I say without hesitation. "Matthew would never forgive me if he had to spend the next seven years listening to her plan the biggest thirteenth birthday party any child who regularly converts her religion based on presents has ever had."

"I'm sure you were bad enough at that age."

I pretend not to hear her as I pull in the driveway.

"Anyway, I've gotta run. Boss man is going to be unhappy I'm late so I need to make this quick."

"All right, all right. I guess I'll go find some more eggnog." She sighs. "I'll talk to you next week so we can hash out those updated ad rates for the new year."

I turn the car off, effectively disconnecting the Bluetooth and grab the book from my bag. It's the same book my mother gave me as a kid when I wanted to make my own decorations and needed step by step instructions. I even brought some extra construction paper and new markers. I'm really excited that Calypso has taken an interest in this. Even if she doesn't decide the Jewish faith is for her, the fact that she wants to know more about it is pretty cool.

Racing to the front door, I knock quickly and wait. No one answers, and I don't hear any movement inside. Weird. Matthew's truck is in the driveway, and I know he doesn't work today.

I opt to ring the doorbell, thinking maybe he's in the garage working out and just left the garage door down. This time, the door unlocks and opens but it's not Matthew who answers. It's a woman.

She's tall and lithe with the perfect hourglass shape. Her long blonde hair is disheveled in that sexy way that makes you think of "just had toe-curling sex" hair.

And she's wearing nothing but Matthew's T-shirt.

The same one I wore the last two times I've spent the night. I know because it still has a small black stain on the hem.

I drop my gaze to her bare legs and wiggling toes painted red. As my eyes lift, I can barely focus on her beautiful face, my vision hazy through the emotions building inside me. Instead, I glance past her into the living room and that's when my heart stops completely.

There on the floor, completely forgotten and being played with by Olaf is Calypso's stuffed squirrel, Kristoff.

"Can I help you?" She asks pulling my attention back to why I'm here.

"I was… is—?"

"Are you here for Matt? He's not available."

Swallowing down the lump in my throat, I hand over the book. "Um… can you please give this to Matthew?"

The unknown woman takes it from me and looks down, questioning what it is and why I'm giving it to her. ""How to Make Hanukkah Decorations"? He's not Jewish. Or crafty."

Licking my lips, I force myself to breathe normally, even though my lungs have essentially stopped working. I feel like I can't get enough air, and I just want her to take the book and close the door so I can leave without looking like the freak I feel like I am right now.

I should have seen this coming. I should have known. Technically we've only been on one official date. Hell, we've never even defined our relationship. There was no discussion of exclusivity. So then why do I feel like my heart has just been sliced in two?

"No, I know. Spri… Calypso wanted to do the crafts so I brought it for her to see."

"Oh." That seems to make sense to her so she stands up straighter, the shirt riding up so I can see even more of her perfectly tanned legs. Legs that I'm sure were wrapped around Matthew's waist because mine never have been. "Is that for her too?" She points to the plastic bag with the supplies I'm holding.

"Huh? Oh, yes." I hold it out awkwardly, still stunned enough I can't seem to make words make sense.

She takes it out of my hands slowly, then cocks her head at me in question. "Is that all?"

I fight back the tears that want to fall because they have no right to be there. It's my fault I fell for Matthew. It's my fault I let my guard down. This is why I don't put out. Because these emotions would be a hundred times worse if I'd given that part of me to him.

"That's all," I whisper, my voice practically giving out.

"Okay then." She backs into the house, eyeing me cautiously as she slowly closes the door. "Bye." And the door is shut. With me still standing there staring at it.

I am so stupid.

I guess I was right to believe the first impression people make. Because I got snowed. Again.

# Chapter 29

*Matthew*

It doesn't matter how many times I tell her, my daughter refuses to accept that while Olaf found Sven it doesn't mean his barking always equals more squirrel babies. Of course, it doesn't mean there aren't any either, but I won't tell her that. Since I'm a sucker for her big eyes and how worried she was for the potential dangers unknown animal babies may encounter, I'm on my hands and knees crawling around in the dirt. Again.

"Dammit," I shout as a stick pokes me in the knee.

"Daddy, don't say bad words like that. You could scare the babies."

"Honey," I begin as I stand and brush the dirt from my legs. "There are no babies. I told you, Olaf was being beat up by a bird. She probably didn't like the way he was poking around and was afraid he was after her nest."

Disappointment is written all over her face as she kicks the ground. I can't wait to tell Carrie about her little wildlife rescuer in training. Maybe I should talk to her about letting us come hang out with her one day so Sprite can see other rescues at Critter Keepers.

"Can I go shower now? I'm still sweaty from my run earlier and now I have a layer of dirt on top of that."

"Sorry, Daddy. I thought we were going to save a life today."

Shaking my head I motion for her to move toward the house. "Again, your Papa and I are having a talk about your screen time. No more live rescue shows."

Chattering away, she jumps through four different topics before we make it back inside the house. Since I refused to let her join me on the ground, she doesn't need to do anything except wash her hands, which she rushes to do while I kick my shoes off outside.

The sound of another female voice in the house startles me for a minute, especially because it isn't Carrie. I almost forgot Delilah was here. When I woke this morning, intent on a quick workout in the garage gym, she was already up meditating in the middle of the living room. At least I think it was meditation. She was sitting on a towel with her legs crossed and eyes closed as her lips moved like she was speaking. Only, there was no sound, not even a whisper.

As soon as I completed one set of bicep curls, she

appeared in the garage and told me she was here if I wanted to go for a run. I happily took her up on the offer and pounded out a solid six-mile trek.

"Olaf, no!" I shout as the four-legged monster runs through the room with Kristoff in his mouth. Chasing him, I catch him long enough to pull the stuffed animal from his mouth. "Out! You're a bad boy."

"Is that not his toy?"

Turning, I don't reply as I take in her ensemble.

"Why are you wearing that?" My tone conveys my displeasure in her choice of clothing. Or lack thereof.

"I needed to do some laundry and didn't have anything to wear. This was on the bed in the guest room so I threw it on. I was just going to put my things in the dryer. I should've asked but you were gone. I'm sorry."

Closing my eyes, I release a long breath before I respond. It isn't her fault that I now consider that Carrie's shirt. Or that I hadn't washed it yet because it smelled like her. Hey, I've read some of the books I'm on the cover of. Men can sniff laundry too.

Centering myself I try to refocus. It isn't a big deal that she's wearing it. It's only a shirt. I can wash it. And if everything keeps going the way it has been, Carrie's scent will be back on it soon enough.

"A woman came by and dropped that off," she says, pointing at the kitchen counter. "She was a little odd, not really talking and just standing there."

I don't bother to hide the smile on my face as I see

the book and bag of crafting supplies. "Carrie. Sprite will love this. Did she say anything else?"

"No. I told her you were busy and then she just kind of stared at me. I didn't realize it was Carrie, but by that look on your face I guess it was."

"Yep."

"I wish I had known. I would have invited her in. Calypso couldn't stop talking about her. She sounds fantastic. Well, except the pet squirrels. Who does that?"

Chuckling I can't help but agree with her. Although, I can't imagine her having any other sort of pet. "Only my girl." And then it hits me. "Wait. You didn't answer the door like that, did you?" I ask my eyes wide as I realize exactly how little she's wearing and how bad this could look.

"Matt, I just told you I was doing laundry. What's wrong with you? Your color is looking a little off. It may be your aura."

"Tell me you told Carrie you were here for Sprite. That she didn't see you dressed like that," I accuse, motioning toward her lack of clothing.

Seeming to only realize how she's dressed and what that may look like, she gasps. "Oh heavens. You don't think she thought…?"

"Of course she did," I try hard not to roar. "You're a half-naked dancer who answered the door and said I was unavailable. Did you tell her your name or anything so she *wouldn't* assume the worst?"

"It never occurred to me. Matt, you must go to her. Or I can—"

"God no! I think you've done enough. Okay. I need to think. Shit. We haven't even defined our relationship. I mean, obviously we're together. There was the mistletoe. And Christmas Eve. Christmas morning. The dreidel smack talking."

"What's wrong with Daddy?" a sweet voice asks. "Why is he walking in a circle like Olaf when he has to go out? Does Daddy have to pee?"

"Honey, your dad seems to be having a breakdown. Why don't you go grab my bag? I have some crystals in there we can use to help him."

Glaring at her, I stop and look at Calypso, who is staring at her mother like she's grown two heads.

"You're not doing anything but hanging out with our daughter while I go and talk to my girlfriend. And maybe confirm she actually wants to be called my girlfriend."

Without another word, I head straight for the shower and say a little prayer Carrie isn't spiraling.

Pulling into the parking lot of Critter Keepers, I notice immediately how empty the place is today. Only a few cars are in the parking lot, Carrie's parked in front of the main door. The entire time I was in the shower and during my drive here, I've tossed around how best to approach the topic of Delilah.

It never occurred to me to call her or even text her last night to let her know I had an impromptu house guest. Hell, I don't even let my own mother know unless it comes up in conversation. That's just how long it's been since I've had to think of anyone else or their feelings other than my daughter, and how insignificant her drop-ins are. The reality is, I don't even think of Delilah as anything other than an acquaintance. We were never in a relationship, and while it was a struggle to accept her choices early on, we've grown into a mutual respect for our roles in our daughter's life. For years, she's dropped hints that I needed to find someone special, and I have no doubt she'd love Carrie.

Kind of like I'm starting to do. She's everything I didn't know I needed for my little family, and I don't want to lose that over the randomness that is my baby mama.

I know my girl well enough to be fairly certain she's inside listing every worst-case scenario about Delilah and me. Here goes nothing. Pulling the key from the ignition, I step out of the truck and walk toward the large gray building and the two large glass doors. Tugging one open, I take a deep breath and step inside.

"Well, well lookee who's here."

"Good morning, Jamie."

"She's losing her shit."

That's not encouraging. To be expected, but not encouraging. "I figured. It's not what she thinks, I swear. Delilah is Calypso's mother. She's here for my daughter. Nothing more."

Nodding, Jamie picks up the phone and pushes a button. Her eyes squint like she's attempting to glare at me, but the small lift of her lips tells me she believes me. Thank goodness someone will be on my side.

"I need you up here. Uh huh. No. Nobody cares if you have snot on your shirt, Carrie. This is a rescue facility. Tell them it's squirrel poop. I have to pee and you need to cover the desk. No, you can't use the phone back there. Be a team player and get up here."

Jamie rolls her eyes as she returns the receiver to the cradle. Not saying anything, she just stares at me. Assessing. It's unnerving, which is strange since I spend much of my spare time with someone holding a camera staring at me. Unable to take the awkwardness, I turn my back on her and stare out the window.

When a door opens, I hear a gasp and a mumbled "crap on a cracker" behind me. Slowly, I spin to take in my beautiful girlfriend. Her hair is piled on top of her head haphazardly and there is a large spot on the front of her blue scrubs top. But it's the sadness in her eyes that I really notice. Crap on a cracker is right.

Carrie sniffs and slowly turns to her friend. At least her sadness changed to menace. "You are dead to me, Jamie."

"Sorry not sorry."

I stand with my hands in my pockets as Jamie leaves us alone, slipping through the door Carrie just closed. Offering her a small smile, I take a tentative step forward and when she doesn't move, I take another. Seemingly safe, I close the distance between us and rest my hands on the counter.

"Thank you for the book. Sprite already had it spread out on the table when I left."

"I'm glad. My mom gave me that book when I was about her age. It's very special to me."

"Carrie, about Delilah—"

"That was Delilah?" she interrupts, and I can see the wheels turning in her head. Maybe I have a shot to clear this up after all.

"Yeah. She showed up late last night out of the blue. Apparently, her dance tour is on hiatus for the holidays."

Carrie nods and folds her arms over her chest. Okay, maybe this won't be as easy to fix as I hoped.

"She called you Matt."

Confused, I furrow my brow.

"When I was there, she called you Matt."

"That doesn't surprise me. No matter how many times I tell her I don't go by a nickname, she doesn't listen. There's nothing going on." I'm practically begging her to understand. "I'm sure it looked bad, but I swear she's only here to see Sprite. I didn't even know she was coming, and she never has a place to stay."

"Come on, you can't be serious. I saw how she was dressed. In my… I mean, your shirt and nothing else. She's beautiful and you have a child together…"

Rounding the counter, I step into her space and grab her hand to turn her toward me. Her bottom lip is tugged between her teeth, gaze to the floor.

"Babe, listen to me. I swear to you she is only my friend, and I use that term loosely. It's important for Sprite to see her mom. I believe that. Do I wish she was more reliable and called in advance? Absolutely. But like the name thing, Delilah does what Delilah wants. I promise I'll talk to her and tell her she has to call first. No more just dropping in."

"You don't have to do that. It's not my business. We're not even—"

"What? Together? Yeah, we are. I want to be with you. We want you to be part of our life, Carrie. My life really is simple even if it looks complicated from the outside. I'm just a single dad who has an amazing little girl and a dog that fancies himself a squirrel saver. Until I met you, I had no idea something was missing. I'm so sorry you were hurt."

She grants me a smile. It's barely there, but I'll take it.

"I swear if you don't accept his apology I'm going to dump Chris and take him for myself."

We both stare down at the phone on the desk. While I bark out a laugh, Carrie groans and picks up the receiver.

"I cannot believe you put it on speaker to listen to us. You're an awful person, Jamie!"

I laugh again as she rolls her eyes and not so carefully puts the phone back on the receiver. I'm sure her inability to hang up right away has more to do with the obnoxious noise it'll provide on the other end of the line than it does with clumsiness.

"Look, I know you're conflicted, but I want you to know that Delilah will never stay at the house again. Or, if she needs to I'll have my mom come over, and I'll stay at her house. Or yours. It's about boundaries and something I should have done long ago. I just never had a reason to think about it until now."

"That's a lot to ask of you," she says as I take her hand again, lifting it to my lips and placing a kiss to the knuckle.

"You're not asking. Besides, it's what you do when someone you love is hurt. I should let you get back to work. Call me when you want to talk. Delilah will be gone by dinner."

Not giving her an opening to question what I've said, or the fact that I just dropped a little word I never planned to speak out loud, I move quickly from the space and out the door. I never said I wasn't a little bit of a coward.

# Chapter 30

## *Carrie*

As predicted, Delilah left town before I could meet her beyond that one awkward encounter. Part of me was disappointed she was gone. I would have liked to feel her out more, preferably while she was wearing pants. And a parka. Maybe a snowsuit. Anything to cover up her long legs and tiny waist.

The majority of me, though, is still glad she left. No matter how hard I try, no matter how much I remind myself that she gave birth to Calypso, it still feels like she took away something that's mine.

Crazy, right? I don't own Matthew or his family. I'm not a part of it. But a small piece of me was enjoying pretending I was. And now it feels like I'm back on the outside.

Add onto that, the entire incident has forced my thinly veiled insecurities to rear their ugly irrational heads. I know logically that Matthew isn't the same guy I mistook with all of those rumors, but logic tends to take a backseat when a barrage of negative emotions have been triggered. And boy, do I mean triggered.

Matthew and I still talk and text every day, but it feels different somehow. Like I'm forcing myself to play the role of happy girlfriend, when really I want to hyperventilate and cling to Matthew's shirt begging him to not break up with me. Not to break my heart.

I have no idea why my inner child is the age and maturity level of a middle school girl. But I really wish she would grow up and be the independent woman we've been working on for all these years. Instead, she's currently sitting on the couch by herself on New Year's Eve.

I know Matthew has something model related going on tonight and Calypso is with her grandma, but it still sucks to be sitting here wallowing in my own ridiculous thoughts. I would much rather be spending time with them. And clinging to his shirt.

*Stop it, Carrie. Focus on the good things—you've got your boys Ben and Jerry, your boys Luke and Sven, and your boy Ryan Seacrest on the boob tube. Life could be worse…*

The doorbell rings, which is odd for this time of night. It shouldn't be my next-door neighbor yet. He isn't typically drunk this early on New Year's Eve. I don't expect him to wander up to my doorstep, thinking my house is his for at least another three hours.

Ryan Seacrest announces yet another musical guest

who catches my eye, so I'm only halfway paying attention when I open the door—until I see who it is.

Matthew is standing a few feet back holding a sign that says, "Don't talk. Just wait." I furrow my brow because this is odd, made even odder by the fact that Calypso is trying to take a video with his phone. From this angle, it looks like he's doing a live video, but I can't really tell since Calypso keeps moving the phone around. For their sake, I hope this isn't actually live and Matthew can edit out the motion sickness parts later.

Holding up his finger to me, Matthew turns to the phone. "Hey Sprite. What number is on the top of the screen?"

She pulls it closer to her, no doubt making someone need some Dramamine. "One, four, three, five."

"Thanks, baby girl. There are one thousand, four hundred thirty-five of you out there witnessing my declaration. Pay close attention, though. This next part is going to require some reading."

I cock my head because I'm so confused as to what's happening right now. And then he drops the poster board on the ground revealing one behind it. It says, "This is my public declaration."

"Ohmygod, he's doing the *Love Actually* thing," I mutter, throwing my hand over my mouth in shock. I can only imagine how wide my eyes are at this moment. Is this really happening? Am I dreaming? Did I drink more than my neighbor and am having a hallucination and any moment someone is going to wonder why the crazy lady is standing outside of her house staring at nothingness?

But then he drops another poster board, never taking his eyes off me, and I know this is real. I can only imagine the number of red hearts that are floating across the screen. This is the type of model behavior his followers love.

Looking down at the poster board it reads, "Because I am officially a taken man."

Another drop.

"You have impressed me…"

*Drop.*

"You have beguiled me…"

*Drop.*

"You have loved my child like your own."

I'm not sure if he's referring to Calypso or Sven but either way, happy tears start rolling down my face, until he drops another sign revealing two pictures… one of his human child and one of our rodent child. I can't stop the laugh, and the tears keep coming. Especially when he tosses aside yet another piece.

"And now you have taken my heart."

*Drop.*

"No sex required."

Fingers crossed none of our mutual friends are watching because I will never live that one down.

*Drop.*

"Since tonight is the end of one year…"

*Drop.*

"And the beginning of all things new…

*Drop.*

"And because I know how much you need to know I'm serious…"

*Drop.*

"I solemnly swear in front of all these people…"

*Drop.*

"I"

*Drop.*

"Love"

*Drop.*

"You."

My whole body is shaking, and I can't stop the tears, but in a weird way, I don't want to. What I'm feeling now isn't fear. It's the feeling of my heart breaking wide open, spilling out with all the love I feel for this man and his beautiful daughter.

I try hard to speak, but nothing comes out so instead I just mouth, "I love you too."

The last of the signs goes fluttering to the ground as Matthew races to me. His fingers dive into my hair as he pulls me to him and devours my lips with his. His tongue invades my mouth in the most intense, passionate, welcome kiss I've ever had in my life. He kisses me like he's been starved for me and I think in many ways, he was. For our entire relationship—from the bar at the NANA awards until now—I've held back. I've guarded my heart and a piece of myself.

No longer. There is no doubt Matthew is in this relationship for the long haul. Any final reservations I have fade away.

Finally pulling away, Matthew rests his forehead against mine and I whisper, "Just to be clear... I'm still not putting out."

I feel the laugh rumble through his body. "I never expected you to. But what do you say we officially go public with this relationship anyway? No hiding. Just us, shouting from the rooftops that we're it for each other."

I smile and nod, because that's exactly the confirmation I need.

Somehow, his smile is even bigger than mine. Turning to Sprite, he reaches his hand out for his phone and then frowns. "What are you doing there, kiddo?"

She's pointing the phone straight at the ground, attempting to zoom in and out.

"There's an ant, Daddy. I wanted all the people to see him go marching one-by-one."

I nuzzle my face into his neck, laughing at her randomness. Matthew chuckles, too, and flicks his fingers at her impatiently.

"That's really amazing but I need my phone real

quick."

Calypso sighs but complies and goes right back to observing her new friend, this time with her naked eye. Matthew, on the other hand, struggles to get his phone positioned since he's only using one hand. The other one is around my waist and securely holding me to him.

Eventually, he gets situated and the screen flipped around. "Sorry about that folks. She was the only cameraman I could get at the last second. Not bad for a six-year-old, but my apologies if you got motion sickness from all the movement."

I lift my head and look at the screen, noting that there are even more people watching now than there were a few minutes ago. I'm not surprised. People love a good romance. Add a hot single dad with abs to the mix and we're all goners.

"Some of you recognize this beautiful woman." He glances at me and quickly back to the camera. "Or you might just recognize her name. This is Carrie Mibooks, and she runs the Literary Arts website and blog, which you've probably heard of. If you haven't, you need to get on her website immediately. Her reviews are fantastic."

I shake my head, not embarrassed but not really sure what I'm supposed to be doing right now. I'm not usually the one in front of the camera. This is all new to me. It feels good. It feels transparent. But it also feels a little out there for someone like me.

"I just want to publicly say," Matthew continues, "that I love her. She's amazing. She's perfection. And she's mine."

I watch as the heart emojis go crazy, floating across the screen by the dozens.

Which is exactly how I feel right now too.

# Epilogue

*Twelve Months Later*

## Matthew

It amazes me the things a person will do for love. Some will scale mountains while others will watch a movie that normally they would never give the time of day, all out of the gesture of love.

Of course, there are different types of love: platonic, parental, and romantic. When it comes to friends, I have found myself bellying up to a bar to celebrate a birthday and even a retirement.

For my daughter, there is no sacrifice large enough. I will slay a dragon for Sprite or let her paint my fingernails. No matter how grand or simple the request, I'm always there to show her how much I love her.

Then there's the romantic gesture of love. How we

show the woman, or man, the depth of our love for them. Most of my past relationships have been short and honestly not falling into the "relationship" category in the first place so my experience is limited. Sure, I've watched my share of romantic movies, both the serious and the funny, and I can usually predict the way a character will express their feelings and commitment to the other. I've been accused of ruining a perfectly good movie with my need to "rip apart a beautiful and romantic moment." That's Carrie's opinion. I think these screenwriters need to read more books and step out of their comfort zone with expressions of love.

When I decided to claim Carrie as mine, I went about it in a very public fashion. Something she gave me grief over for a few weeks. Specifically whenever one of the social media followers would tag her in a comment or post. The love of my life, or second love after my daughter, is a private person. Putting herself out to the world has been difficult for her, but she also accepts that it's part of my job as a cover model. More importantly, she knows I would never do anything to hurt her. Although, when she not so subtlety asked me about how many views the video had received, I knew she liked it a little more than she was letting on. That's why when she proclaimed *she* would never do anything to embarrass me like I did to her with my live video, I decided to put all my cards on the table anyway. In an epic fashion.

"Daddy, I don't think Olaf is happy."

I turn my attention from the mirror and take in my

little princess and her sidekick. Well, he would be her snowman but he seems to have figured out how to remove his costume. Great. I have spent weeks fixing our costumes from Halloween for this night and in just five minutes he's already messing up my plan.

"Looks like we're going to have to do this without him."

Calypso gasps and her eyes widen to the size of half dollars. Or not.

"Okay, maybe he can still come with us, after all it was because of him we found our way to Carrie."

"Olaf you are a bad boy, and Sven is going to throw nuts at you for messing with the costume."

She's not wrong. At Calypso's request, when Sven was old enough to be released into the trees, we did it in my front yard. We toyed with releasing him in the back, but it takes some time for young squirrels to stay in the trees and we didn't want Olaf to mess with him.

As predicted, Sven came back every day for a few weeks to be fed while he got settled. And then one day, just like Carrie warned, a flip switched in Sven's brain and he turned into an ornery menace of a rodent. I think he purposely found an old nest in the backyard, close enough for Olaf to find him and bark incessantly. And I know for a fact I've seen him standing on a branch, flicking his tail and taunting my dog. Apparently he learned more from Luke than we gave him credit for.

I adjust the sleeves of my ensemble and turn to motion Sprite out of the room. My phone vibrates with a message from my mom.

Mom: We're leaving now.

Me: Us too.

Mom: I am so excited. Don't forget the precious cargo.

Rushing Sprite through the house toward the front door I check my pockets to make sure everything is secure before snagging my keys off the counter. Before I can open the door she stops abruptly and spins on her heel. "Be right back!" And in a flash she's running through the house with Olaf hot on her heels. Sliding the back door open she sticks her head outside and shouts, "Sven, wish us luck!" Before closing the door again and meeting me at the door.

The drive across town isn't long but it's enough that I have to flip the air conditioning on. It's actually chilly outside, but I don't even think the breeze would cool me down. I'm so nervous the sweat is running down my back like some sort of faucet is sprouting out of the back of my head. Calypso doesn't seem to have the same issue as she sings at the top of her lungs in the back seat, bundled up in her coat. I should have sent her with my parents. They think her singing is adorable. It's also why I suggested they both have their hearing checked.

"Oh, we're here! I wonder if Luke is still up."

Turning off the ignition, I kill the lights and turn to face Sprite but instead get a face full of Olaf's tongue.

"Gross. Get down, Olaf. Okay, remember the plan.

You have to be quiet until the door opens. Then Grandma will signal when it's your turn to talk."

Rolling her eyes she releases a heavy sigh. "I know, Daddy. We practiced so many times. Geez."

I thought the tween phase would start when she hit double digits. Who knew seven was the new ten? Opening the door, I hop down from the truck and open the back door and scoop Sprite up and out of the cab. Taking her hand, we walk toward the house, my parents exiting their car and joining us. I quickly tap a few icons on my phone before handing it to my dad. With a deep breath, I nod to my mom and then exhale as she knocks loudly on the door and then rushes to the lawn.

"Here goes nothing."

My dad lifts the phone to start recording just as the first beats of the song waft through the little speaker my mom has on the ground. Slowly I rise from the ground and start lip synching to the song, and I know beyond all things my face is the color of a tomato but humiliating myself for this moment is absolutely worth it.

## *Carrie*

"Here ya go, Lukey. Do you want another acorn?"
My boy takes it, sniffs it, and tosses it down.
"I guess that's a no. You want another pecan, don't

you?" He snatches it out of my hand, startling me. "Oh. I guess so. It seems Matthew really did pick your favorite."

Luke attacks this nut with the same kind of vengeance every man uses on their favorite foods. It's not surprising. In the last year, he's gained at least a pound, which is not a lot unless you only weighed one pound to begin with.

I really should start taking videos of him and posting them. If that Thumbelina chick can become an internet star, surely my boy can too.

Petting his head while he eats, I remark, "It's just you and me tonight, buddy. Wanna catch up on some *Jane the Virgin*? She's our kind of people, huh? Yes she is."

I have no idea what Matthew and Calypso are up to tonight. When I asked, he got kind of shady about it, so I let it go. With any other man, that would have freaked me out. What I've come to know about my two favorite Roberts though, is it usually means they have some kind of surprise up their sleeve. A couple months ago, it was matching ugly Christmas sweaters for all, including the pets. The time before that, a pink and purple squirrel box for Sven to get used to before he was released and the box was nailed to a tree. The surprises are always random and each makes me smile. So I just bide my time until they're ready to show me what madness they've come up with this time.

Luke's eyes suddenly roll in the back of his head and he falls over, asleep.

"So much for any companionship," I mumble, and gently place him back in his cage. At least I don't have to worry about him falling asleep in a random place tonight. Last time it was on top of the fridge which I didn't know until Matthew opened it and Luke fell on him.

I may have laughed way too hard at how loud and shrill my boyfriend screamed.

Matthew is much more comfortable with Luke now. And by comfortable, I mean he doesn't automatically assume Luke is going to attack him anymore. But he still startles whenever he jumps. At this point I think Luke does it on purpose.

I gather all the pet supplies in one pile, ready to put them away when a knock at the door distracts me.

"Hmm," I say to no one since I'm by myself. "I wonder if my little schemers are finally ready to share their latest idea."

Beating feet to the door because I'm always curious what they're about to do, I swing it open and find Matthew and Calypso, fully decked out in the same Elsa and Anna costume they wore the first time I met them.

I laugh because, come on. Matthew looks funny in drag. "What are you guys up to this time?" That's when I notice they aren't alone. And I don't mean Olaf, who is also with them, although without a carrot nose. No, what makes this time different is the addition of Matthew's parents. His mom is standing off to one side with a large box in front of her and his dad is on the other, holding up Matthew's phone. That can only mean one thing—whatever is happening is live on Matthew's social media. This is about to get interesting.

Before I can think more about it, Meghan Trainor's *Dear Future Husband* begins playing, the beat catchy. Then Matthew begins to shimmy. Badly.

Now I'm really confused. And highly entertained because this dancing really is atrocious. The blond wig is barely holding on to his head as he twists and turns and pops his manly hips. I'm almost surprised the dress isn't ripping open from all the random high kicks. RuPaul needs to give him some lessons on dancing in heels and glitter.

As the song continues, Calypso dances her way to her grandma, clearly trying to keep in step with whatever pre-planned moves they've been practicing. She then turns and dances to me, handing me a bouquet of flowers.

"Thank you, Sprite."

"Shh," she reprimands. "No talking yet." And then she dances away, but not for long.

Through the entirety of the song while Matthew is shaking his groove thing, or at least attempting to, Calypso keeps getting more gifts from her grandma and bringing them to me—a bag of pecans, a signed JR Ward book (which almost made me scream regardless of the performance in front of me), a pizza…

And then, as the song begins to wrap up, Calypso surprises me one last time by holding up a giant sign that reads, "Will You Marry My Daddy?"

It's right about this moment that I stop breathing. Yes, my mouth is open, but there's nothing going in or out. I suddenly understand how people pass out at moments like this. *Because no air goes in or out!*

Trying desperately to curb my internal freak-out, I focus on Meghan's words as she belts out, "Buy me a ring. Buy, buy me a ring."

*Ohmygod. This is really happening. THIS IS REALLY HAPPENING!*

As if he can read my thoughts, Matthew begins doing some weird cha-cha movement towards me, a huge grin on his face. His father is following his movement with the phone, and I can barely believe what is happening.

Dropping down on one knee, Matthew pulls out a velvet box and opens it, presenting a princess cut diamond ring that I can't see very well through the tears that have suddenly sprung up in my eyes. But I don't care what it looks like. This moment is about so much more than a diamond.

"Carrie, there is no one I want to publicly humiliate myself for more than you."

That makes me laugh and the squinting of my eyes forces the tears down my cheeks.

"While this is a public declaration about wanting to spend my life with you, some things should be kept private, between the two of us. So I'm just going to ask one thing."

I nod vigorously, probably answering the question he hasn't asked yet, but trying very hard to be patient.

"Will you marry me? Be my wife and the person to tame Sprite's unruly curls? Will you move in with us and bring your scary squirrel? Will you keep me grounded and make fun of the neighborhood gawkers every morning and let me show you every night why how they see me means nothing compared to how you see me? Will you say yes?"

I take a deep breath now that the air is finally moving again and get ready to answer the most important question of my life. This man has proven to me over and over who he is and how he treats those he loves. And for some reason, reasons that are never real clear for any of us in situations like these, I'm one of those people.

Finally feeling calm and sure, I smile. "Yes."

Calypso and Grammy cheer as Matthew stands up, slides the ring on my finger and goes to kiss me, the faint sounds of hundreds of social media notifications blowing up his phone in the background.

Matthew leans in to kiss me but stops with an "ow."

"What?"

"Maybe you should put the pizza box down first so it doesn't jab me in the rib again."

Giggling, I toss all the presents aside, to hell with

the thought that went into them. This moment is worth so much more than that.

"You know that was more than one question, right?"

"Is this how it'll always be?" he asks, wrapping his arm around me.

I meet him halfway and smile with a nod before his lips drop to mine. It's gentle yet full of passion, every emotion expressed between us in the most earth-shattering, soul-scorching kiss. Sure, we keep it somewhat family friendly for the little eyes currently twirling around my yard.

This moment. This relationship. This commitment.

*This man.*

It is everything I've ever dreamed of and more.

*He* is my ultimate book boyfriend.

And he's totally getting laid tonight.

## *The End*

Want to know more about Carrie's friend Celeste and if she will ever meet her celebrity crush? Find out in **Better than the Book** available at all retailers!

Turn the page for a sneak peek.

# Better than the Book

Carrie dances her way toward me, a huge smile on her face. Why wouldn't she be smiling? She is marrying one of the most eligible bachelors in the world of cover models.

Honestly, it still kind of blows my mind. I know I figured out she had a crush on him a long time ago, but it's still hard to reconcile that my friend who has often shared very specific details of her latest book boyfriend, is marrying Matthew Roberts. The man who represents many of those same book boyfriends and is the leading man in many book nerd fantasies. It's a little surreal.

Throwing her arms around me, Carrie pulls me into a giant hug. "I'm so glad you could make it. It's a long flight from New York City."

"Are you kidding? I wouldn't miss this shindig. It's like the hottest event in the book world right now."

"You think?"

I look at her like she's lost her mind and point at the couple Matthew is talking to. "Your cover model boyfriend, sorry *fiancé*, is chatting up best-selling author Donna Moreno and NANA award winning narrator Hawk Weaver. Yeah. I'd say this engagement party is a big deal. By the way, why are the guys wearing those weird shirts?"

Both Hawk and Matthew have on black T-shirts that are covered in what looks like pictures of boutonnieres. The only difference is Matthew's says, "I am the groom" and Hawk's says, "I am not the groom."

"That's Hawk's thing." Carrie stares longingly at her fiancé. It's kind of nausea inducing, to be honest. If she really does eat him up like her face indicates she wants to, I'm outta here. "He buys these ugly shirts for charity or something, and since Matthew loves charity as much as the next guy, he always requests one whenever they see each other."

She giggles. Carrie actually fucking giggles. People in love are so weird.

Suddenly she gasps and grabs my arm. "Did you see what Matthew got me for our honeymoon? Tickets to Australia! Can you believe it?"

"I actually can. I'd have to put a stop to this relationship if he didn't realize it would be the perfect place to spend a couple weeks consummating your new marriage."

Carrie's face turns a bright pink and my eyes widen.

"Carrie Myers, you bad girl," I chide playfully. "You gave up the goods already."

She flips her dark hair over her shoulder and tries to play off her embarrassment. "We are engaged. It's almost like being married."

"Oh no it is not," I say with a laugh. "But I'm not judging you. The whole point of your celibacy was to make sure the next man you were with was completely and utterly serious about you, no matter what. I think waiting for over a year to get in your pants and publicly humiliating himself to propose means Matthew's pretty solid."

I shudder when I think of the dance I watched him perform for his proposal. He may be a decent dancer in pants, but in heels? Not so much.

"Yeah. Oh hey," Carrie blurts out shifting gears, "did you get your tickets for the con?"

Taking a sip of my wine, I shake my head. "Nope. And I'm not going to try this time."

"Why?" she whines. "You've been trying to get there for three years. You deserve to go."

"Exactly. I've tried for three years and something always stops me at the last minute. I don't feel like wasting the money just to be disappointed again."

"Disappointed about what?" a deep voice asks, interrupting our conversation. I guess I should give him grace. He is the groom to the bride standing next to me.

Carrie wraps her arms around her man's waist and proceeds to answer for me. "She's been trying to go to the Prince of Darkness con for a few years and every time she buys tickets, she ends up having to cancel last minute."

"Because the universe doesn't want me to go," I insert, not that I'm bitter or anything. I'm more, trying to keep a silver lining or something.

"Or it could be coincidence," she argues back and turns to look up at Matthew. "She's been a huge fan of Hunter Stone since she saw him in some off-off-Broadway show."

"Hunter Stone?" Matthew sounds confused, but I'm not sure why. Hunter is practically a household name these days. "I just had that cover shoot with him a few weeks ago. We hit it off. I bet I can just ask him for some."

He looks down at his phone, completely oblivious to the fact that my jaw has just hit the floor. Matthew knows Hunter? My blog partner's fiancé is friends with my celebrity crush? How is this happening? More importantly, how did I not know this sooner?

"Oh I forgot about that!" Carrie announces, and I throw my hands out.

"You forgot? How could you forget about something like that? That's like me forgetting that, that... that you have that weird squirrel or something."

"Luke is not weird," she shoots back. "Just disabled. And I didn't think about it because it was like a one-day job or something. Matthew didn't even leave town."

I open my mouth to keep playing this tit-for-tat game with her, but Matthew speaks before I can argue.

"Done. You have tickets to... hang on..." He zooms in while I blink rapidly a few times, in serious disbelief that this is happening. "Looks like it's an all access pass to the event, all the pictures and one round-table of your choice. Will that work?"

I'm not sure how it's possible, but my jaw drops even further. I turn quickly to Carrie and point at her. "If you don't marry this man, I will."

# Acknowledgements

Megan A., Ally M., Marisol S., and Rachel G. Thank you for always giving honest feedback and making sure we don't get too ridiculous (just enough to be the most fun authors you work with!).

Kayla Ann. Thank you, for, your eagle eyes, and hard work, to find the lack, of commas. See what we did there? Really, thank you so much for taking the time to help us polish our words.

Aly H. Thank you for your vast knowledge of Christmas and Hanukkah traditions. You saved us from looking more ridiculous than we do on our own anyway. If we made any errors it's not your fault. It's our parents for not being Jewish.

Alyssa with Uplifting Author Services. Don't forget to save that other font for the next book entitled "Because We Like This Font". Thank you for always joining our level of insanity and never judging us for being "complicated".

Karen with The Proof is in the Reading. Thank you for giving us resource information. At least one of us read up on the Oxford comma. We likely won't use it but we read it. (Or at least Andrea did.) We're so sorry for all we put you through with Matthew's sacrifice.

Jennifer Van Wyk and Mary L. Thanks for not making us beg and indulging our neurosis to be our last set of eyes.

Thank you cover models for all your hard work and

smoldering looks. Please accept our sincerest apologies for any inappropriate ab touching you've experienced from romance readers (and authors).

Bloggers. Just know we fangirl over you as much as you fangirl over us. Without you this book community would not be the same. Our wish for you is that you find your own Matthew, complete with abs.

Wildlife Center of Texas. Thank you for saving all the animals, especially the baby Lukeys of the great state of Texas.

It goes without saying, Carter's Cheerleaders, Sassy Romantics, and Nerdy Little Book Herd, you all are the best readers and supporters around. We love you as much as Luke loves a pecan.

We've forgotten at least three people in this section. None of you are surprised and if you are, you aren't those three people.

# About the Authors

M.E. Carter and Andrea Johnston are romance writers who share a love of the written word. Combining their sense of humor, beliefs in love, and sarcasm, this writing duo has joined forces to create the Charitable Endeavors series. With the sole purpose of bringing laughter and love to their readers while tapping into their charitable hearts, a portion of the release proceeds will be donated to charity.

# Other books by M.E. Carter

**Hart Series**
*Change of Heart*
*Hart to Heart*
*Matters of the Hart*

**Texas Mutiny Series**
*Juked*
*Groupie*
*Goalie*
*Megged*
*Deflected*

**#MyNewLife Series**
*Getting a Grip*
*Balance Check*
*Pride & Joie*
*Amazing Grayson*

**Charitable Endeavors**
(Collaborations with Andrea Johnston)
*Switch Stance*
*Ear Candy*
*Model Behavior*

**Smartypants Romance**
*Weight Expectations*

# Other books by Andrea Johnston

**Country Road Series**

*Whiskey & Honey*

*Tequila & Tailgates*

*Martinis & Moonlight*

*Champagne & Forever*

*Bourbon & Bonfires*

**Military Men of Lexington**

*Promise Her*

**Standalones**

*Life Rewritten*

*The Break Series*

*I Don't: A Romantic Comedy*

*Small-Town Heart*

*It Was Always You*

**Charitable Endeavors**

(Collaborations with M.E. Carter)

*Switch Stance*

*Ear Candy*

*Model Behavior*

CPSIA information can be obtained
at www.ICGtesting.com
Printed in the USA
BVHW041028131221
623917BV00009B/202

9 781948 852233